HISTORY OF THE HOUSE NEXT DOOR

Peter Tiernan

DEEPWOODS BOOKS

Copyright © 2018 by Peter Tiernan

Published by Deepwoods Books.

ISBN 978-1-7325717-0-9

To all my childhood friends…
and my best friend, Michelle.

HISTORY OF THE HOUSE NEXT DOOR

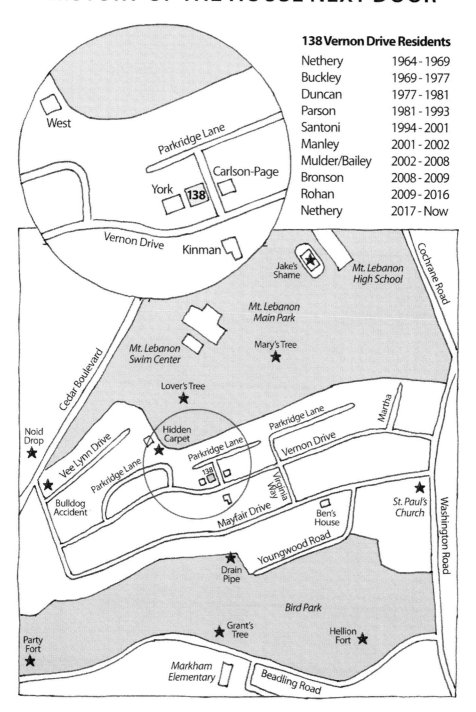

138 Vernon Drive Residents

Nethery	1964 - 1969
Buckley	1969 - 1977
Duncan	1977 - 1981
Parson	1981 - 1993
Santoni	1994 - 2001
Manley	2001 - 2002
Mulder/Bailey	2002 - 2008
Bronson	2008 - 2009
Rohan	2009 - 2016
Nethery	2017 - Now

CONTENTS

PREFACE

I conducted these interviews over a five-month period in 2016. They are presented in chronological order, from the interview relating to the earliest known resident of 138 Vernon Drive in Mt. Lebanon, Pennsylvania, to the most recent. The interviews themselves, however, did not take place in this order. I would have preferred to conduct them that way, but the logistics of tracking down subjects, coordinating schedules, and arranging travel made this impossible. Readers may notice instances where this difference between when the interviews occurred and where they're placed in the book make for unexpected interactions.

Early readers of this manuscript—in other words, my mom— suggested that I should say a word about how the tape recordings became the interviews you're about to read. She observed that most people don't talk as articulately as these interviews portray. They muddle their speech with an assortment of verbal pauses and stock phrases. It's true. In the interest of readability, I've removed these distracting tics, except where they give a better sense of a subject's personality. I've also cleaned up the way many of my interview subjects related conversations they had. It was only in the process of transcribing my tapes that I realized how inelegantly people convey what other people say. Trust me: you would quickly tire of reading phrases such as *I'm like*, *then he goes*, and *so I'm all*. In the interest of increasing my odds that you won't chuck this book across the room, I've smoothed over the dialogue.

Finally, I want to make clear that I did not sit quietly during these interviews. Some of these people, as you'll discover, were near-unrestrainable talkers; others were less-willing subjects. Sometimes, to break long silences or steer the interview back to the matter at hand, I asked questions, interrupted tangents, and gave gentle prompts. None of those comments made their way into the final manuscript, except in the last story.

The one question that everyone I met with invariably asked me was, "Why *this* house?" I would not answer them, at first because I wasn't quite sure myself, and then after I was, because I didn't want them to know. It's my hope that the interviews themselves, the history they piece together of the last half century, reveal the significance of the house at 138 Vernon Drive, or any home any-where, for that matter.

Grace Page, October 2017

138 VERNON DRIVE
Mt. Lebanon, PA 15228
FOR SALE, 4/28/16: $630,000

A BEAUTY! Impressive 5-bedroom, 5-bath stone home with slate flooring in the entry, arched doorways, beautiful wood trim and hardwood floors. Inviting formal living room with crown molding and fireplace flanked by built-in shelves. Large dining room has French doors that lead to den. Den offers full wall of built-in shelves and access to new enclosed patio. Gorgeous updated kitchen with stainless steel appliances, unique tile on walls, beautiful cherry cabinets, breakfast nook with seating and pendant lighting. Oversized master bedroom with skylights, spacious master bathroom and two walk-in closets. Sunroom with large windows on three sides, large laundry room with storage and laundry chute. Fabulous enclosed patio with skylights leads to outdoor stone patio and wonderful level back yard.

NOBODY

I don't want to beat this to death, but I still don't get why you're here. When we first talked, you said we could do this by email. Then when you told me you'd be in Anchorage, I said I'd come meet you. You didn't have to fly all the way out here. Hiring a floatplane to land on this nowhere lake had to cost five hundred bucks. Bet the pilot hadn't heard of Stevens Lake Lodge, had he? If he'd known how narrow that pass was by the mouth of the river, he would've charged you more. Whatever. I agreed to help you out and I won't go back on my word. You want me to tell you what I remember about our house in Mt. Lebanon. You just want me to talk. No questions. No interruptions. And you're reaching out to everyone else who ever lived there. What is it, some *all meaning in a potato* kind of thing? Fair enough. But this isn't any old potato to you, is it? I know: you never lived there. Still, you have your reasons for picking 138 Vernon Drive. Grace Page…is that even your real name? Never mind. I'll let it go.

I assume we're still the oldest residents you could find, eh? So I did what you asked: I talked to my dad. Like I said, he's not all there. But he did remember the guy who sold him the house. Name was Woolson, Henry Woolson. He doesn't recall much about him, just that he was an old guy, nearly ninety, and he always wore a real Civil War cap—you know, with the round flat top tilting forward.

He claimed he was the son of the oldest living veteran, a Union officer who died in the fifties. I don't know if that's true.

As far as our family is concerned, I don't know how much you should take my word for things. Vernon Drive was the beginning of my memory. I was six when we moved there. Everything before then—where I was born in Iowa, then Cleveland, and Philly—that's all a dream. I have a few hazy visions: chewing fur off my stuffed bear's ears; clomping around in an oversized cowboy costume; going headfirst down a slide and driving my front teeth through my lower lip. But I'm not sure where those came from really—my own head, my parent's stories. I don't know.

I can tell you precisely the moment I woke to this world, though. It's the first day in that house. The Mayflower truck is unloading. I'm behind the hedge that runs along our backyard down Parkridge Lane, lying on the ground, hiding. On the other side, big kids are playing, boys 11 or 12. I'm six. There's a Charles Potato Chips tin upside down in the middle of the lane, a few steps away from me. One kid is chasing the rest up and down the lane and around the yard next door. I want to play so badly it aches. But I'm afraid. There's a girl on the porch swing next door, perched above the lane, pointing at me, right into the gap in the hedges I'm spying through. "Get him," she's crying out. "Get *him*!" She's younger than me, small and slight, with a head of bright, blond wavy hair, and wide eyes that flicker and dance. "Right there, Bobby!" she shouts to the boy chasing everyone. "He's playing too."

"No, he's not," Bobby says. "He's out of bounds."

"Dad said you have to let everyone play!" the girl shouts after him as he runs off. And now she's motioning to me. "Come on," she's saying. *"Come on!"*

I just want to run inside and hide. But when I stand up, I see a cluster of boys out by a light post in the front yard. And they see me. "Kick it!" one yells, pointing at the can. The others join in. "Kick it!" Then I understand. If I do it, they'll be free.

I step out into road. "Hurry!" the girl says.

Behind her, Bobby's coming around the far corner of the house. "He can't do that!" he yells across the backyard.

I kick the can. It rolls and clanks down the lane. The kids by the post roar with glee and race off. The girl smiles down at me, eyes bright, face aglow. Bobby comes stomping my way. "That doesn't count," he barks. "You're nobody. You don't count!"

That was 1964, 52 years ago. Today, that old house is bright gold sandstone. Back then, it was dark and forbidding. Everything was: the hills, the tunnels, the rivers, the skies above Pittsburgh. The stone exterior of 138 Vernon was smoky grey, stained with decades of soot from the steel mills. And that road next to our house, Parkridge, it wasn't the quaint, landscaped lane it is today. It was an alley, trespassing between our house and the Carlson's. My dad hated that lane. Our garage door couldn't have been more than a foot from what should've been a curb. Dad must've griped about that a thousand times. "We're the only people who have a goddamned road through our property," is what he used to say.

I don't want to come off negative. Truth is, I never felt more in control of my world than I did when I lived on Vernon Drive. Isn't that sad? I'm talking about when I was 10 years old like it's the best it ever got. Maybe it was. Maybe every kid that age goes through the same awakening, gains the same sense of a world ripe with adventure. Maybe it wasn't my age so much as the time. We think back on the Sixties as a decade of turmoil—Vietnam, race riots, dead leaders, failed ideals, lost souls. That's not how it felt to live through. We bought our first color TV in that house. I watched Saturday cartoons and *Batman* and *Get Smart* and *The Monkees*. I got the first GI Joe that ever came out and a wheelie bike with a banana seat. And we played with chemistry sets and cooked up Creepy Crawlers, and no one ever worried about toxic fumes. My mom bought me a 45 record player and I had *Hello Muddah, Hello Fadduh* and *The Name Game* and *Crimson and Clover* and *Build Me Up Buttercup* and Tommy Roe's *Dizzy*—and the first single I got of The Beatles was *Strawberry Fields* with *Penny Lane* on the B side. Then there were all the cards we collected—Green Hornet and Batman and Beatles cards, Classic Monsters and Odd Rods and Wacky Packs. I can still feel the indescribable thrill of opening a pack of baseball cards, smelling the cardboard gum. I had a dozen shoeboxes full. We used to put our best Pirates cards—the Clementes and Stargells, the Mazeroskis and Alous—in the spokes of our bikes so they'd rattle like machine guns as we rode. We ruined them and thought nothing of it. There'd be more the next year, and more after that. The past was disposable.

Back then, kids played outside. That's what playing was. And where we lived, up on that hill between those two valleys, couldn't have been a better place for a kid. You've been there. You know. Behind us, all we had to do was walk to the end of Parkridge, cut between the houses, and we were looking down into Mt. Lebanon Park. And on the south side, we could wend our way through the neighborhood down to the sprawling hillside of untamed woods that seemed like our exclusive paradise. What do they call those woods now? Bird Park? I'll bet there aren't many kids whose parents let them walk through there to Markham Elementary anymore. If I had a kid, I wouldn't. Different times. How easy would it be for some sicko to hide there and wait for a kid walking alone? I'm amazed my mother let me do it, even without the threat of molesters. The way to Markham was over a mile—up Vernon, down the sharp decline on Virginia Way, along Mayfair, then down another tier again on Youngwood, until you entered the woods and took a winding path up the hill, farther and steeper than you'd already gone. Only then would you pop out of the woods, cross the traffic on Beadling, and climb the drive to Markham.

No way my mom would've let me do it if the Carlsons hadn't made Bobby take me. He's the kid I pissed off playing *Kick the Can*. It was one thing to have to take his sister Ilsa; now he had to watch over this little nobody next door. Ilsa Carlson: she was the bright-haired girl who called me out from the porch. And she was a first grader. I was in second. You know how it is when you're young; one grade is a Richter scale difference. Bobby was in fifth. He may as well have been an adult. For him to be seen with us was an unbearable humiliation. We tagged along a dozen steps behind as he hurried down the sidewalks and up the switchbacks to school.

One day, Bobby stopped at the top of Youngwood and said, "You know the way," staring me down. I must've looked at him cross-eyed or given some sort of mutinous scowl. He poked me in the chest. "If you tell, I'll knock your block off, you cake." That's what they called you back then if you were somehow different: *cake*. So that became the new routine. Bobby would lead us out their front door to make a show for his mom, stay close until Virginia Way, then leave Ilsa and me on our own. I couldn't race ahead of her like Bobby did; there was no one else to watch her. Besides, with all the kids on the trail, I couldn't risk word getting back to Bobby that I'd abandoned his sister. So I went the same pace I always did and let her walk beside me.

I make it sound worse than it was. Truth is, in those early days, I didn't know anyone else to replace her. And she wasn't half bad to talk to. I still remember our conversations. We debated the existence of Santa Claus. She had it on Bobby's authority it was a trick parents played on kids; I was doubtful myself, but less willing to give up on the myth. I corrected Ilsa on the proper term for when parents split up. She thought it was "orson"—possibly short for "divorcin'; I told her it was "dorsic." And I believed that right into seventh grade, the day my mom told me she was getting a divorce from my dad. Ilsa informed me what the numbers were on the wrist of our librarian, Mrs. Fishman. She said they burned them on in Germany when she went to jail for not believing in Hitler. I taught her a song I'd learned at school. *Whistle while you work. Hitler is a jerk. Mussolini bit his weenie. Now it doesn't work.* Have you heard that one? I have to say, the country might've been in the middle of Vietnam, but kids our age were still consumed with World War II.

Sorry. I'm rambling. It's this place, the expanse of it. The solitude. We haven't had a guest up here all spring and won't until the salmon start running. It's just Randall the guide and me here by ourselves. I still cook breakfast every morning—it's my job. But Randall doesn't always show. Sometimes I won't see him for days. He'll be down in his cabin or checking out our bear camp across the lake. I don't read much anymore, and the internet comes and goes, so there's a lot of time to think, to sit here on this deck, look out on the water, around at all the mountains, up at the clouds racing away from Denali. Know what Randall says when people who want to hike ask for bear spray? Know what he tells them? He says, "I'll give you spray if it makes you feel better." That generally stops them, and they wind up sitting here on this deck drinking beer. That sort of remark doesn't exactly set the mood our owner wants. But it's true. If you're going to wander these woods, you have to accept you might run into something sudden and over-whelming, something you can't handle. That's the way I feel about all this thinking I get to doing. You start circling back through memories, trying to find the sense of things, you're bound to run into something you don't want to face, something you can't escape. There isn't any spray for that.

Where was I? Oh yeah: walking Ilsa to school. Like I said, I didn't mind. Not until I started getting teased about it. "There's the cake with his baby girl." That's what Ralph Brink would say. Ralph was this gangly, summer-toothed punk of a kid who was always dirty and allegedly ate his boogers. It's not hard to gain that reputation when you're constantly showing off how you can pick your nose with your tongue. My guess: Ralph is incarcerated some-where. Anyway, he didn't bother me all that much, except when he was with the kids I wanted to be friends with. Then, the teasing hurt. Ilsa took it harder. She'd yell back at Ralph, throw sticks at him, threaten to tell her big brother. One day, she said she didn't want to walk with me anymore. She could go with her own friends, she said, Trish and Laurie. I told her if it was because of Ralph, it wasn't her he was teasing; it was me. She said she wanted him to stop. I tried to follow behind her the first time she walked with her friends, but she saw me and yelled back, "Why are you doing this?" That hurt me more than any of Ralph's teasing.

By Halloween , Ilsa's rejection didn't matter. I'd fallen in with a gang of kids my age. Joey Jansen, Cal Peoples, Lips Chadwick, Ralph (whether I liked it or not), and my best friend Ben Fishman, the same Fishman as the librarian who survived Auschwitz. She was his mom. We played together practically every day. He lived on Mayfair, but we spent almost all our time outside, in the woods. I still remember the way I felt there—wild, unafraid, certain the world held boundless promise. I'd wake up weekend mornings practically jumping out of my skin to meet my friends there. In those woods—our woods—we could be warriors and martyrs, builders and scientists, explorers, philosophers. We could try on any mask we wanted, and nobody was there to judge us. No parents, no teachers, and, for the most part, no big kids.

What a difference the woods were from the other valley our neighborhood overlooked. Back then, Mt. Lebanon Park was this big, open expanse, a landscaped hillside scattered with towering trees that tumbled from the backyards along Parkridge down to the public pool, then bottomed out at the ball fields bordering Cedar Boulevard. If the woods were our refuge, the park was our trial. That's where the bigger world began for us, where we faced strangers and had to behave, where we weren't allowed in the deep end of the pool, and big kids played in full baseball uniforms on manicured diamonds we couldn't step on. At the far end of the park, there was the high school football stadium, where everyone came together to watch the Blue Devils play, where the town's full and true character was laid bare, and we could only be who we really were. You know what I'm saying. You know the lay of that land. Perched there on Vernon, teetering between our possibilities and limits. It was exhilarating, but frightening as well.

Once, in fourth grade, our gang was walking up Vernon to the game, and a car came rolling up behind us. I can still see it, a sleek fifties car with tailfins, painted blue and gold: *Go Devils. Seniors 67*. Leaning out every window, even the driver's side, were high school kids, boys and girls, waving their arms, roaring and laughing. I'd never seen anything like it, never imagined you could act up like that in a car. It was rebellious, criminal. We gaped at them as they passed, crowing all the way up Vernon. There, ahead of us, drifting out of sight, was our future. One day we'd be making up our own rules like them, loudly celebrating our freedom. Only an hour later at the stadium, I saw one of those kids from the car in the bathroom. He was in a stall with the door open, kneeling beside the toilet, getting sick. His buddies stood to the side, laughing.

That same night, I saw Ilsa by herself near the end zone, sitting on the bottom step of the long stairway that led from the field to the school. She had her head bowed, knees tucked under her chin, and she was rocking back and forth. I asked where her friends were. She shrugged. I asked what was wrong. She shook her head. Her blonde hair was hanging over her face. I asked again, "What happened?" She shook her head harder. I begged her, "Come on. Please!" Finally, Ilsa looked up. Her face was smeared with dirt and tears. She straightened her legs, and I saw the stain. It was on the bottom of her shirt and spread across her lap: a big brown blotch on her white pants. Someone had spilled Coke on her in the bleachers. She wanted to go home and change. But Trish and Laurie didn't want to lose the good seats they had. So they let her go by herself. She was embarrassed and angry and lonesome. I would've felt the same way. She couldn't walk around like that without getting razzed.

I had my CPO jacket on, an oversized sort of flannel shirt, and I offered it to her. She put it on. It went down to her knees. I thought she'd head back into the stands then, and I'd go find the gang. It wasn't even halftime. But she said she was going home and started walking away. I watched her go all the way around the track, through the swarm of kids behind the end zone and over to the visitor's stands. Then I started running. I don't know why—whether I felt sorry, responsible or worried. I caught up to Ilsa near the exit off the park. I didn't say a word, just fell in with her. She didn't say anything either. We walked up the hill to our houses, through the shadowy scattering of trees, and didn't see a soul.

It was only when we crested the hill, not far from the backyards of Parkridge houses, that we saw anyone; a boy and a girl, high schoolers, maybe older. They were on the far side of the park, beyond where we had to cut through, but close enough to see them. If they'd bothered to look up, they would've seen us too. But they were absorbed with each other. The boy was lying on his back, head near the trunk of the tree, feet pointing downhill. The girl was on top of him, face raised up but close to his, eyes glinting in the fading sun. And she was smiling. Beaming. I'd never seen two people so close together, so intimate. Not even in my own home. It was love. I didn't call it that back then. But that's what it was. Ilsa and I stood there, silent and still, watching this young couple, just down the hill, whispering and laughing. Then kissing.

I looked over at Ilsa. She turned slowly to me, either sensing my gaze or expecting it. For the first time since I caught up to her in the stadium, our eyes met. And held. The moment got stuck. We went on staring at one another, nine and 10 years old, with the lights of the football game far below and those lovers so close. It was Ilsa who finally looked away, hanging her head, like she was suddenly ashamed. She slipped off my CPO and handed it to me. "Thank you," she whispered. Then she ran off between the houses. If I could only keep one moment in my life, that might be it—there on the crest of that hill, glimpsing a small clue to the giant mystery that was only beginning to involve us.

But things changed. By sixth grade, we weren't chasing fireflies; we were lighting firecrackers. And we weren't rifling through packs of baseball cards; we were sneaking into Ben's brother's room and pawing over *Playboys*. We replaced crew cuts with hair that grew into our eyes, and cuffed jeans with outlandish bell-bottoms. Instead of building forts in the woods, we were going there to smoke the Lucky Strikes I stole from my dad. And instead of wielding plastic machine guns, we were thrashing at electric guitars. When Ben played *The White Album* for me, I wrote down the lyrics to *Back in the USSR* on a scrap of paper. My mom found it in my pants, thought I wrote the song, and wondered where I'd learned such communist drivel. I was flattered she thought I could write something like that. We were growing up, testing boundaries. And, even though it was the beginning of an end we didn't recognize, there was a sweetness to it. Innocence over-ripening. I could blame puberty or pass it off as the consequences of the time. After all, it *was* the summer of '69. But those aren't the real reasons for why all the trouble started. Truth is, I don't know if there is a reason. Just a series of circumstances. One thing after another.

The day I finished sixth grade, my dad called me into our living room. My mother was there, sitting beside the fireplace with that look that said, *You're in trouble*. They told me we were moving. To Detroit. I cried right there and then. I told my dad I didn't want to go, I *wouldn't* go. He said we had to. "When you get offered a better job at Westinghouse, you take it," he said. "Or you don't have a job." I stomped off and hid away in our basement. I stayed there brooding all day and even after the windows went black. My mom called down for dinner. I didn't answer. Didn't even come up when it was time for bed. Just slept there, without a blanket, in the strange, cold darkness. For days, I didn't talk to my dad and only grumbled at my mom. They tried to pull me out of my funk. My mom bought me the Wellington boots I'd begged for since Christmas. My dad dredged up an old *Sports Illustrated* with Denny McClain on the cover and said the Tigers were defending champs. I refused to give in. They were traitors. They'd brought me to Mt. Lebanon, let me conquer this world, and were now exiling me.

I didn't tell my friends I was moving. How could I? If I had, I'd become a kind of ghost they would either abandon or feel compelled to mourn. If I didn't tell them, I could still share in their dreams; and I'd be nothing worse than an imposter, faking excitement for a future I'd never reach. It seemed easier to stay included and let them think I still mattered.

We were hanging out a lot with the girls that summer. That seemed to be the only thing Ben and Ralph cared about anymore. One day, we convinced Ilsa, Trish, and Laurie to meet us down where Youngwood dead-ended. We hardly ever ventured into that side of the woods. For one thing, it was out of the way to school. For another, the sides of the valley folded in closer to each other and the underbrush was heavier. With fewer paths, steeper footing, and a darker canopy, there was something eerie about those woods. I thought this was some crazy idea Ralph had cooked up. But it was Ben who led us down the dried-up creek bed. I was behind him, then the girls, then Ralph. We went deeper than I'd ever gone into that side, leaving behind the ridge of houses up on Mayfair, until it was dark and wild all around us. Finally, we came to a clearing beside the phantom creek. There was an old stone fire pit there, encircled by a rotted bench. It seemed like the place where we'd stop. The girls even sat down. But Ralph marched past us and started up the far slope, pushing through tangles of branches that whipped back at us. After five minutes, he tunneled into a cave of bent brambles. We followed. Ben scrambled back to where the brush closed up and pulled out a grocery bag. There were three Iron City beer cans inside. Ralph took a can from Ben, snapped off the old-style ring, gave the beer a quick swig and held it out for Trish. She didn't resist. No one did. But when the second one came around, Ilsa shook it off and said she didn't like the taste. Everyone else took their turn.

Before Ben opened the last beer, Ralph was waving a fat cigarette in front of us. At least that's what I thought it was until Trish blurted out, "Is that grass?" Ben hushed her and scanned the wall of branches, like some narc might burst in at any moment. I was already uneasy, but Ben's darting eyes scared me. I'd never seen him so jumpy, so worried he was doing wrong. Ralph took the first hit, inhaled deeply, then coughed it right out. Laurie giggled. The smoke rose and left a wicked sweetness in the flimsy cave.

When Ben took the joint, I scooted back to the opening. "I'm not going to," was all I said, and I stood up outside the brambles.

"Nethery," Ralph called out, ducking down to glare in my eyes. "Get back in here, you cake." I said I wouldn't tell and hurried off.

Not long after that, it started drizzling. The woods twitched and crackled, and those looming slopes got darker. Then I heard my name. Ilsa was running to me through the rubble of the creek bed. When she reached me, she was out of breath. "I wanted to go with you," she said. I can't remember exactly how I responded, only that it wasn't what I really felt. I should've told her it wasn't right, admitted I was afraid. Those were the days, after all, when every drug was alien and evil, when the news showed crazed kids sniffing glue out of lunch bags and sticking needles in their arms. I'm sure Ilsa was just as scared as I was. Instead, I said we should get home before the rain came down too hard. We continued on in silence, the only sound the gathering clatter in the trees. The rain did get heavier, but I didn't change my pace. And Ilsa didn't seem to mind. The truth was, I was glad she had come.

By the time we got to where the valley unfolded, our clothes were sticking to our skin. Still, we took our time. Now and then,

we'd even catch each other's eye and smile. Then the skies opened
up, a roaring downpour we could barely see through. We were out
from under the thicker canopy, close to the path that went from
the dead end at Youngwood, up the hill, to the backs of the Mayfair
houses. It was the shortcut home, and we took it. But the path was
slippery. Ilsa fell before we even got to the steepest stretch. The
whole front of her shirt got smeared with mud.

There was a drainage pipe nearby, just across a swale of thicker
underbrush. It was big enough that you could stand in it if you bent
down. Ben and I had gone in there a few times, but never ventured
far. It got dark really fast and the noises in there were spooky.
Besides, you could see it from the houses down on Youngwood.
Still, with the rain and treacherous footing, I pointed Ilsa that way.
We sat just inside the opening, facing each other in the round pipe,
legs crossing over the trickling runoff. And we looked out from
the shadows of that circle we were in, through the cascading
shroud of rain, down into the valley. It seems like we sat that way
in silence a long time, or else it's one more moment that got stuck
in my head. After a point, Ilsa said, in a voice that resounded
through the pipe, "I don't want you to go." I didn't know what she
meant until she added, "Why didn't you tell me you were moving?"

I was thinking of what to say—that I didn't want to go either,
that my dad was making me, that I was sorry to keep the secret—
but before I could speak, a shout rose over the torrent. "Get outta
there!" Below us, a man was standing on his back deck, pointing
our way. I leaned into the shadows. Ilsa did the same. That only
made him angrier. "I see you!" he roared, stomping across his yard,
through the downpour. It wasn't much further from us than the
drop of a staircase. But he would've had to jump his fence and
scramble up the ravine to catch us. Still, we retreated into the pipe.
I don't know what we were thinking. We couldn't hide there forever or escape out the other end. And if we didn't already realize
that, the man made it clear. "You're not going anywhere," he
bellowed, his words reverberating in the tube.

We scurried deeper into the dark. When I looked back, it was
like what you'd see through the wrong end of binoculars, a small

bright circle of stormy daylight at the end of a long, black barrel. Only I got it turned around in my mind, maybe not at the time, but ever since. It wasn't that we were holding the binoculars backwards looking out, but that someone was holding them, staring in. "I'm calling the police!" the man's threat bore in on us. Ilsa retreated further. I scuttled after her. Soon, we came to where the pipe split right and left to follow the line of houses up and down Mayfair. Ilsa stopped just around the left corner, away from the receding light. She leaned back across the far arc of pipe and let out a shivering sigh. I crawled over to her, but not so far around the corner that I couldn't still see the bright end of the pipe. The stream at the bottom of the pipe was rising and we had to scooch our butts up the side and straighten our legs so we wouldn't get wet.

We were silent for a long time. I can still hear the water gurgling deep in the pipes and the interplay of our breathing, still feel the mounting pressure. "Don't tell anyone I'm going," I finally said. "They won't like me anymore." She put her hand over the hand I had on my knee. When I turned to her, Ilsa's eyes were gleaming, ink in the gloom. And she was waiting. My hand trembled under hers. "I don't know what to do," I confessed with a raw desperation I'd never felt before. She lifted my hand, pinned it to her chest, and held it there. I could feel her heart pounding under her muddy shirt, her heaving rib cage. *Thump. Thump.* She was only 11. She didn't even have a bra. What struck me then, what sticks with me now, was her eyes, that look she gave me. It was tender and true, more naked, even in that dim shaft of light, than anyone ever looked at me. Before or since. I was transfixed, enraptured. She leaned over and kissed me, a quick soft kiss on my open mouth, slick, warm, and secret. Then gone. Gone...

Not long after, the end of the pipe brightened, and we climbed out into a fresh day, sun glinting everywhere off the wet trees, a hush of wind drifting through the valley. Ilsa touched my arm and pointed down to Youngwood. There, right where the trees gave way to the road, Ben and Ralph and Trish and Laurie were coming out of the brush. Ben turned to see where the others were. Then he scanned the hillside, one hand brimming his eyes against the sun. He seemed to stop when his gaze reached us, but it was hard to tell. He didn't wave. Neither did I.

I only saw Ben twice after that, once to keep our friendship, then to end it. The first time came a few days after my desertion in the woods. I'd been waiting for him to come up to my house, rather than going down to his. In my mind, if I went to him, it meant I was weak and anxious for acceptance. If he came my way, he'd decided that being friends was more important than being accomplices. As it turned out, I was the one who gave in. Ben was in his room when I went over, slumped on his bed next to Ralph. They were listening to records and reading comic books. I leaned against the wall inside his door. Ralph taunted me straight away. "Look who's back," he smirked.

I said something like I didn't know I'd gone anywhere, trying to act as cool as I could. The whole time, my eyes were on Ben's, and his were on mine. "What were you doing with Ilsa?" he asked finally, "I saw you coming out of the drain pipe behind Peoples."

I said I was getting out of the rain. Ben didn't buy it. "Come on. You did more than that." I shrugged—and maybe grinned for show. Honestly, I didn't mind the insinuation. It took the attention away from deserting them.

"Did you ball her?" Ralph asked. I didn't know what that meant. I'm not sure he did either. So I said something I did know. I said I'd felt her up. Ben's eyes bugged out. Ralph was less impressed. "Big deal. Ilsa Carlson barely has mosquito bites." I was going to let it go. Who cared what a loser like Ralph thought? But then he added, "It's good to know she gives it up though."

Before I knew it, I was standing over him, fists clenched, trembling. "Don't say that."

"You don't want me to get up, Nethery."

"Just don't," I blustered. "Don't. Say. That."

Ralph gave a huff and went back to his comic book. I should've dropped it then, but I couldn't let the accusation stand. I told them I didn't do it very long. Ilsa made me stop right away. And that was how we left it. Nobody said another word. I snatched a comic book off Ben's bed and flopped down in a beanbag across the room.

Of course, that wasn't the end of it. Kids don't keep those kinds of secrets. I don't know how long it was after that. All I know was I started getting anxious to see Ilsa. But I didn't have the guts to go to her door and knock. So I went out into the lane with my baseball mitt and a tennis ball and started throwing it against the garage door. I stood under Ilsa's window, banging the ball against the wood, sending out a hollow thump. Now and then, I'd let the ball get by me. That way, I could turn and sneak a peek at her window. Anyone watching would've pegged me for a lousy ball player. I had just made a bargain with myself that I'd quit after three more throws when I heard the door to the Carlson's back porch open. "You told," she said before I could even turn around.

I don't know why it surprised me. I don't know why I hadn't fathomed the possibility. I had to admit something. So I told her that Ben had seen us coming out of the drain.

"But he didn't know what happened inside," she said, so quietly I could barely hear. "You told. Laurie said Ben told her."

"I didn't tell them hardly anything," I flailed. "They must've made it sound worse."

She started to cry, not out loud, not openly, just tears streaming down her disappointed face. "I thought you were nice," she said. Then she went back inside.

I thought you were nice.

For a long awful moment, I stood there, frozen. Then I threw the tennis ball as hard as I could over our house, flung off my mitt, and started running. Up Vernon, down Virginia, onto Mayfair. I didn't stop until I was in Ben's driveway, standing in front of him, his Sting-Ray bike between us. He was putting race car decals all over the frame. He looked up at me, heaving to catch my breath, and didn't say a word, just crouched there and gave me a cold insolent glare. "What did you say?" I snarled. "Why did you tell?"

"You told first," Ben hit back. Then he gave a little snuffle.

That did it. Something was going to be the trigger, and that dismissive snort was it. I grabbed his bike and threw it down the slanted driveway. It clattered on the cement and came to a stop in a contorted heap. Before Ben could even stand, I shoved him in the chest. "You're not my friend anymore," I bawled.

"I don't care," he shouted back. I hit him. As he was straightening up. One swing. With an open hand, hard against his cheek. He staggered and fell back on the driveway. Then he gazed up at me. And his expression wasn't heartless or mean. He was stunned, vulnerable, exactly like you'd expect a hurt friend to look. I ran. Up Ben's driveway and all the way back home, tears stinging my eyes, streaming across my face. That was the last time I ever saw Ben.

After that, I never left our house. It was just days away from our move, and my mom was after me to pack anyway. So my parents didn't notice anything wrong. But that time, those long hours hiding in my room, hiding from what I'd done—to my best friend, yes, but so much worse to Ilsa—wishing I could undo it and knowing I couldn't, that was the worst I've ever felt. Now and then, I'd sneak to the bathroom window across from Ilsa's and peek over to her drawn shade. Hour after hour, day after day, the shade stayed down. Toward the end of my packing, I found a penknife. The next time I went to the window, I took it with me. Instead of spying out, I narrowed in on the end of the windowsill. You'd have to be sitting where I was in the corner and focused on it to see what I did. The carving could've fit on a dime. *IC DN*. I never went near the window again. I didn't deserve that hope.

Soon after, the Mayflower arrived, the movers carried out our belongings, and they drove off for Detroit. Then, it was the morning of having to leave. It was so early, the sky was dark. As I shuffled out to the car idling in the lane, I sensed a glow above me. There was Ilsa, silhouetted by her bedroom light. I couldn't make out her face, but something in the way her shoulders heaved and her head hung grabbed my throat. She brought her right hand up, ready to wave, then kept it there, pressed on the glass. I held up my left hand, mirroring her. We stayed like that for a second, then my dad said we had to go. I got in the car and we drove away.

I think of that morning as the end of something vital, something beyond my time in Mt. Lebanon. It was an amputation. Ever since that summer, I seem incapable of believing in my own goodness. What I disabled was any sort of trust in myself. I didn't realize it right away, or for a long time after that. The rest of my school years weren't much different than anyone else's in the Seventies. I had a good time without getting in too much trouble, fooled around with the girls who let me, and got decent enough grades for my dad to pull some strings and get me into Michigan. That's when everything caught up with me. The drugs had something to do with it, sure. But they didn't make the hole inside me; they just tempted me to the edge of it.

I dropped out after my junior year. Didn't tell my parents. Didn't plan it out. Just threw all my stuff in the back of my beat-up '68 Impala and took off. I wish I could say it was some grand quest for self-discovery, an *On-the-Road*-like search for the faith I'd lost. But it wasn't. I came back to Mt. Lebanon. I parked my car down by the ball fields near the pool and walked the long hill up to the houses. I passed the place where Ilsa and I saw the lovers under the tree. I cut through a yard and came up on our old house from the back, right down Parkridge Lane, right up to the point where I'd left, completing a long loop. There was a man in our old backyard, raking under the bushes where I'd hid the day we'd moved in. They were just about to bud. It must've seemed strange to him to see a wild-haired kid standing still in the lane during a school day, gawking at his house. He asked if I was lost. It made me laugh. Not softly or wistfully, but in a kind of mad eruption, like it had been building for a while. I forgot to reply until the man straightened up from his raking, and I saw his hard stare. "I used to live here," I answered, which wasn't an answer at all.

"You're kidding," he said with an odd sort of reverence. "We moved here last fall. I bet you know the house better than I do."

I wasn't going to say any more. All I wanted to do was look up at the high window behind me. But the man kept staring, waiting, it seemed, for something. "Do the Carlsons still live there?" I finally asked. He said yes, that was their name "And the daughter?"

"I saw her just last month," he answered, "playing in the snow." *Playing in the snow.* It seemed so unlikely, so hopeful. But then he added, "They had her all bundled up. She must've just learned to walk. She couldn't take more than a couple steps—"

I interrupted him. I said I meant the daughter. Ilsa. The one my age. He shook his head and said he thought I meant the baby. "Whose baby?" I snapped.

The man stiffened and tilted the handle of his rake like a sword. His voice was suddenly lower, "What's your name?" he asked me then. "I'll let them know you stopped by."

I shook him off and hurried away, back along the lane, down the hill, through the park, and to my car. I drove off, got on a highway west and just kept going. I didn't stop for anything more than food and gas until I saw a help-wanted sign outside of Denver. That was the first of I don't know how many odd jobs I've done— dishwasher, janitor, landscaping, construction, waiter, air cargo supply…now this. In a way, I never stopped driving. Talkeetna's the longest I've lived anywhere. Six years. Maybe that's because there isn't anywhere farther to go. Barrow? No thanks. The only option is to start heading back, and I'm not ready for that. I've been tempted. That's for sure. But there really isn't anything for me anywhere else. Like it or not, this is home. A guy could do worse. Still, I don't trust myself. Why do you think I took this job? If I get a wild hair, I can't just pack up and drive off. And I can't exactly walk out of here; I'd be grizzly chow in these mountains. This is the way I want it, apparently. It's the way it has to be.

Maybe it's better that I don't know what happened to Ilsa. What could I do about it anyway? I do wonder though. That little girl. The Carlsons were older than my parents. They would've been pushing fifty back then. It's more likely the kid was Bobby's. He would've been in his twenties. But what if it was Ilsa's? She would've had it in high school. How could that have happened? And why wasn't she around? I'm not fishing. Believe me. But if you happen to meet Ilsa Carlson on this quest of yours, will you tell her something for me? Will you tell her I'm sorry?

Never mind. I shouldn't have asked.

Let's go call your pilot.

QUEEN

THE BUCKLEYS, 1969-77
Told by Wes Carlson, Villa at Green Lake Estates, West Bloomfield, MI

If it's all the same to you, I'd rather raise the bed and do this right here. Can't the recorder catch what I say from the night stand? It's nice to offer to take me out. But you don't realize how hard it is to get me in that wheelchair. I'm dead weight. No help at all. They get me outside every Sunday, and it takes two aides, big guys, to lug me out of this bed. I've told them: it isn't worth the trouble. There's nothing to see outside but the front lawn and the road at the bottom of the hill. I can open my blinds and see more.

Did I mention you're the first guest I've had? Three years and not a soul. Can't say I'm surprised. I don't blame the family. It's been nearly 40 years since the divorce. Everyone said back then they never wanted to see me again. And they stuck to their guns. You've got to give them that much. I see you've dropped Carlson off your name. Not even the hyphen, eh? I guess I deserve that.

I know I said I wouldn't talk about the Buckleys. I could tell by the way you got quiet on the phone you weren't happy. I'm just worried that having me tell their story isn't in your best interest. It's a question of balance. I freely admit: I have no objectivity when it comes to Bill and Valda Buckley. And let's face it: no matter what I say, it won't change anyone's mind. Nothing short of an apology will, and even that's unlikely. Look: I can see how what I did hurt people, but I'm not ashamed. That's why I changed my mind. I know in my heart I'm not trying to get anything out of this. I don't expect to win anyone back or earn their forgiveness. I just want to tell the truth, as much as I know, as carefully as I can. If I'm going to be damned, I'd rather it was for what really happened than for what everyone thinks.

So I'll talk about the Buckleys. I don't know who you'll get to tell the Nethery's story. I wouldn't have been right for them any-way. I barely talked to the parents and didn't much like their kid, that Derek punk who was always hanging around your mom. I don't know what she saw in him. All I know is she seemed less squirrely after he moved away. Then again, we didn't have the greatest handle on her. I don't have to tell you that.

Is that thing on already? You need me to turn toward it? I can't talk much louder than this. I get out of breath. Okay. So where to start...I think it's fair to say Bill Buckley was the closest thing to a celebrity who ever lived on Vernon. You're, what, late thirties now? You weren't around when the Steelers were bad, back in the sixties, before Bradshaw and Mean Joe Greene and the Immaculate Re-ception. I mean really bad. Laughingstocks of the league. Buckley was a back-up linebacker for three seasons, when the team was at its worst. Not even a starter. But he was a character. Bulldog Bill Buckley. That's what they called him. He got kicked out of a game once for sneaking into the other team's huddle. And he's still the only defensive player in the NFL to attempt a drop kick. He inter-cepted Johnny Unitas toward the end of some meaningless blow-out, broke into the clear and decided to give it a shot. He nearly whiffed, fell flat on his back and sent the ball straight up in the air. It took the refs 10 minutes to figure out defenders couldn't do drop kicks. After the game, Bulldog told reporters he was just trying to have a little fun. That was Bill Buckley—a lousy player on a lousy team. But an absolute goofball, a complete hoot. You couldn't know Bill and not love him. The local media treated him like a big mascot, a loveable loser. Marv Throneberry or Bob Uecker. Those names don't mean anything to you. But you can look them up on your phone. You'll see what I mean.

Anyway, a local station hired Buckley after he retired and put him on their postgame show. He was a riot, especially when the Steelers lost. And that year, they lost a lot. I used to tune in after the final whistle just to hear him rail on the team's ineptitude. After that radio stint, you couldn't turn on the TV without seeing Bulldog Bill. He was in a slew of cheesy ads for car dealers, aluminum siding installers, appliance stores, you name it. But it was his spot for Smokestack Ale that made Buckley more than a local celebrity. Picture a group of guys hanging out at a backyard barbeque. Bill pokes his head around the corner of the house. He's eyeing a beer on the picnic table. When the guys raise their beers to toast each other, suddenly Bill's in the huddle, arm raised alongside theirs. They all cock their heads, then shrug and accept him. The announcer says, "Smokestack: the dark ale that sneaks up on you."

Did I mention Bill was black? I forgot that little detail, didn't I? Oh, and all the friends in the ad were white. If they played that ad now, people would be up in arms. They'd cry racism. They'd march on the brewery. But because it was Bill and because of his famous huddle spying caper—and, yeah, probably because of the racial undertones—people couldn't stop talking about that commercial. It was funny, but for reasons much more subversive than were ever intended. It had a bite to it, like something the Smothers Brothers might dream up. I know: more people you've never heard of. The upshot is, it got noticed in New York. Before you knew it, Bulldog Bill was doing national commercials. Then he was on *What's My Line?* Then he got a bit part on *The Mod Squad.*

I'm pretty sure they were the first black family in the neighborhood. At least, I don't remember any other black kids running around before the Buckleys. He had three of them. Willie was about 12, and he was in your mom's grade. Ike was a few years younger, and they had a baby girl, Hope. Then there was Valda, Bill's wife. I don't remember meeting her until years after the Buckleys moved in. Either she was holed up with her kids or overshadowed in all the excitement over her husband.

For a star on the rise like he was, Bill was much friendlier and more big-hearted than anyone had a right to expect. He'd walk the neighborhood like anyone else, lounge around the public pool, show up at local events. And everywhere he went, he'd go out of his way to introduce himself, like he was the nobody and you were someone special. As if that wasn't enough, he even coached the sixth-grade little league football team, although that didn't go so well. You'll know why in a minute.

I got to know Bill better than most, not so much because he lived next door, but because a buddy of mine who lived at the end of Youngwood, Paul Raymond, let Bill into our monthly poker game. He was fun to have in the group—always brought a lot of booze, told great stories, kidded around like he was one of us. Best of all, he was a terrible card player. He took a lot of dumb risks, was easy to read, and hardly ever came out ahead. He knew he wasn't any good; he just didn't care. If he dropped fifty bucks, big deal. To Bill, poker wasn't about the money. It was about hanging out with regular Joes, feeling normal for a while.

That game was how the trouble started. One night, Bulldog showed up with a couple fifths of Jack and said we had some cele-brating to do. He'd just gotten a full-time part on a sitcom. What's the one that took place in the high school? *Room* something or other. So we started drinking. Hard. And true to form, Bill started losing. He kept peeling fives off a big roll of cash, throwing them in on wild longshots, and laughing off his losses. Toward the end of the night, we switched from blackjack to five-card stud, where everyone's first card's down, then the next four are dealt up so all of us can see them.

I was dealing the hand that set everything off. After the second up card, there were three of us in, Bulldog, me, and Monty Flynn. I didn't know him that well, but his wife was friends with your Granny Emma. He was a rough sort, stone-faced, bitter sense of humor. He owned a car dealership and seemed to be doing pretty well for himself. One thing's for sure; Monty was the card shark of the group. He always won. That pissed a few guys off, and they quit coming. But Monty always found somebody new to sit at the table. In fact, he was the one who invited Bill. His kid played on that little league team Bill coached.

Anyway, we have this hand going, and the pot's pretty big. Bill's showing two tens, Monty's got a king, nine, and I have two threes. Remember: there's a down card, so nobody knows exactly what the other guy has. Bulldog bets twenty bucks. That's a lot for us; we're usually playing 50 cent, dollar bets. But everyone's drunk at this point. Monty matches, and I decide, I'll go in too. On the third up card, Bill gets the three I want, Monty gets another nine and I get a seven, but that's my down card. I'm looking at the table, thinking I've got a pair of tens and nines beat. Then Bill says, "What the hell," peels off a hundred-dollar bill and slaps it on the pot. This is around 1975. A hundred dollars is a lot of money. Five times as much as today. Monty mulls it over, same blank face as always, and matches. Now it's my turn. I don't know odds, but I probably got this. Still, it's a hundred bucks, so I fold.

Good thing too, because on the last card up, Bill gets another 10 for three of a kind and Monty gets a king for two pair. Bulldog can't contain himself. He's whooping and pumping his fist. Meanwhile, Monty's sitting there, still as stone, cold eyes studying Bill. Bill's too drunk and happy to notice. He takes out his wad of cash, counts out three hundred bucks, and throws it on the pile with a big, shit-eating grin. Monty doesn't hesitate. He sees the three hundred and drops two more C notes on the pot. There's over a thousand dollars on the table. Big money. You could buy a Pinto with what's in that pot. Bulldog's grin collapses. His mouth goes slack. He cocks his head, scrunches his brow in numbed confusion, and squints at Monty's cards, trying to figure out how he could get beat. And that's when Monty knew he had him. For the first time ever, he betrays a little grin. The answer's obvious. Monty's down card was a king or a nine. He's got himself a full house. For some crazy reason, though, Bill can't see it. He keeps twisting his head around, like looking at the cards from different angles is going to unlock the secret. Then he finally shrugs and calls. Monty reaches out and turns over a king. Bulldog's eyes bug out like he never fathomed the possibility. Monty leans forward to rake in the pot.

That's when Bill turns over his down card: another 10. Everyone gasps and howls. Everyone but Monty. He's still hauling in the money he thinks he won, doesn't realize he's been beaten. Cool as can be, Bill says, "Sorry, my man." Monty doesn't get it until Bill waggles the fourth 10 in his face. He falls back in his seat, glares at Bill all gape-mouthed. And I'll never forget what he said. "I'll be damned. You fucked me." Like Bill had known what he was doing all along. Like he'd been playing dumb for weeks to make this one score. Of course, nothing could've been further from the truth. Bill fooled Monty not by disguising how shrewd he was, but by blatantly displaying his ignorance. Nobody whoops it up when he's about to lay down a three-hundred-dollar bet. And nobody has to think so long about calling when he has four tens.

"Shit Monty," Bill replied. "You fucked yourself. I couldn't figure how you thought you had me beat."

It was the wrong thing to say. You could see the blood leap into Monty's face. Worse than losing, now he was getting humiliated. But that was Bill; just as bad at reading people as he was at reading cards. The game ended right there. Monty grabbed the bottle of whiskey and polished off the last few fingers. Then he lurched up from the table, mumbled something like, "I guess you're better'n me," and staggered for the door. Bulldog gathered his money and went after him. Then I heard glass hitting the floor.

It took a while to collect my losings. When I caught up to everyone in the entryway, Paul was kneeling, cleaning up a big porcelain cross Monty had shouldered off the wall, and Bulldog was trying to convince him to accept a ride home. "You're going to wind up face down in somebody's yard," Bill argued. "Come on, Monty. Don't do a fool thing just 'cause you're mad."

"That's what I mean," Monty wagged his finger at Bill, swaying above Paul. If Bill had nudged him, he would've gone over Paul ass over elbows, like that prank when someone gets on hands and knees behind you. Monty was too drunk and gloomy to do anything dumb like take a swing. And Bill was feeling sorry. It was dawning on him how much he'd taken Monty for. I came between them, holding a fistful of bills, the money I'd left on the table, easily a hundred bucks. "You forgot this," I said to Monty. That baffled him enough to calm things down and get him in the car.

We would've been better off walking. Bill was in no shape to drive, and neither Monty nor I was sober enough to take the keys ourselves. But this was the Seventies, before anyone paid much attention to drunk driving. Plus, it was all in the neighborhood, a few hundred yards to manage. So we took off in Bill's Continental, and he seemed fine all the way up Youngwood. But once we were coasting down the long slope on Mayfair, Monty started grumbling and Bill started eyeing him in the rearview mirror. I didn't catch what Monty said, but Bill must've. "If it's going to piss you off so much," Bill said, "you can have your money back. It's no big deal. I got a lucky hand."

"I don't want your fucking money," Monty snapped. "Shit. It's all the same with you people, playing dumb when it suits you."

There was an ugly silence. The car floated down Mayfair, gathering speed. I looked over at Bill. I knew what I thought Monty meant; I was hoping Bill didn't think the same thing. Finally, in a voice that was lower and more menacing than I ever heard out of him, Bill said, "What the fuck's that supposed to mean?"

We rounded the curve on Mayfair that led down the steep hill to Cedar. Monty's street, Vee Lynn, was near the bottom, angling off to the right. I remember thinking when we made the curve everything was going to be okay. Monty would be out of the car before things got out of hand. I was wrong. "Whatever you think it means," Monty answered.

Bill glared at him in the rearview. I could feel the force of the hill pushing up in my stomach. Vee Lynn was coming up fast. It suddenly dawned on me we weren't going to make the turn. I figured Bill had decided to sail past and double back. Next thing I knew, he was wrenching the steering wheel. The Continental hit the far curb on Vee Lynn and went airborne. I don't know how many times it flipped. It happened so fast. There was a sensation of spinning and falling, this sudden fracturing from the moment. Then we landed hard on the driver's side to a burst of glass, teetered, and went upside down onto the roof.

We managed to climb out of the car and found ourselves in the driveway of the last house before Cedar. We'd been thrown around pretty hard, but no one was badly hurt. Monty kept clocking his arm and rubbing his neck. I did get an ugly gash on my forehead—you can still see the scar up here by my hairline. If Bulldog was hurt, he didn't show it. He just circled the car, rubbing his chin like an insurance assessor. Before we had a chance to talk between ourselves, the driveway lit up and the owner of the house was standing above us, staring at the retaining wall we'd knocked over. "Holy shit," he kept saying. "Holy shit."

I have to give Bill credit. He was pretty fast on his feet. He gave the guy a line about swerving to miss a deer and he bought it. Monty kept grumbling in the background, but he was the drunkest of us, and the owner didn't pay him any attention. By this time, he'd figured out who Bulldog was and had softened up. When someone crashes in your yard, it's a problem. When a celebrity does it, it's an occasion. Still, Monty wouldn't shut up, so Bill told me to get him out of there and walk him home.

I got back in time to see Bill handing the owner a wad of cash—most of the winnings from that last hand, I'm sure. They shook hands and Bill crossed the lawn before I could join them. As we walked home, Bill gave me a few sketchy details of what transpired. He said he couldn't convince the guy not to call the cops. There was too much damage to the retaining wall. But he got him to see that it wouldn't be good for Bill to have to talk with the police that night. So he gave him some money to wait until the morning, like he'd just woken up and discovered the car there. I asked a few questions. It didn't seem to me like leaving an accident was all that much better for Bill's reputation than just owning up to drunk driving. But I didn't get any real answers.

A couple days later, an article came out in the *Pittsburgh Press* about the accident, buried a few pages deep. Bill admitted it was his car. How could he not? But he said a friend had been driving when they jumped the curb. He told the reporter he wasn't going to say who it was because he still felt responsible and didn't see the point in dragging someone down. There was no mention of the police, no speculation of drinking, no statement from the home-owner. And, amazingly, that was all that came out in public. Imagine that happening today. Imagine Ben Roethlisberger leaving his car upside down in someone's driveway. You think he'd get away with a three-paragraph story buried in the local paper?

But Bill did. He never suffered for it. I told Granny about the accident the next morning. I had to say something; there was that gash on my head. Besides, I didn't think there was anything to hide. It wasn't me driving. Sure, I was drunk, but it was poker night. Granny was ticked off. What wife wouldn't be? And she didn't like that I refused to go to the hospital because it might cause problems for Bill. She couldn't fathom why I felt the need to protect him. His celebrity never impressed her. More than once, she complained it wasn't right that someone could afford a house on Vernon just for playing football—and being pretty bad at it to boot. Still, even for Granny, the accident was no more than a dumb but dismissible case of boys being boys. That was until the article came out. Then she started harping on me: what if the police insisted Bill give up the driver's name? Maybe he already had, and it just didn't make it into the papers. What kind of a friend was I protecting who was so quick to blame others? For a few days, I wondered the same thing.

It didn't help to run into Monty. He was waiting for me after a Lebo basketball game. "Can you believe that black son of a bitch blamed us?" he fumed. Then he dredged up the poker game. "I know that bastard cheated me." Next, he went on about what a lousy coach Bulldog had been. "He stopped playing my kid at QB, gave every snap to that lazy-ass Ike, and we never scored again." Finally, he took aim at Valda. "She's a piece of work. At the games, she'd always sit off by herself, with this uppity look on her face, chin jutting out like some African queen. Couldn't make it any plainer that she didn't want to be around us."

I should've said something right then, should've had the guts to call Monty out for his bigotry. I have no excuse. Some people my age say it was just the times. Back when we grew up, if you were Irish, you were a mick. If you were Italian, a wop. A Jew was a kike.

And black? Well…that's just the way it was. Nobody got worked up about it. Maybe that's true. But that was 60, 70 years ago. Today, it's either the license of a bigot or the excuse of a coward. We live in the here and now. And as long as we're alive and have all our marbles, we have to grow with the times, do what's right at the moment. I'm not a big one for political correctness, but I am for moral correctness. It wasn't right for Monty to say those things. It wasn't right for me to stand there and let him say it.

Worse than that, Monty's smears had their effect. The first time I really talked with Valda, not just saying hi from across the lane, but up close, I had that picture Monty painted in my mind—high and mighty, contemptuous. Can you imagine? Six, seven years and I'd never bothered to approach her. Anyway, there used to be a public mailbox in the front yard of the Buckley's house. One day, I was out there when Valda came striding across the yard. Right off, I noticed the tilt of her head. I remember thinking, so that's what Monty means. There really was a prideful jut to her chin. I could see how someone might say it was regal. And I'd be lying if I said I didn't notice the color of her skin. It was smooth and shiny, like the buckeyes that fell off the tree in our backyard. The idea Monty had planted in my head didn't go away until she was just on the other side of the mailbox, eyes locked onto mine. I saw then the fear they held, the strain it took to keep them still. I realized that what she was doing there, out in broad daylight with me, and what she was about to say, was an act of bravery.

She held her hand out over the mailbox. "All this time, and we haven't really met," she said. I laughed and took her hand. "Bill was really sorry about the accident," she added as we shook. "The article too. But he had to say something." I said I understood, though I really didn't. "And he still feels bad he let you drive." The words rushed out like they'd been pressing on her the whole time.

"Let *me* drive?" I was incredulous.

"He said he should've known," Valda went on, "drunk as he was, that you were too." I told her I wasn't that drunk. She must've read it as defensiveness. "I'm not judging," she said. "I just wanted to say, Bill won't give you up. He's a man of his word."

By this point, I wasn't even trying to disguise my annoyance. I think I grumbled something sarcastic like, "Isn't that a relief."

"He would've told you this himself," she said, "but he had to fly out yesterday and won't be back for a month." Her eyes broke contact and drifted away. Mad as I was, I could still see her pain. I ascribed it then to the prospect of missing him. Maybe if I bothered to commiserate, I would've discovered it was more than that.

I asked if it was for the show. At least I did that. She nodded and gave me a weak smile, almost as an afterthought. I should've felt compassion, but her distress made me anxious. I just wanted to end things. "You must be very proud," I fumbled.

She sniffled and smiled again, this time with no effort to hide her sadness. "That's what everyone tells me," she said. Then she was the one hurrying away.

That was also the first time Granny saw me with Valda. When I came inside, she was looking out the window that faced the Buckley's yard. "What was that all about?" she asked.

I had no reason to lie at that point, so I said, "Get this: she told me how bad Bill felt for asking *me* to drive that night." Emma gave a told-you-so snort. It bothered me. "So he fed his wife the same story he told the papers. What's so surprising about that?"

She leveled me with that glare of hers. You know the one. "He lied to her," she said. "He *lied* to her." All I could do was shrug my concession. That seemed to appease Emma. She changed subjects. "It looked like you upset her."

And here's where I can see someone might've thought that I— I won't say "lied"—but maybe wasn't entirely forthright. There's a difference. I just said, "Oh?"

"You didn't see her walk away," Granny said. "She was on the verge of tears."

"Maybe I didn't disguise my anger well enough," I offered.

Your grandma eyed me through a long silence. "Good," she finally pronounced.

Things went quiet after that, not settled so much as held in suspense. Winter came. Bill was still filming in California. You'd see the kids now and then. Their oldest was a senior like Ilsa. He took out the garbage, got the mail. And Ike played in the yard once when it snowed. But I rarely saw Valda, just glimpses of her coming and going. It worried me. After one snowfall, they didn't shovel. No big deal. Once the plow comes down the lane, there's just a little strip left. But it stayed there for a week. And their walkway wasn't done either. So next time we got a dusting, I took care of it for them. Easy. Fifteen minutes tops. When I came inside, your grandma asked, "What'd you do that for?"

"It's what neighbors do," I fired off a ready answer, even though I'd never done that for anyone before.

When I finally saw Bill and Valda together again, it was this otherworldly April weekend. Everything had just started to bloom, but the temperature was pushing 90. I came home from work to find the lane crowded with cars. There was a party going on at the Buckleys. The backyard was overrun with kids, and a handful of couples were sitting around a grill, drinking beers and whooping it up. They were all black. That didn't bother me so much as how loud they were. Then again, I'd heard the same sort of commotion at other neighbor's parties. So maybe it was that they were black.

Rowdy as things were, I wondered if Bill had gotten some old Steeler pals together. I invented an excuse to go and check. It was time to set up the outdoor furniture anyway. I could've done it in a couple trips. But I took five. Each time, I spied over the hedges. These weren't buddies from Bill's playing days. He was standing off by himself, glaring at the gathering with folded arms. Valda was behind a man and woman near the grill. She had a hand on each of their shoulders and she was laughing. Her face was tilted to the sky, mouth open and wide, teeth flashing. These were her people. Her family.

Once it got dark, the party got louder. The adults strayed out into the yard, chasing each other, colliding in drunken barks and shrieks. I couldn't tell who was who and whether it was all in fun or hostile. It didn't help that Granny Emma was out of sorts about it too. As night wore on, she went from suggesting "We should do something about this," to insisting, "You need to call the police. Now!" I started coming around to her way of thinking. But it wasn't even 10 yet. And I was hoping old Dan York on the other side of the Buckleys would cave before me and make the call.

Then we heard gravel kicking up in the lane, and your grandma was sure she saw shadows drifting through our hedges. I had the phone in my hand—but suddenly car doors were opening, and kids were piling into the backseats. We watched from our darkened kitchen window as Valda hugged her children before they too climbed into the cars. Bill stood behind everyone, fists on hips, flashing waves when he had to. One by one, the headlights swung away, and it was as quiet as any other night. Granny let out a relieved sigh. "I wonder what *that* was all about," she said, before heading upstairs. I kept watching a little longer. Valda stayed in the lane well after the cars had gone, her back to Bill. Then she turned and went to him slowly. When she was beside him, she put her hand on his chest and held it there. His fists stayed on his hips. His face was stone. Valda dropped her hand, bowed her head, and walked with a slump toward their house. Only after the back door closed did Bill turn and follow. I backed away, into the protection of our dark house and repeated to myself what Emma had said, only for very different reasons. What *was* that all about?

Next morning, I was up early, in the dim light of dawn. I had a cup of coffee and was standing on the porch above the lane, when I heard this clamor over at the Buckleys. I turned to see Valda getting shoved out the double doors that led to their den. She was completely naked, struggling against Bill to get back inside. I didn't see his face, just his huge arms and outstretched hands. She was begging as she clawed at him. "Please, honey, please!" Then, with one hard shove, Valda staggered backwards. The doors slammed shut. She yanked at the handles, but the doors never opened. Finally, she stopped and hung her head, her back to me like that, naked and exposed in the hazy morning sun. It was an electric moment, so out of place, so surreal. It might surprise someone your age, with everything that swirls around the internet, but we didn't have much occasion to see nakedness back then. I can't deny, that was part of what captivated me. But it was more than that. It was the unexpectedness of it, the sheer singularity, like some otherworldly creature had appeared out of nowhere in our sleepy neighborhood—and I was the only one graced to witness it. To this day, when I think of that morning, I think about how beautiful Valda was, how suddenly I was taken by that beauty.

I don't know how long I watched her standing there, head hung as in prayer, back muscles shuddering. At some point, she straightened and cocked her head. Then she turned, at first just glancing over her shoulder. But once she noticed me on my porch, Valda swung all the way around. She tilted her chin up—the same way, I'm sure, that set Monty off—and stared me down, unflinching, unashamed. Maybe I should've hid my face and hurried into the house. But it didn't feel right. Finally, though, and without any forethought, I bowed my head, as if in deference, and went inside, leaving her the dignity of suffering in private.

I've never told anyone about that moment. I suspect Valda hasn't either. But if the fact of her banishment was never known, the reasons for it became public only weeks later. Stories started circulating in tabloids about Bill's involvement with the lead actress of the sitcom he was on. Then came news that Bill had filed for divorce and planned to marry the starlet. None of these reports said a word about the damage Bill's desertion had done to his ex-wife and children. The family's plight was nullified in the glare of celebrity. None of our other neighbors expressed any concern about the jilted family's misfortune either, at least not to me. But Granny recognized how hard Valda and the kids would have it. The first time we heard the news, she sighed and said, "That poor woman and those poor kids. How could someone do that?"

I appreciated Emma's instinct for sympathy. And I used it as license later in the spring. We decided to have a party for the kids who were graduating from high school that year. It wasn't the sort of party they have now, catering to one kid with elaborate displays from kindergarten to the cap and gown ceremony, and the heavy expectation of college donations. It was just a simple get-together among close neighbors whose kids were all sharing the same rite of passage. One day, when I saw Valda clipping blossoms off the lilac bush in her front yard, I hurried out and pretended to be surprised to run into her. It was the first time we'd talked since I'd seen her naked. If Valda was harboring any embarrassment, she didn't show it. On the contrary, she gave me a wide smile and answered my awkward greeting with what seemed like a considered reply. "All in all, everything's just fine, Wes. And you?"

Imagine that. She called me by my name. And she looked right at me. Straight into my eyes. There was nothing of herself in that look, none of the pain I imagined she'd been suffering nor the bitterness she had the right to hold. I told her we were having a party to celebrate the kids' graduation and invited her and Will to stop by. She stared at me blankly. I couldn't tell if she was surprised, offended, or moved by the invite. She had a better poker face than Bill. "Ilsa says everyone likes Will," I threw in. I had no idea if that was true. The only change in her expression was a slight tilt to her head. I started to worry. Maybe Will hadn't graduated. Maybe he and Ilsa didn't get along.

"Thank you," Valda said at last. She mustered a soft smile and headed inside with her lilacs.

I broke the news to Granny right after that. She couldn't very well argue over a simple friendly gesture. Still, there was a bite to the way she said, "How thoughtful of you." I let it go. She had a right, I figured, to be suspicious. After all, it wasn't like me to be extending social offers.

When people started showing up to the party, I was so busy setting up chairs outside, getting the beer on ice, and making drinks that I didn't stop to think about who all was coming and what might happen when we threw them together. I remember running into Monty outside. He slapped me on the back and said they missed me at poker. Even still, I never considered that I ought to shield Valda from him. I blame myself for that.

She surprised me by knocking on our front door. Everyone else had just come around back. It was lucky I happened to be inside. When I opened our door, she was turning away. I caught this fleeting disappointment in her eyes, like she'd nearly escaped, but was trapped now. "You came!" I gushed, grateful and welcoming, throwing out my arms. I was trying to put her at ease.

"Will went around back," she said, ignoring my enthusiasm. "But that isn't proper."

"Probably not." I laughed, waving her in. Valda wasn't exactly dressed for the party. She had on a white button-down shirt and a pair of black pants, creased and flaired in a fashion that was restrained for the times. She could've been going to work. I shouldn't have said it, but I did anyway: "You look nice." It was a simple observation—a polite compliment, I thought—and it happened to be true. I could see I'd embarrassed her. She kept glancing to the back door, like she couldn't wait to reach the refuge of the party. In hindsight, it was a mistake to oblige her. "Why don't you head outside," I said. "I'll make you a drink and join you in a second." She seemed relieved and asked for a rum and coke.

While I was making the drink, it dawned on me how awkward Valda might feel to walk into a yard of people she barely knew, all of whom were white. So I was hurrying. But I didn't get out there fast enough. Valda was standing alone at the far edge of our porch, looking out over the yard, behind a handful of laughing men. One of them was Monty. My chest seized even before he stepped away from his circle and put a hand on her back. It all happened so fast. "Hey, I didn't know Wes had hired help," he bellowed, holding out his empty glass. "Here, sugar. I'll have another Seven and Seven."

Next thing I knew, Monty and I were toe to toe. "What's your problem?" I barked.

"What do you mean?" Monty said with a smirk.

I poked his chest. "You know exactly what I mean."

He threw up his hands. "Hey, it was an honest mistake."

"Like hell."

By this time, I was aware we were drawing attention. So was Monty. "Leave it alone," he growled, his voice low and menacing. If he meant to scare me off, it had the opposite effect.

I put my hands on his chest. "We're going to talk," I said.

And I pushed him, not hard, just enough to let him know we needed to have this out somewhere else. He slapped down my hand. Then I really shoved him. I wish I could say I didn't know he was so close to the top of our porch steps. But I did. I have no excuse, other than blind anger. The force of my blow knocked Monty back. His foot missed a step. He toppled off the porch, banged his head on the cement below, and didn't move. I didn't fully realize what I'd done until I saw blood behind his head. There was a moment, after someone cried out to call for an ambulance, that I was worried I'd killed him. But when he started groaning, I wheeled around and went inside, walked upstairs, shut myself in our bedroom, and waited for everyone to leave.

I knew I was going to catch hell from Emma. I didn't care. I figured once I told her the full story, she'd see my way of thinking. The party broke up soon after I shoved Monty off the porch. For about an hour, I heard muffled voices coming from our living room. One of them was your mom's. I could've listened to what they were saying if I'd put my ear to the vent. But I threw a pillow over it instead. I didn't want to know what people thought. I knew how I felt. That was all that mattered. The house was silent for a long time before Emma came upstairs. I burrowed under the covers, hoping she'd think I was asleep. She stood over me for a while before saying, "Do you realize what you've done?"

"What *I've* done?" I shot back, coming up out of the blankets.

"What were you thinking?" she cried out then, her voice thick with despair.

I was unmoved. "I was thinking that no guest of ours should have to be subjected to the kind of slur Monty made. I was thinking we were the kind of people who stood up to that."

Your grandma defended Monty. "He said it was an honest mistake. He was thrown off by what she was wearing. He didn't mean it to come out the way it did."

I huffed in the darkness. "That's all bullshit," I told her. "Monty knew exactly who she was. And he knew exactly what he was doing. Trust me."

"I can't believe that," Emma declared.

"Well, there's a lot you don't know," I said. "A lot of shit. Ever since that car accident."

She fell silent, and I remember wondering if that was the end of it. But then she said, "None of it excuses what you did. You split his head open. In front of all our friends. They'll never look at us the same way again."

"I don't care about them," I yelled.

"But you care about her," Emma said in a broken whisper.

I thought of denying it. But I didn't. "I guess so."

The air went out of her. She backed away and collapsed in our corner chair. "How will we ever get past this?" she wondered.

All I said was, "I don't know."

We *did* try that summer. We really did. I booked a hurry-up trip to Venice. We spent a week cruising the canals, wandering alleys, seeing relics, drinking wine. It was like a dream, one sad, beautiful dream. There we were, surrounded by the whole allure of romance, immersed in it, seeing it, touching it—yet somehow incapable of feeling it. Don't get me wrong. We enjoyed ourselves. But everything was tinged with a weary melancholy. Between the heat and our misery, we seemed removed from the moment, tourists in the purest sense, taking it all in yet not belonging.

Then we were cruising down Vernon again, coming back from the airport. Like nothing ever happened. As I turned into our driveway, the *For Sale* sign in the Buckley's yard swung across the windshield. I paused on it for hardly an instant, just enough to register the *SOLD* sticker, then lurched up the drive. While we waited for the garage door to open, Emma said, "I knew it." I wasn't sure if she meant that she knew they would move or that my hesitation showed I was still stuck on Valda. Either way, I didn't care. I knew what I was going to do—and the damage it would bring.

The only criminal act I committed was bribing our mailman. And you could argue even that was an innocent exercise is cutting out the middleman. When I intercepted him a day after our return and asked for the Buckley's forwarding address, he said I should send a letter to the old address with the words "Return Service Requested" on the envelope. I said that seemed like a pretty round-about way to do it since he was standing right in front of me, and would 10 dollars help expedite the process? He said more like 20. I paid it and got the address. 74 Dwight Avenue, Pontiac, Michigan. I made the decision right then to go. I was selling radio spots at the time for a company that repped stations all over the country. We had WJR in Detroit. Every year, I'd go up there and give a pitch. This wasn't the right time—until that moment. When I told your grandma I had to fly to Detroit for a last-minute meeting, she must've known I was lying. I never had to make emergency trips. But she didn't call me on it.

So one afternoon in the dog days of August, I found myself puttering down Dwight Avenue in a rental car, scanning houses for addresses. It must've seemed odd for the kids playing in the yards and the adults fanning themselves on the porches to see a white man cruising slowly down their street. I know how I felt, doors locked, sitting up straight, peeking under the visor. Valda's house was between an empty lot and a boarded-up apartment complex. It was small, but it had two vaulting gables, and the brown brickwork was done in a parquet pattern. If you had placed it on Vernon Drive, no one would've looked twice.

As I got out of the car, people on the porch across the street stood to get a better look. I didn't know what else to do but nod. Valda's front door was caged with iron bars. There wasn't a door bell, so I fit my fist between the bars and knocked. Nothing stirred. I had this sudden dread I'd come all that way for nothing. I pounded harder. Finally, I heard steps coming, the door unlocking. It opened on a heavy-set man I recognized from when Valda's family visited. He thrust out his chin. "Who're you?" I told him I was Valda's neighbor in Pittsburgh. He glared and said, "So?"

"So I need to talk to her about something," I started. Then it came to me. "About Bill."

He stared me down then stepped away and shouted for Valda. I wish I could describe the look on her face when she saw me. She was at once surprised, bewildered, and moved. At least, that's what I thought. "What in the world are you doing here?" she wondered.

I didn't have a good answer. "We never said goodbye," was the best I came up with. She folded her arms with wary regard. "And there was something I never told you," I tried again. "About Bill. Something you should know." She waited. Like I should tell her right there. "Can we go somewhere?" I pleaded.

Valda's eyes wandered past me. When I turned, there were more neighbors watching now. That must've made up her mind. "Wait here," she said, leaving me at the door. I heard a short, muffled squabble, then Valda came hurrying back. "Half an hour," she said, pushing open the iron frame and bounding past me down the steps. As I hustled over to unlock the passenger door, she waved to her neighbors. I scurried around to the driver's side head down, started the car, backed out, and sped away. Valda burst out laughing. "You can slow down now, Wes," she said. "There's no mob coming for you." I must've still looked rattled when I glanced over. She howled again and rocked in the seat. "You should see yourself!" she said, practically in tears. "You're the whitest white man I ever saw." I couldn't help but laugh along.

We went to a dim, swanky bar on the outskirts of town named Brandy's. It had those red, half-circle leather booths, and we slid into the one farthest back, out of sight from everyone. The place was busy, considering the work day wasn't over. And I couldn't help but notice it was a pretty even mix of black and white. I figured this was why Valda brought me here—and not for some devotion to spirits, although we did order some pretty stiff cock-tails. As we waited for them, Valda an arm's length away on the arcing seats, me fiddling with the ash tray, she said, "You came all this way to tell me something about Bill..."

I tried to shrug it off. "I was in town anyway. On business."

"Like I give a damn about Bill," she interrupted.

Our drinks came. Valda gazed hard into hers. "You remember that car accident Bill and Monty and I got in?" I started.

She stopped swirling. "So Monty was the other one?"

You didn't know that?" She shook her head. "I know Bill told you I rolled the car, but the truth is, he was the one driving."

She was silent for a while. Then she took a long drink and shook her head with a bitter sigh. "Why aren't I surprised?"

"I thought you should know," I replied. And suddenly there was nothing else in front of us but what I really came for. "And I felt...bad. You know," I stumbled, "with the whole Monty prob-lem. At the party. We never got a chance to talk about that."

"What's there to say?" she challenged me. I was at a loss. I tried a couple times to explain but ended both with exasperated huffs. "Were you looking for me to thank you?" Valda pushed. "Is that it? You want me to tell you what you did was brave? That you were righteous?"

"No!" I barked, slamming my fist on the table. Valda's eyes shifted away and across the bar. "That isn't it," I insisted. Then I got quiet and thought about it. "I don't know. Maybe that *is* it. God knows nobody else is happy with me."

Valda put her hand on mine. "I didn't mean to come off ungrateful," she said. "Bad as things were, it *was* nice to have someone stand up for me."

I seized on what she said. "That's the point, Valda. That's why I came. Because I care. And it makes me feel good. Yeah, part of it *is* probably selfish, just being proud I had it in me to do what was right. But it's more than that. It's more."

The waitress interrupted then, poking her head around the high booth. Valda motioned for another round, and the girl was gone before I could even weigh in. "You don't have to say this, Wes," she said, downing what was left of the drink in front of her.

"Yes, I do. I won't get past this if I don't. I care about you. I can't help it. I can't stop thinking about you. And I knew I wouldn't until I came and told you."

Valda sat there eyeing me, lips sucked in, head shaking. Then she shoved my shoulder. "What do you think's gonna happen?" she asked.

"What do you mean?"

"Come on Wes," she said, getting to the point I couldn't. "I mean you and me. Isn't that what *you* mean?" Of course it was. "Let's be real," she went on. "We're 10 years apart and hundreds of miles. You're married, I'm divorced. You're white, I'm black."

The waitress reached in quickly with the drinks, like she was afraid she'd heard more than she should. "I know," I conceded when she left. "It's impossible. Still…"

Valda shifted closer. She put her arm around me. "Are you my friend, Wes?" I nodded. "I've never had a white friend. Went to school with them, worked with them, partied with them. But never got close enough to think one was a friend." She leaned her forehead against my temple. "Now here you are," she whispered.

"Friends," I agreed.

She heaved a long sigh. I could feel it radiate through me. "Hell," she exclaimed, pulling her head away. "You're the only white man ever to see me buck-naked."

I glanced sidewise at her and grinned. "Lucky me."

She smiled back. "Lucky you."

We took our time with that last drink. Just sat there together, enjoying the silences as much as talking, meditating apart as much as laughing together. And when we left the bar into the soft blaze of that setting sun and I drove her back, kids were still running in the yards and elders were still watching from the porches. But when we eased to a stop in her driveway, Valda didn't get out right away. I looked over at her. She was already looking at me. Then she put her hand on my knee. I welled up so fast, it caught my breath. "I'm going to miss you," I said in my anguish.

Valda heaved a sigh and smiled sadly. "Stay brave," she said. Then she leaned over and kissed me. I reached for her face. She broke free, got out of the car, hurried up her porch steps, unlocked the door, and disappeared. I sat there for a long moment. Then I drove away, utterly shattered. Yet strangely, blessedly, alive.

There was no going back after that. Nothing could put me back together the way I'd been. Emma and I didn't break up right away, as you know. We stayed together another year or so, looking after you until your mom was ready to come home. Don't take that the wrong way. You weren't a burden; you were a Godsend. Both of us needed to love—everyone needs to love—and since we couldn't love each other, Granny and I poured all our love into you. You might've been too young to appreciate that, and I'm sure it was too long ago to remember. But you should know it now. You were greatly, greatly loved by your grandma. And by me. You still are.

I have a lot of trouble sleeping. It's a terrible curse for someone like me, bedridden, alone, undistracted. Sometimes, I wonder if it would've been better if I'd lost all my marbles. Sometimes, I wonder what would've happened if I hadn't fallen for Valda. Maybe Emma and I would've made it. Maybe I'd still be in the house on Vernon, closer to you and Ilsa and everyone else. But there's no point now in wondering.

I never did see Valda again. I tried a couple times, made a few phone calls, chased a few clues. I couldn't find her. I wonder about that sometimes too. But in all my brooding, through all these dark, inescapable nights, I always circle back to the same question: if I had to do it over again, would I change anything? And the simple, hard truth is, I wouldn't. I'd do it again.

I'd do it all again.

HELLION

THE DUNCANS, 1977-1981
Told by Beverly and Clay Kinman, The Korner Pub, Mt. Lebanon, PA

Y ou're saying you had no idea what the Duncans meant to our
family. And you expect me to believe that. Well, you might've
fooled my mom on the phone, but I don't buy it for a second.
Know what the giveaway was? Asking to speak with my brother.
Let's be honest: you look like someone who does her homework;
you know about the fire. You found out Clay was there with Lionel
Duncan and you want to talk to him. Because how can you resist
a fire? Never mind Clay barely knew the Duncans, and Dad forbade him from seeing Lionel. You're not really interested in docu-
menting the history of that house. You're digging for scandal.

I can appreciate that. Now let me be clear about why I'm here:
I don't want my family hurt in this. Clay has a certain viewpoint
that I don't share, and that would cause my mother a lot of heart-
ache that she's too old to revisit. Put it this way: if my father were
alive, you never would've gotten Clay's phone number, and I
wouldn't be sitting in this dive bar, drinking mystery wine and
trying hard to be polite. He might've told you something about the
Duncans, but it would've been vastly different from what Clay had
to say. And the conversation would've been over in a minute.

So. I'm all you're going to get. Clay won't show. Once I told
him I was tagging along, I knew he'd back out. We don't get along.

Never did, really. I'm eight years older, more of a third parent than a sister. And I was in college when Clay was going through his really serious troubles. Then we lost touch.

Never mind. We're here for the Duncans, right? You must know something about them. They were around in the late-Seventies. Just before Lionel would've gone to high school. I remember how relieved Dad was when they moved. He had a nickname for Lionel. Hellion. The first time I saw him, he was standing in the lane between your houses. I was looking out our bay window, and there he was, holding a gas can, a line of fire trailing behind him. He'd doused that road and lit it. He wasn't even watching the fire. His back was to it, like he was leading a procession, staring, almost defiantly, at the houses that faced him. At me. I backed away from the window. I was eight years older, and he even scared me.

But not Clay. He was fascinated with Lionel. I'm sure Dad's reaction had a lot to do with it. Kids are naturally curious about what they're forbidden. Still, when it came to Lionel Duncan, what parent wouldn't be overprotective? And what boy wouldn't be captivated? It all was there, right across the street—the seduction and danger of unbridled youth. When he wasn't lighting the driveway on fire, Lionel was racing his mini-bike around the yard, throwing rocks at the hornet's nest in our tree, climbing up on his roof and shooting off arrows. That actually happened while Mr. Duncan was mowing the lawn. He didn't do a thing. That bothered Dad more than Lionel's misbehavior.

You know about his hair, right? It was white. Not grey. Not blonde. White. I'm sure it was some sort of disease. I should've had more sympathy for him, but I didn't. It was such a part of who he was. I never thought of it as an affliction he couldn't help. It was more like something he'd done on purpose, another bad thing.

So let's talk about the fire. I take it I don't have to rehash the facts. I'm sure you found the article online as easily as I did. Lionel burned down part of the woods when he shot off a homemade potato launcher and it exploded. The potato hit Curtis Stallard in the face and broke his nose and eye socket. Clay helped Curtis out of the woods to St. Paul's, where they called the hospital, the fire department, and the police. That's about all you got out of the article. It came off like three kids goofing around. Clay was even the hero of the story, leading his friend to safety. There was more to it than that. Dad got the full story when he got Clay home. He found out Lionel had sucked Clay into building a fort in the woods, pressured him to sneak tools out of our garage. This was after Dad had told Clay he couldn't play with Lionel. That's what I mean about the hold this kid had on my brother.

That was part of the reason Curtis Stallard showed up. He was Clay's true friend, his protector in a way. Curtis was a year older but might as well have been 10. He was bigger than most adults, better than anyone at sports, and popular with nearly everyone—kids, parents, teachers. Curtis wouldn't have hung out with Clay if our fathers didn't work together. Dad had a lot of respect for Mr. Stallard. He was a gung-ho kind of guy and he'd clearly done the right thing with his kid. I'm sure Dad was hoping it would rub off on Clay. He invited the Stallards over all the time, helped the dad coach the boys' little league team, encouraged Clay to go down to the Stallards whenever he was bored. He might've pushed too hard. But the amazing thing is, it worked. Curtis took to Clay. They were good friends. At least before everything went crazy.

Curtis didn't like Lionel and the way he kept dragging Clay into trouble. The truth came out that Curtis went to the fort to get Clay before anything bad happened. As fate had it, Clay was the one who saved Curtis. Know anything about these potato launchers? Spud guns, they call them. They're made out of plumbing pipes, PVC. There's a long barrel that barely fits the potato, and a wide chamber you fill with hair spray. You put a hole in the chamber and fit a special lighter switch in it. Then, when you turn the switch, the hair spray ignites, and the potato rockets out. Like a cannon shell. You can't see anything until the potato hits something. Then it basically pulverizes. Imagine that hitting a boy's face. Imagine someone wanting to make a weapon like that. You know how easy it was for Lionel to build that gun? He told the police he got everything from the hardware store uptown and made it in his garage. Again, where were the parents? That's what Dad always wondered. Where was this kid's moral grounding?

　. . .

Well, look who decided to show up! I said you wouldn't come, Clay. I said my coming guaranteed it. But apparently some occasions matter more than family conflicts.

Nice to see you too, Bev. Have another chardonnay.

Oh, is that what this is? It just said "white" on the menu.

If I knew you were going to worm your way into this, I would've picked a spot more befitting your sophisticated tastes.

I was just starting to tell Ilsa here—sorry; that's your mom's name—Grace. I was telling Grace about how Lionel Duncan nearly blinded your best friend and burned down the Bird Park woods. But now that you're here—

Oh no. I was just a kid. I can't be expected to remember what happened the right way. That's what Dad always said. Please. Continue.

Suit yourself.

I will. And while you're telling the story, I'll go get a pitcher of beer. Grace, you look like you could use a refill.

What do you know? He actually showed. See what I mean about being difficult? He can't help it. He enjoys it too much. Let's get through this before he gets back. So. Curtis confronts Lionel at the fort. Lionel points the spud gun at him, and it goes off. That's what Lionel told the police. He didn't mean to shoot it. It just exploded in his hands, out the front *and* back. The potato smashed Curtis's face at the same time the chamber burst open in flames. Before they knew it, there was a fire and it was too big to stomp out. Curtis's face was bloody, and he could barely see. Lionel ran off and left Curtis and my brother to themselves. He told the police he was scared. He wasn't thinking straight. I don't doubt it. So with Lionel gone and the fire spreading, it was left to Clay to get Curtis to safety. Can you imagine? Someone so small and insecure leading someone that strong and confident out of harm's way? It *is* sort of hard to believe.

What's hard to believe?

Your heroics.

Ah yes. My heroics. You know what else is hard to believe? Guess what Lionel Duncan is doing with himself these days?

Not this.

Why not? Didn't we come here to talk about the Duncans? Isn't that why you called me? I would think you'd be interested in how Lionel ended up.

She wants to know about when the Duncans lived on Vernon. What happened after doesn't matter.

So it doesn't matter that Lionel was the brains behind every Microsoft operating system since Windows 95 and is worth, oh, nearly a billion dollars? And it doesn't matter that Curtis was a phone support monkey until he got fired last month, or that I've been a janitor my whole life? Good. What a relief. We can talk about our formative years without having to worry about what they formed. Because that's the way Dad would want it, right? That keeps the story in line with what he always believed. Lionel Duncan was the hellion who corrupted me. And that's the root of all my problems.

This is exactly why I told Mom I had to be here. You're bringing Dad into this.

No, I'm trying to keep Dad out of it. The story is bigger than he thought. If he were alive and knew what became of Lionel, don't you think that would change his mind about what happened—and how he reacted to it?

No. I don't.

So he wouldn't think twice about accusing Lionel of taking me down the wrong path. He wouldn't look at where that path led and conclude maybe he made a mistake?

You have no right to wonder what Dad would've thought. You wouldn't see him for 25 years. You couldn't even bother to be there when he died.

And why do you think that is?

I don't know, Clay. You tell me. What possible reason did you have to punish him?

Because I'm sick, Bev. I know it. Mom knows it. Dad would never admit it. And that's why you won't either.

We all know you're sick, Clay. How can you not be with all the shit you've pulled?

Yeah, but here's the difference. You think I did that shit because I wanted to. You and Dad never understood. I did it because I couldn't help it. Let me tell you something about Lionel Duncan. That's why we're here, right? People remember Lionel for all the crazy things he did—burning his driveway, dying the kid's pool red, blowing up Don Grierson's locker with an M80. No one remembers the crazy things people did to him. There was a whole gang of them. And Curtis was the ringleader. They used to sneak up behind him and drum on his head. One time in art, someone squeezed Elmer's Glue in his white hair. Another time in sixth grade, they took everything out of Lionel's desk and filled it with tampons. Mean shit.

But here's the thing. He never got mad over any of it. He'd just laugh it off. I used to tell him when we were alone, I'd say, "Let's get those assholes back. Let's fuck them up." And he'd just smile and shake his head. "Aw, they're just having fun," he'd say. There wasn't a mean bone in Lionel's body. Now, do I think it was just a coincidence that Lionel chose to plant that M80 in Don Grierson's locker, one of the guys who'd been riding him the hardest? No. But the weird thing was, Lionel didn't do it out of malice. It was more like a friendly game. You got me, I'll get you. He didn't realize his capacity to scare people. That's because he didn't think the things he did were all that scary. To him, they were more like little experiments. He knew what he was doing, whether people thought so or not. Sure, he walked the line between thrills and danger. All the time. But he never stepped across it.

Except when he burned down Bird Park woods.

That was an accident.

Pointing a homemade potato cannon at Curtis Stallard and shooting him in the face…that was an accident?

Alright. I wasn't going to go into it. I was just going to come here and stick up for Lionel, tell the truth about who he really was, and spare Mom any more pain. But you have to keep pushing, don't you, Bev? You're good at that. So screw it. Besides, none of this will come as a surprise to Mom anyway, assuming you ever tell her, or she ever hears this.

You want to know what really happened in the woods? I'll tell you. First off, the fort was my idea. We used to watch Hogan's Heroes *after school— you know, the show where the POWs dug all those tunnels? One time I said, "We could make something like that." Lionel would've let it go if I wasn't so insistent. He didn't need a hiding place. I did. So I took Dad's shovel and started digging a hole. It was a few days before Lionel joined in. By the time we were done, we'd dug a pit deep enough to stand in and big enough to lie across. We covered up the hole with two-by-sixes and big sheets of particle board, then piled a bunch of dirt and leaves and twigs over top so it blended with the ground. But the best part was the entry. We found this big stump by the church, cut clean on both sides, and hollowed it out, just like the entry they had on* Hogan's Heroes. *Lionel had to sneak his dad's chainsaw out of their garage for that job. I remember how scared he was we'd get caught, what with that chainsaw whirring way up in the woods. But we got it done. And nobody came to check out the noise.*

I loved that fort. We rigged up a bunch of flashlights, so we could read comic books there and play cards or Stratego or Mastermind. Lionel dug out a little space in the wall to fit a tape recorder, and we'd play cassettes—the Clash, Joy Division, Ramones—over and over. I had my first beers down there, stole them out of Dad's mini-fridge in the garage.

That was the summer before eighth grade, about the time Dad started going on about heading down the right path. That's when he reached out to Mr. Stallard and asked him if Curtis could take me under his wing. I didn't want to play baseball. Dad made me. I didn't want to catch—I was afraid of the ball for god sakes—but Mr. Stallard gave me a mitt and put me behind the plate. I think Dad put him up to that too.

Funny thing is, as big a hard-ass as Dad thought Mr. Stallard was, he actually had a soft heart. Too soft when it came to Curtis. But you'd never know it unless you saw them alone together. This one afternoon, we're lying around watching Lost in Space *when Mr. Stallard comes home and starts trying to get us outside to take batting practice. He had a cage with an automatic pitching machine, nets, and everything rigged up in his backyard. I get up off the couch like we have no choice in the matter. This is back when I had the same impression of Mr. Stallard Dad did: that he was a my-way-or-the-highway Roger Ramjet kind of guy. But Curtis doesn't budge, just goes on watching TV like his old man wasn't even there.*

"Come on, Sport," his dad says. "Let's knock the old ball around."

"I don't want to," is all Curtis says.

Mr. Stallard looks at me, puts on that robust man's-man winning grin of his, and slaps me on the back. "Okay," he says. "More swings for Clay then."

"Like that's going to help," Curtis mutters.

"That's enough!" Mr. Stallard barks. I think to myself, uh-oh, now the old man's going to drop the hammer.

But no. Curtis just glares at us and huffs. "Lay off, Dad. Okay? I don't need to practice. I don't want to practice. I'm not going to fucking practice." That's what he says. Just like that.

There's this long, tense silence, with Mr. Stallard staring down at his son, working his jaw, Curtis looking off at the TV, and me standing there between them. Then Mr. Stallard claps his hands and says, "Awright. Your loss then. Come on, Kong. Let's go." That's what he called me. Kong Kinman, after Dave Kingman, the all-or-nothing slugger for the Cubs.

So you can understand now why I didn't want to hang out with Curtis. I hated Curtis. The feeling was mutual. When it was just us, he'd tease me, punch me in the arm, give me purple nurples. And all along, Dad thought everything between us was buddy-buddy. Shows how much of a handle he had on the real situation.

The same is true of Lionel's home life. He always thought Lionel's dad— good, old Fred—was a pushover. Couldn't control his kid. Wasn't hard enough on him. He had no idea. Once when Lionel and I were alone, he took me into his dad's office, that room in the back off the patio. He had a bunch of memorabilia there—rare beer steins from a factory that had gotten bombed in World War II, a rifle from the Civil War, a couple old pistols, and this sword, from all the way back to the Revolutionary War. Lionel said it was his dad's prized possession. He kept it in a glass case mounted to the wall. I asked if I could hold it. Lionel was nervous about taking the sword out of the case. But he did it anyway. When I got hold of it, I pulled the sword out of its leather scabbard and started waving it around. Lionel begged me to stop. He said if anything happened to that sword, his dad would know. He took it from me and slid it back in the scabbard. The whole incident couldn't have taken more than three minutes. But our timing was bad. As Lionel was setting the sword on the hooks in the case, his dad came bustling into the dining room on his way to the kitchen. When he saw us through the glass doors, he stopped dead in his tracks. I noticed him before Lionel did and gave him a nudge, but there was no time to hide what we'd done. Lionel was still holding the sword.

"What are you doing?" Mr. Duncan asked with an odd sort of disinterest, like he didn't much care what the answer was.

"I was just showing Clay your sword," Lionel said.

Mr. Duncan twisted around his lips, picked at his ear, looked at what he'd found there on the end of his finger. "But didn't I say that no one should touch that sword without my permission?" Again, the way he said it was with this numbed distraction. He could've been asking Lionel to clarify what his favorite color was.

"We didn't take the sword out of the scabbard," Lionel lied.

"No?" Mr. Duncan said, with the barest hint of curiosity. He came up beside Lionel and took the sword from him. "That's interesting. Because you see this tape here?" He pointed out a piece of Scotch tape on the scabbard. "And then this other piece right here" He tilted the sword, so we could see the underside of the hilt. "That used to be one piece. Now it's two. And you know what that tells me?"

"No, sir," Lionel played dumb.

"Lionel," his dad said, with a smile that under any other circumstance might've been described as kind. "I'm surprised at you." Then he unsheathed the sword, pointed it at Lionel and twisted the blade against the light. "You're a smart boy. I would've thought you'd know exactly what this told me."

As Mr. Duncan examined the blade for marks, Lionel glanced at me. I would've expected to see fear in those eyes. Or dread. Some sort of worry. But he was just as calm and indifferent as his dad. "No..." he answered, looking down at the floor.

"That's unfortunate," Mr. Duncan said. And then, in an instant of fury, he swung the sword inches above Lionel's head, as hard as he could, and planted the blade into the corner edge of the bookshelf behind him. The anger drained from his face just as fast as it rose. As he worked the blade out of the gouged wood, his subdued demeanor returned. For his part, Lionel stood stock still, blinking at the wall in front of him with a placid mask of a smile. The way the two reacted, it seemed like a routine moment in the lives of the Duncans, their unique way of measuring Lionel's growth up the corner of the bookshelf.

"I would prefer if you didn't lie to me, son," Mr. Duncan said. Then he nodded at me and added, "Hello Clay," before he left the room. I was stunned. I deflated like I'd been holding my breath the whole time. Maybe I had. Lionel kept smiling that flat, plastered smile at the wall. Then he shuddered, gave a little snort, and looked around as though he'd just woken up. No wonder nothing bothered Lionel at school. That was Mr. Duncan. That's how wrong Dad was about him. You didn't know that, did you, Bev?

Now don't get me wrong. Just because Dad couldn't see Mr. Stallard or Mr. Duncan for who they were doesn't mean he didn't have me pegged. Truth *is, Dad was right to be worried about me. I was the one who made the spud gun. I know what Lionel told the police. It wasn't true. I found the instructions in some magazine, got everything I needed at Rollier's, and built it in the fort. It was a surprise for Lionel. I thought he'd think it was cool. But he didn't. He lectured me like a little kid on how dangerous those kinds of guns were. He said we shouldn't keep it in the fort. I got mad. I told him I didn't care what he thought. He just didn't like it because it wasn't his idea. Lionel up and left, without a word. That was the only fight we ever had. And when he didn't come back the next day, I cried about it. After a while, though, I started thinking maybe Dad was right; Lionel Duncan was the wrong kid to follow, a kid who made you think bad thoughts.*

Of course, none of that stopped me from wanting to shoot off the gun. But I was too chicken to do it alone. So I told Curtis about it. That's why he came to the fort. It wasn't because he had to rescue me. I told him I had a cannon that could fire a potato all the way across the woods, maybe to Markham. He wanted me to prove it. I never expected Lionel to be in the fort when we showed up. He had this box he'd made out of particle board. It was longer than a coffin, but no wider than a shoebox. He was digging a hole to fit it flush with the floor of the fort. The box had a top on it that was hinged and half open, and the spud gun was inside. I got mad. I thought Lionel was trying to hide my own gun from me. I yelled at him and kept yelling even after he explained he was making a hiding place, so we wouldn't get in trouble. By then, it was more about showing off for Curtis than arguing with Lionel. I wanted him to see how tough I could be. But he wasn't even paying attention. While I was busy getting after Lionel, Curtis picked up the launcher, swept it around like a machine gun, and said, "How's this thing work?"

Lionel said, "It doesn't," without even looking at Curtis. He was staring me down, waiting for me to back him up.

"Yes it does," I said. And I fished the hairspray out of my backpack. By the way, Bev, I got that hairspray out of your bathroom. Then I led Curtis back above ground. Lionel followed us out of the hole, begging me not to do it. As I was spraying the aerosol into the canister, he said something about how the igniter didn't look right, how the spud gun he read about had it in a different place. Curtis kept telling him to shut up. Then we went to put in the potato. But I'd forgotten one thing. I was supposed to bring something to jam the potato into the tube. Curtis saw the shovel in Lionel's hand and told him to give it

over. He wouldn't. They started fighting over it, tugging the shovel handle back and forth. Curtis was so much stronger he was whipping Lionel around like a flag. But Lionel wouldn't let go. I felt sorry for him. I told Curtis to go easy, but I didn't say to stop. I still wanted to see the gun go off.

Then everything changed. Curtis kneed Lionel in the balls. Really hard. He dropped to the ground and curled up, gasping like a beached fish. I was stunned. I don't remember Curtis taking the launcher away from me. But I must've given it up, because next thing I knew, he was forcing the handle of the shovel down into the barrel. Then he started swinging it around, making blasting sounds. "What should we shoot?" he roared. "We gotta hit something!" I didn't answer. I kept staring at Lionel, writhing there on the ground.

"I know what," Curtis decided. "Let's lob one down there." He pointed the cannon out across the valley at the houses on Youngwood. I was too numb to react. Not Lionel. He lunged out and grabbed Curtis around the ankle. It surprised him. He nearly went down. Things might've been different if he had. Instead, he kept his balance. Then he got angry. He kicked out of Lionel's grasp, stepped back and pointed the gun down at him. "You want to be the target? Okay, start running!" I don't know if he was serious or kidding. I'd told Curtis how powerful that gun was, how far it could shoot, how the potato exploded on impact. Maybe he didn't believe me. All it would've taken is a flick of the igniter and Lionel's skull would've been crushed. So when Curtis looked down and felt for the igniter, everything went black.

I don't remember picking up the shovel. I don't remember swinging it. Then the blade hit Curtis's face and I jolted awake to everything all at once. The blood. The explosion. The fire. Lionel shaking me. Somehow, when Curtis spun to the ground, the gun blew apart and flames shot out the back of the chamber. I saw fire in the wild grass. I saw Curtis lying there, hands over his face, blood leaking through his fingers. Strangely, none of this was shocking to me. It just seemed...done—the aftermath of what had to happen. That's how unphased I was. You see the problem? That's not right. Not for someone so young. Not for anyone.

I didn't get scared until Lionel was screaming in my face. He said I had to get Curtis out of there. I had to get him help. He said, don't tell anyone what happened. Say he was the one who did it, that he shot Curtis with the gun. Say it was an accident. Curtis didn't hear any of this. He was so out of it, we were afraid we'd never lift him off the ground. And all this time, the fire was spreading. When we did finally get him to his feet, Lionel told him the gun blew up and shrapnel hit him in the face. But we weren't going to tell anybody that. We were going to say Lionel shot the gun and hit him. Curtis didn't get it. He kept asking why. I didn't get it either, but I wasn't about to question someone else taking blame.

So I led Curtis away and we left Lionel there. Last I saw, he was half-naked, stomping at the flames and beating them with his shirt. By the time I got to St. Paul's, I was exhausted from Curtis leaning on my shoulder, struggling against my grasp. He finally collapsed when we were halfway across the parking lot, but by then people were hurrying toward us, pointing up at all the smoke gathering above the trees. Before long, an ambulance came and took Curtis away, and the fire trucks went wailing down Washington.

Then the police came. They took me into the church and asked me what happened. I told them the things Lionel wanted me to say—that we had this gun and it shot potatoes and something went wrong when Lionel tried it and the whole thing blew apart. I told them Curtis got hit by the parts flying out and flames shot out the back of the gun and lit the grass on fire. They told me to slow down. Then they started firing off questions. Where was Lionel? Was he hurt? Did I see him get away? What was in the gun that made it explode? How did we make it? Who did it? That was the only tough one. I lied and said it was Lionel. He was taking on everything else; I figured he wanted to keep me out of trouble on that too.

Then it was over. At least that part of it. Really, though, it was the start of everything else. Dad picked me up, took me home, yelled and screamed, said how disappointed he was, grounded me, threatened there'd be changes coming. It was bad, the worst I'd ever gotten it to that point. But you know what? None of it affected me. If anything, I came away relieved. I kept thinking how much worse it would've been if he'd gotten the truth out of me, if he found out I made the gun, I took a shovel to Curtis's face, the fire was my fault.

But I got away with all that. Lionel took the blame. For everything. More than he needed. I don't know what he told the police when they found him, like the article said, twisting on a swing at the Markham playground, shoes half melted, legs blistered and scorched. But he confessed to pointing the gun at Curtis and me because we got too close to his fort. He only meant to scare us, but somehow the gun went off. The potato or something hit Curtis in the face and the backfiring flames lit the dry grass. To this day, I can't fathom why he went so far. He could've just said it was an accident, that he was showing off the gun, and it blew up. He didn't have to come off like such a nut job. When the story came out, the first thing I thought was Lionel made it up so everyone would think he was a badass and leave him alone. Part of me was mad at him for taking the credit. For building the fort. For making the gun. But when I saw how much trouble it brought him, how much hate he stirred up, and how isolated he became, I was glad it wasn't me.

Lionel never did come back to school. His parents must've decided it was too dangerous. He was the first kid I ever heard of being home schooled. It sounded terrible, a permanent grounding. I rarely saw him after that, not just because Dad forbade it, but because Lionel hardly ever stepped foot out of the house, at least where I could see. And, believe me, I watched for him.

Once, when I was alone at home, a month or so before they moved away, I saw Lionel scrambling around on the roof outside his room. Dad would've killed me if he knew I did this, but I couldn't help myself. I snuck across Vernon, went up to the Duncan's house, right under where Lionel was, and called out to him. He shuddered at my voice, but when he turned and recognized me, his face broke into a big smile.

"You're out of your cage," he joked. I laughed and asked him what he was doing. "My dad's pretty steamed about all the eggs," he said, waving his arm out. There were white and yellow splatterings and broken shells all over the dormer window to Lionel's room, on the stone walls nearby and running down the roof. "It's the third time they got us. But I figured out a way to block most of them." He lifted a big metal frame in front of the window. It was one of those pitching nets that bounces the ball back to you. "I've got a rope in my room," he explained. "Every night, I give it a pull, and this net covers the window." It was classic Lionel, ignoring the cruelty aimed at him, devising a way to protect against it. "And look at our front door," he added. "See that camera above it? It's pointed out at the street. I turn it on before I go to bed, and it captures everything that goes on overnight. Whoever's doing this is going to get caught on tape."

I was impressed. But at the same time, it made me sad that he was still getting picked on, long after the fire. And for something I'd done. I was about to bring that up, to thank him and ask why he'd taken so much on himself. But before I could, he said, "You should see this computer system I set up in my room. It's all connected."

I told him I better not. He wouldn't take no for an answer and told me to meet him at the front door. When it opened, though, it wasn't Lionel. It was his dad. "Clay," he stated with drowsy indifference.

Lionel came up beside him. "I just want to show him my computer."

"I don't know that that's such a good idea," his dad said.

"Please!" Lionel begged. "Five minutes."

Mr. Duncan looked at me with those blank eyes. "Let's call your father and ask."

My heart sank. "That's okay," I said and gave Lionel a little wave.

"Why does he have to know?" he cried out.

"Are you talking back?" Mr. Duncan mused, just before the door shut.

And that was the last I saw of Lionel Duncan. At least on Vernon Drive. So I never did get the chance to ask him why he decided to spare me all the punishment. What I did was vicious, deranged. It scares me now just to think of it, that something like that's inside me. Maybe Lionel recognized that. Maybe he figured the trouble I'd be in would be much, much worse. The kind that never went away. A scar you couldn't hide. I'd like to think that. I'd like to think Lionel was trying to do me a favor. But I'll never know. Hell, it might not have been much of a favor anyway. If the truth had come out right then, I may have gotten the help I needed earlier. Things might not have had to get so dark. But I refuse to see the bad in anything Lionel did. I refuse to question whether he was right or not. How was he to know what would happen? At the time, he was looking out for me. That's all that matters.

I say that was the last time I saw Lionel before he moved. But I did see him again when he was older. One of the companies in the old building I cleaned was a software developer named Crowdware. You might've heard of them. They were in the paper a while back for some ugly scandal. Anyway, one morning when I showed up to work, the monitor in the lobby had a message: "Crowdware welcomes Lionel Duncan, Microsoft." I decided to wash the windows in the lobby that morning, even though I'd done them two days before. As I was climbing up the ladder, Lionel came breezing in with an entourage of young go-getters scurrying behind him. I called out his name, louder than I'd ever dared speak in that cavernous lobby. He slowed up and looked around, but I was behind him.

"Hey Hellion!" I shouted out. Lionel stopped dead in his tracks. This time, he scanned the whole lobby. When he found me, I raised my hand and

held it up like I was waiting to be called on. Lionel whispered to his colleagues then came over my way. I stepped down off the ladder. Neither of us said a word at first, just stood there, taking each other in. I don't know how I seemed to him, but Lionel looked the same. His white hair hadn't changed; it was just longer. And he was as thin as ever. In fact, with the loose suit he was wearing, Lionel looked strangely younger than I pictured, a kid playing grown up.

"Clay Kinman," he said finally. "I'll be damned."

"Lionel Duncan," I said back. "I never thought I'd see you again."

"How are you?" he asked me, not in the casual way you might greet an acquaintance, but like he'd been worried about me for a while.

It seemed right to give him an honest answer. "Better. I'm getting help."

He nodded. "That's good to hear." I told him then I'd been following his career for years. I'd always wondered where he went and how he got where he was. I explained that I'd dropped out of high school and told him what had become of Curtis. I said I'd never married and asked if he was. And I wondered, was his dad still alive? All this came flooding out in less than a minute.

Lionel put a hand on my shoulder. "I have to do this meeting," he said. "But if you have time when I'm done, maybe we can grab lunch and talk."

I was speechless. I couldn't tell if he was kidding or not. "Yeah. Sure," I finally managed.

He smiled. "It's really great to see you, Clay," he said. And he repeated the word "really."

Then he left me. I watched him walk back to his entourage. One of them asked him something, and I barely heard Lionel's answer: "That was my best friend when I was a kid."

I didn't finish the windows. I waited until Lionel and the rest of his crew got into the elevator, then broke everything down and took it to the janitor's closet. When I got there, I shut the door, turned off the lights, and cried. I never did meet Lionel for lunch. I couldn't bring myself to do it. It wasn't that I was ashamed of what I'd become. I just didn't see the point. It wouldn't take away the pain I'd suffered or change how I felt about the past. If anything, it would open those old wounds. I was Lionel Duncan's best friend. That's what he said. He was mine too, maybe the only true friend I've ever had. And Dad took him away. If you're looking for the trigger, that was it. I'm not saying it's justifiable. I'm not blaming Dad. But that's what I latched onto. That's what got stuck in my head. And I couldn't let it go.

Couldn't? No, Clay. You *wouldn't* let it go. You still won't. You've turned teenage angst into a life's passion. It's your badge.

I was sick. Okay? Clinically. I needed help, and Dad wouldn't admit it. To him, my problem wasn't anything more than what could be fixed by good parenting. I was his failure. That's it.

God, you are so full of shit. This whole new story of yours, it's so typical. So convenient. The big secret only you can tell. Lionel gets exonerated. Dad gets demonized. And you get to be the dark rebel you've always wanted everyone to believe you were.

Damnit! I'm not demonizing Dad. Did you heard a word I said? He was doing the best he could. I know that now. That's the point. I'm trying to explain, Bev. I came to tell the truth, not just about Lionel and the fire, but everything. It's not Dad's fault. It's mine. It's the wiring. Up here. You'll never grant that possibility. Doesn't matter what I say. Doesn't matter if I tell you I wanted to kill Dad, that the urge became so overwhelming, I lied awake at night concocting ways to do it. You weren't even there. You just know what Dad told you. Yeah, I got into drugs. Sure, I dropped out. And, yes, I ran away and never came back. All of those are facts. But why did they happen? What made me decide it was either poison Dad or leave? How did I come to the conclusion my best option was to hitchhike downtown and hide away in the back streets? Eighteen years old, a hundred and five dollars to my name, half a dozen Snickers bars, and a backpack that was barely half full. It's a wonder I didn't get killed. Who knows where I'd be if the owner of that bakery hadn't found me in his alley, taken pity, and got me to talk to his psychologist friend. I was schizophrenic, Bev, and I had violent impulses because I wasn't getting treatment. I'm still schizophrenic, only now I have medication. So go ahead. Question the story. Question my motives. Question my character. I know why I came here. And it wasn't to absolve Lionel or blame Dad. I came to confess.

Good for you, Clay. I'm sure you feel much better now that you've unburdened yourself. It's great to see you going out of your way to be so selfless. You must've had to change shifts with the day janitor to pull this off, right? And I guess you finally found the energy to figure out the train schedule out to here. It's a shame you couldn't have made a fraction of that effort to see Dad when he was dying in a hospital that wasn't five minutes away from where you work. You say you don't blame Dad. You say you understand he was doing the best he could. You act like you forgive him. But when you had a chance to tell him that to his face, to give him that small measure of comfort, you didn't do it. You know how many times he asked for you? Mom kept saying, "He's coming. He's coming." So Dad waited and waited. And I knew you wouldn't come. You know how hard it was to watch him fighting to hang on, fighting for that last shred of hope that you'd show up, so he could tell you he was sorry, so maybe you'd free him with your forgiveness? Don't tell me about Lionel Duncan and what a great friend he was. Don't tell me about the demons in your head and how crazy they make you. Don't pretend now that you care.

I do care, Bev. I do! Please. I was still struggling then.

I don't care. And I don't care about your story, whether it's true or not. None of it changes a thing. You had a chance to do something good, to redeem yourself. And you couldn't do it. *That's* what matters.

Wait. Come on. Don't go like this.

Here's a 20. That's more than enough for this crappy wine.

It does matter, Bev! It does! The story says everything. She knows. You know, right?

JUDGE

JACK PARSON, 1981-1993
Told by Elizabeth West, Hilton Garden Inn, Charlotte, NC

O h no. That's terrible. You two were so…so close. That's what my sister Julie said. I'm sorry. I didn't mean to upset you. It's none of my business. I just thought, since you were doing these…interviews, you had a chance to talk to Mary. I shouldn't have said anything.

See what one martini does to me? If I were staying here and didn't have to drive, I'd have another. For a cheap hotel drink, it's not bad. But don't let me stop you. You just need to operate an elevator. That's one thing I learned from the Judge: caution. My ex had other words for it. Repressed. Holding back. Shielding myself off. I can't argue with that.

I met Jack—that's what he insisted I call him—gosh, back in 1992. I was 14. You know where we lived, down on the Vee Lynn cul-de-sac. I used to cut through his yard on my way to Missy Vidmer's. I don't know why I did it. I could've taken the extra two minutes to walk up Parkridge and down the lane between your houses.

I was going home one night before dark and just coming up to the gap in the hedges at the back corner of his yard when this voice rose up, "So that's why those bushes won't grow." I nearly jumped out of my skin. Not that there was any reason to be scared. Judge

Parsons wasn't yelling. More like thinking out loud. But I couldn't find where the voice came from in the fading light. "My neighbor was sure the deer were doing it," he added. "You're lucky he didn't catch you. He'd call the police."

I spotted him then. He was propped up in a lounger on his patio, bundled in a heavy coat with a blanket around his legs. It wasn't that cold. I said I was sorry, no more timidly than I usually talked to adults. I should say men. I was 14 then, and too mature for my age. I already had boobs that drew stares. And not just from boys in my class, but high schoolers and teachers, even some of my friends' dads. It made me awkward. To be wanted…to see that want in other's eyes.

The Judge didn't know any of that when he stopped me. I doubt he could see much more than my silhouette in the shadows that stretched across his yard. I could barely see him, and he was in a sliver of light. He mistook the tone of my apology. "Don't be scared," he said. "Your secret's safe." Then he lifted a bottle over his head, and rusty liquid flashed in the slanting sun. It might as well have been apple juice for all I knew then.

A couple days later, I met him face to face in broad daylight. He was standing in the alley like a defeated statue, pondering his overgrown hedges, the ones closest to you. He had clippers in one hand, hanging open at his side, and a glass of what looked like lemonade in the other, frozen up to his mouth. I'm sure now it was something stronger. He seemed lost, caught between the two tasks. I'd come the long way because I was rattled from our first encounter. When I saw him, I gasped. Still, it took him a second to react. He gave this cartoonish jolt and spilled the drink down his shirt. "Why are you coming this way?" he said. He seemed irked about it. I hung my head and mumbled something. It seemed to soften him. "There I go again, scaring you. Do I look like someone you should fear?"

I raised my eyes. No, he didn't. Pity maybe, but not fear. There was a sadness about him I noticed straight away. It didn't take any great powers of perception. The hurt in those eyes, the way his mouth fell, the slouch in his shoulders. Sorrow was wearing him.

I'm saying that now, with the benefit of hindsight. But there was a part of me that *did* feel sorry for him at that moment. Mostly, though, what I felt when I first saw Judge Parsons was attraction. Despite his haunted look, he was a handsome man, with a sheepish smile, thick salt and pepper hair, and those piercing blue eyes. It was the eyes that got me. They seemed to radiate from within, singeing the edges of his face with vulnerability.

"Maybe I *am* a little scary these days," he allowed, after I didn't answer his question. "Sorry for that. You can cut through my yard any time. Okay?"

I nodded and hurried off. Still, for a while, I went the long way around. I don't know how many days it was before I noticed his handiwork on the hedges. In that corner where he'd seen me, Jack had pruned out a perfect half door. I didn't have to slip through sideways or duck. After all his effort, how could I not take it? And when I did, there he was, leaning back in his lounger, head cocked to the hedge opening, as if he'd been waiting there for days. He let me get halfway across his yard before he spoke up. "I was beginning to think I'd have to roll out a red carpet." It made me smile. He sat up and grinned back.

I told him I hadn't noticed the opening until then. He eased back in his lounger. Then he said, "Be careful tonight. You never know." It was the kind of thing a father might say. I didn't think anything of it at the time. But over the next few weeks, all through that spring, whenever he saw me, he'd tell me to be careful. Then he started asking me to promise I would. And I did, even though I didn't know what I had to be careful about, what threat could possibly be lurking in our little cloister of Mt. Lebanon.

I didn't see him every time I cut through, but more often than not. That was partly because he spent so much time in his lounger. But I also started timing my trips for later in the day, when he was more likely to be there. I wanted to see him, sometimes more than my friends. And after a while, always more. Our—what should I call them?—exchanges got longer and longer. He asked what grade I was in, which teachers I'd had, what my favorite subject was, whether I had a boyfriend. He didn't push, and I didn't resist. There was a kind of innocence about the way we talked.

The only time things got uneasy was the night I asked him why he wasn't married. He didn't say anything for a long time. Then he dragged himself out of the lounger, paced that sunken patio, turned away, and gazed up the back wall of the house. "I was," he said, "I was." He downed that night's bottle and flung it onto the lounger. I expected him to say more. But he never turned around. After a while, I quietly went away.

The next day, when I came through the hedge, Jack was in my path by the side of the house. He had a shovel slung on his shoulder and was glancing my way. As soon as our eyes met, he snapped his head down. "My wife was going to make a garden here," he said when I came close. "It was going to start in the back, wrap around the house, and end in a big circle in the front." Then he went on, quieter. "She would've liked that I finished it. She died two summers ago. She and my son. Rachel and Jared. They went sailing on Lake Ontario and a storm came up. They tipped. And the wind was blowing the wrong way." He stopped and turned to me, mustering a smile. Then he swung the shovel off his shoulder, set the blade into the grass and stomped down. That's as far as he got before he spoke again. "Maybe you could help me do this, and I could pay you," he said. "Would 10 dollars an hour be enough?"

I don't know what kids get paid for chores like that today, but 10 dollars was a lot back then. Some college grads didn't make that much. It was the only thing that bothered my parents when I asked if I could work for the Judge. Of course, they knew who he was. But it surprised me how much and how highly they regarded him. Especially my dad. You must've done your homework. You know Jack was no ordinary judge. His penchant for meting out unusual justice made him somewhat of a celebrity. The robber who had to live bedridden for a week in the old folk's home he burglarized. The guy who had to wear a pig mask on a street corner for spitting at a cop. Dad knew them all. When I asked if I could work for the Judge, he recounted every one. I don't know why, but I resented that he was going on about someone I knew better. So I told the story of the boating accident. My dad got quiet. My mom stopped what she was doing. "Don't say anything about that to him," she said. "I'm sure it's still very painful." My dad told me just to do the work and mind my own business. They assumed I'd read about that in the paper or saw it in the news. They didn't know he'd told me himself. That's when I realized the way I knew Jack was special, more personal than most everyone else.

So that summer before high school, I helped the Judge make his wife's dream garden. I edged the bed, killed the grass, pulled up sod, spread mulch. It was a lot of work. Still, it shouldn't have taken as long as it did. Nearly every time I came over, he found a reason to sidetrack me. Sometimes, it would be another chore; sweeping out the garage, washing window screens. Other times, he'd ask me inside for advice—the woman's perspective, he called it; I liked that. How to rearrange furniture, which pictures to keep out or mothball, what plants to put in the garden. He had this encyclopedia with photos of trees and shrubs and flowers. We'd sit side by side at his breakfast table and comb over it.

Our best times came before I left for dinner. Jack fell into the habit of coming out to the garden and praising me for how hard I'd worked, whether it was true or not. Then he'd say I deserved a break and invite me for a drink on the patio. He'd give me Coke or lemonade and have a glass that looked the same, but I knew it was spiked. By the end of those nights, he wouldn't bother hiding it. He'd get the liquor bottle from inside, set it on the far side of the lounger, and top off his drink. Over and over. I knew Jack was getting drunk, but it didn't bother me. It didn't seem dangerous. If anything, he got gentler, more thoughtful. I'd sit next to him in the chair he brought out for me, and we'd watch the world go by. A lot of times, we wouldn't talk. It got to where I was used to being silent with him. He liked to listen to birds. When he heard one he knew, he'd name it and imitate the song. I still remember the northern cardinal: *schweet, schweet, schweet, schweet, switchoo, switchoo...*

When we talked, it usually started with Jack asking a question, something personal I hadn't thought much about. Was I happy? Did I have any dreams? What was I good at? My answers were halting, confused. They came out like apologies. At least to me. If Jack thought so, he never let on. He'd listen to every word I said, without interrupting. He took me seriously and was careful not to offer advice before I had a chance to work out my thoughts. Those talks are a big reason why I'm doing what I am today. The one thing I knew I was good at back then was numbers. Math just came naturally. When I told him that, he squinted, like it was hard to see me in this new light. Then he slowly grinned. "I'll be damned," he said. "There you go, Liz. That's your ticket."

"I said I was good at math. I didn't say I liked it."

He gave it some time, hoping to draw me out. I kept still. Finally, he asked, "Why not?" I had all sorts of reasons. None of my friends liked math. There weren't any other girls in advanced calc. The boys teased me when I asked dumb questions. The teacher didn't like me. There was too much homework, too much pressure. I didn't see the point of it. He sipped his drink when I was done and let me calm down. Then he said, "What's the point of anything? What's the point of this house and the electricity that runs through it? What's the point of TV or my car or the planes in the sky? What's the point of the bridges in the city? I'm not the best person to defend the point of things, Liz. But if there's anything that has a point, it's math. Math builds things. Math keeps us safe. Math moves everything forward. You have a gift. And you shouldn't give it up because the boys don't like that you do. Most people don't have any gifts. Think of how pointless our lives are."

Our lives. That's what he said, meaning him too. This famous judge. This kind, broken man who meant so much to me. To this day, whenever I feel down about my job, whenever the crap at work gets too deep, I think about what the Judge said. And I feel grateful, grateful that what I do helps people, that I have a purpose. I wonder what he'd think if he saw me now. Would he be happy or disappointed? At least I don't wear makeup. That's more advice of his I took to heart. It's also what changed everything.

Even after high school started, I'd make time to see the Judge. I'd done as much as I could on the garden. All it needed was plants, but Jack never got around to picking up the ones we'd chosen. Still, he found other chores for me; dusting the house, cleaning rooms he was closing off, keeping his paperwork from taking over the dining room. That was how I learned why he had so much time on his hands. He'd been suspended since back in the winter. From what I could piece together, he had handed out a harsh sentence on a debatable rape case, and it came out later that the victim's mom was his wife's college roommate. Something like that.

Anyway, one night, walking back from a football game, I decided to stop and see him. He wasn't in his usual place on the porch. And he didn't come to the back door when I knocked. But I saw him through those double doors that went to the den. His head was rolled back on top of his favorite chair. I knocked again, louder. His head wobbled but didn't rise. I let myself in. Nearly every light in the house was on. The kitchen was a mess of dirty dishes, scattered papers, empty bottles. Nothing unusual, though I do remember thinking as I wended my way to the den, that I'd cleaned things up just a few days before. He wasn't any drunker than I'd seen before either. But he was very drunk. An empty bottle of vodka was tipped over at his feet, and a half-filled one was next to the hand that hung off the armrest. I leaned in and called out his name. He stirred and blinked and fought to keep his eyes from rolling back in their sockets. "Jack?" I repeated. "You okay?"

Finally, his focus locked on me, and as it did, his face contorted. "What happened to you?" he asked, his voice thick and anguished, like I'd suffered some terrible disfigurement. "Your face is so red. Did someone hit you?" I thought it was just him looking through bloodshot eyes. Then he let go of his squint and leaned back. "Oh," he muttered. "Makeup."

I might've laughed it off had the timing not been so bad. My dad had been getting after me lately about my makeup too. "This is how we wear it now," I told Jack. "This is the look."

His hand spidered around in search of the fifth. "*This* is the look?" He huffed and latched onto the bottle.

"I'm sorry I'm not wearing gaudy red lipstick and a poodle skirt," I snapped. "Would that do it for you?"

"Is that why? For boys?" He leaned forward, like he'd only begun to grill me.

I'd had it. "What's wrong with that? I want someone to like me. Nobody likes me."

Saying that caught me as much by surprise as it did Jack. My breath stuck. Then I started sobbing. He was out of the chair, and I was folding into his arms before either of us could think. "Hey-hey-hey," he whispered. "Don't think that way. Don't think that." He took me by the shoulders and pushed me away, so he could see my face. "You don't need to make yourself up for anybody," he said. "You are who you are. And anyone who deserves you, anyone who matters, will want you for you."

I nodded and wiped away my tears. Then another wave hit me. "But what if there isn't anyone?" I bawled. "What if there isn't *ever* anyone?"

He touched my face, held his hand on my cheek. "Oh Liz," he said, with such an overcome voice. "Don't you know how beautiful you are?" His eyes kept seeking mine as I shook my head. "Do you know you're beautiful?" All at once, I kissed him. I'd never kissed anyone like that before, and I've never felt that from a kiss since. It stung and burned and shook through me. The Judge pulled me in tight, his bottle falling to the floor. We stumbled onto the chair, clinging to each other. My face was above his, hair hanging around him like a shroud. I leaned down and kissed him again, this time softly, ending as soon as he started kissing back. I don't know what possessed me. I'd never really made out with a boy before, let alone a man. But at that moment, it felt right, like everything we'd been moving toward for weeks. He was mesmerized. His mouth hung open in a kind of dazed wonder. He reached out and touched me. I closed my eyes and leaned back. That's when he pulled his hand away. "Wait," he said. "Just—just wait." I asked what was wrong. He shook his head and said, "No." Then he found my eyes. "No," he repeated in a hoarse whisper.

I asked why not and bent down to kiss him again. He pushed my leg off and tried to slide out from under me. I keeled back and hit the floor. "You have to leave," he said. "I don't want this."

I wouldn't listen. I crawled to him, reached up his leg, and begged. Please. *Please.* He unpeeled my fingers, squeezed my hands and tried to pull me to my feet. I went limp. He staggered. I fell back, and he nearly tripped over me. "We can't want this, Liz," he said. He was breathing hard, begging me as much as I was him. "It's wrong. For a man my age. For you."

I started shouting. If he didn't want me, why had he been leading me on all that time? "I didn't mean to," he protested, snapping his head back and forth. It set his whole body weaving.

I scrabbled away and got to my feet. "Yes, you did," I snapped. I accused him of playing games from the start. Hiring me. For a job he could've done in a week. And dragging it out. With all the breaks. All the praise. Then I really twisted the knife. "Did your wife even want that garden," I said, "or is that just something you told me, Jack? To pity you, to make me care?"

"No!" he cried out, coming for me, wobbling. "It's true. Everything I tell you is true."

I backed into the dining room. He kept coming. I told him to get away from me. I called him a pathetic drunk. I screamed the words. I wanted them to hurt. It was the first time I'd been betrayed, the only time, really, I've ever left myself so exposed. He rocked away like I'd punched him. I ran out of the house and never looked back, not even when I heard him wailing and things crashing. I ran all the way home, went straight to my room, and buried myself under the covers. That night, I dreamed the Judge came for me. He stood out on Vee Lynn and called my name in a voice that was clear and strong. I went to the window. The instant he saw me, he charged our front door.

For days, I avoided his house. When I crossed the neighborhood, I went out of my way, cutting through unknown yards, climbing fences. But as fall wore on, I found myself drawing closer. At first, it was just to catch a glimpse. Then, when the nights came earlier, I'd hurry past on Vernon. Early one morning on my way home from a sleepover, I noticed the Judge's garage door was broken. It was closed but bulging out, the folding panels cracked and unhinged from each other. By the looks of it, he'd backed into the door from the inside. I didn't do anything about it right then. Backing into the garage door didn't seem all that unusual for a man who drank like Jack.

It was only later, when I was eating lunch with my dad, that I started to worry. He asked if I'd heard about the hit and run on Washington, if I'd known either of the boys, the one who died or the one in the hospital. I knew the last names, Caffey and Benson, but didn't know the kids. Then my dad said it ought to be easy to find a silver Mercedes with a broken hood ornament. There'd be paint in the dents from the bikes. The bastard wasn't going to get away with it. I knew right then it was the Judge. Lots of people had silver cars, and I wasn't even sure his was a Mercedes. But there was something about that bulging garage door that scared me. I didn't say a word to my dad. We finished lunch. Then when he went to mow the lawn, I hurried out to see the Judge.

I took the shortcut through his hedges. After all the time away, everything felt different. First, there was the carpet. He'd laid a new red runner through the opening, just like he told me he'd thought of doing at first. Then there was the garden. All the plants were set right where we'd decided. It seemed so hopeful. But there was more. The blinds on every window were down. I'd never seen his house so closed. And his lounger was folded up when I went to the back door and knocked. Nobody answered, and it was locked. The Judge had shown me where he'd hidden his house key. It was inside this garden pagoda he had in his front flower bed. There was an opening in the back where you could scoop the key out with your finger. Why else would he show me than for a time like now?

On my way out front, I passed the broken garage door. A stream of water leaked out from under it and wound down the alley into Vernon. I got the key and hurried around back. Inside, the kitchen was spotless. I'd never seen it cleaned that well. That shook me as much as anything else. The only thing that looked out of place was the liquor cabinet. The doors were open, the shelves completely bare. I called out for Jack. Nothing. I went to the garage. Down the hallway, a hose snaked from the laundry room to the back door. When I opened it and flipped on the light, there was the Mercedes, front smashed in, red paint scars in the dents. The hose was beside the wreckage, feeding a pool that slid away to the alley. Jack wasn't there. I went back inside, turned off the faucet where the hose was attached, then headed upstairs.

When I heard bottles clinking, I didn't feel relieved. I felt panic. I bounded up the steps, shouting his name. "Jack! Jack! Jack!" With every room I checked, every room he wasn't in, my dread grew. Then, at the end of the hall, I saw the door to the sunroom closed. That was the room where his wife used to paint. It had windows all the way around three sides, and you could look out over the trees and see the shape of the hills. He told me once he couldn't bear going in there, and only a month back had made me clear everything out, right down to the hardwood floors. I tried the handle. Locked. I listened. Dead quiet. I knocked. "Jack? Jack?" Still nothing. I was turning away, when I heard a groan. "Jack!" I cried out, shaking the handle. "What did you do?" There was more clattering, a whole chain of clanking bottles. "What did you do?"

Then he spoke. At least tried to. I'd never heard him so slurred, so unintelligible. It took a few times asking *what-what-what* before I made it out. He was saying he was sorry. For the boys. Those poor boys. I shook the door knob. I told him he had to come out. This was something he couldn't hide from. He mumbled that he wasn't trying to hide. Then he paused and took a couple big swigs before announcing the sentence he'd imposed on himself. "This is my prison," he declared. "I have to drink myself to death here."

"What sort of hell lets you drink yourself dead?" I argued. "Isn't that what you want? Isn't that what you've been doing ever since your wife died?" It was quiet for a long time, not even the slosh and gulp of booze. Then I heard this muffled heaving, like a cough he couldn't keep down. I thought he was about to be sick. That was until I heard the one long groan, that mournful howl that kept going.

"She'd be so ashamed," he moaned out. "So ashamed."

"How much more ashamed would she be if you killed yourself like this?" I said. I'm amazed it came out of me at 15 years of age. I knew I'd gone too far, so I tried to soften things. I told him I'd seen what he'd done outside. I'd seen the garden—that he'd cared enough to finish it for her. He said he didn't do it just for her. Then he asked if I'd seen the "other thing." I knew he meant the carpet. But I didn't say so. I didn't want to make it about what happened with us. This was too big for that. He kept at it. *Did I see? Did I see the carpet? Did I remember that first day?*

I lost it. "Damnit Jack! I don't care about the carpet. It doesn't matter anymore. If you don't open this door and call the police, I'll hate you. I'll hate you forever!"

I don't know if it just came out, or I realized at some level I could use his feelings for me against him. It seems cruel when I say it like that. Just remember, though: I loved him as much as he loved me. There was a long silence. I was going to tell him it didn't matter what he did. I was leaving, and I'd call the cops anyway. But before I could make the threat, he started for the door, crawling by the sounds of it. A couple times, his body must've hit the floor. There'd be this big thump, a long moan, then quiet, long enough to worry, before he'd start crawling again. When he did finally unlock the door, I had to push against him until he rolled out of the way. I shouldn't have been surprised by what I found. I knew he'd brought every bottle he owned up there. I just never realized he had so many. He could've drunk himself dead 10 times over. There was nothing else in that bare room, just the Judge lying there in front of those huddled bottles, that silent jury.

It took a while to help him over to his room. He couldn't walk, and I wasn't strong enough to hold him up. We managed it by following the walls, bracing against them until he got close enough that he could collapse on the bed. Then I helped change his clothes. He'd peed himself and started to cry when I discovered it. I told him it was okay. I wiped a wash cloth over his face and brushed his hair, then gave him a drink of water. He choked on it. I had to hold him by the shoulders while he coughed, or he would've doubled over and hit the floor. A couple times, he lost his breath, his face got red, and the veins bulged out of his forehead. It was bad. For a minute there, I thought of calling an ambulance. Then, just like that, he shook his head, blinked his eyes wide, and settled himself.

It took less time to guide him downstairs than to drag him out of the sunroom. He seemed resigned to his fate now, determined to face it. We didn't talk much. I'd tell him to watch this step or put that hand on the railing. Jack kept saying how sorry he was. I never replied. I didn't want him to explain all the things he was sorry for. I pulled a swivel chair into the foyer next to the front door and sat him down there. Then I got the cordless phone. I didn't give it to him right away, just stood in front of him, gathering my breath like it was me who was making the call. We spent that whole time looking each other in the eyes. I don't know how mine looked, but his were the saddest I'd ever seen. And, oddly, the clearest. Like he was waking up from a long nightmare, only now coming to grips with it. "Ready?" I said at last. He nodded. I dialed 911 and handed him the phone.

He straightened up and put the phone to his ear. "Yes," he answered the tinny garble, "I'm the one who ran over those two boys. My name is Jack Parsons, and I'm at 138 Vernon Drive." He hung up on the squawking and dropped the phone. We stared at each other, unsure what else to do. "I know what'll happen," he said. "I've sentenced these cases before. I'm gone for 20 years. At least. I'd give me more." I didn't know what to say. I wanted to be hopeful for him, but what hope was there? He answered that himself. "At least I'll stop drinking." He blurted out a gallows laugh. "Aw, Jesus. How am I going to hold up?" he moaned. "Would you do me a favor? Get me one last shot. Just to get me through. Please?"

I actually considered it—running to the kitchen, getting a glass, hurrying up to the sunroom, pouring a shot, and bringing it down. What was one more swallow? But I was worried about getting caught there when the police showed up. I couldn't risk that. "I have to go," I told him. "Before they get here."

He looked at me like he didn't understand. Then tears started streaming down his face. "Stay with me," he pleaded, pain and despair strangling his voice.

I looked out the front window. "Just a little longer," I whispered. "A little longer."

Then out of the blue, the Judge said, "Please don't hate me. Don't think the worst. Did you see the garden? I was trying, Liz. I was trying."

"You're a good man," I said. "You just got lost."

"I did it for her," he went on. "And you. I never thought I'd feel…happy again." He paused just like that to find the word. "Then you came to me. This miracle." I started crying. "If I thought you still believed in me," he went on, "if I had that much, I could get through this. I could see myself wanting to keep going. Do you? Do you believe in me?" He raised his eyes and looked at me like a frightened child.

I nodded and said, "I do." It was all I could manage. He let out a relieved sigh. His head fell back on the swivel chair. We didn't say another thing to each other. Moments later, the patrol car passed by the bay window. I hurried to the kitchen and gave him one last glance in the hallway. He waved. Then I snuck out the back door and ran for the gap in the hedges. I didn't look back until I got through. There was no one chasing me and no one out on Parkridge. I bent down and rolled up the carpet runner, reeling it in, a fiery red tongue. I tucked it under my arm and took it with me, down along the edge of the park toward home. There's a strip of woods that runs behind the houses on Vee Lynn all the way to Mayfair, a steep tangle of briars and scrub trees. I fought my way in far enough that it was hard to see from the park and set the rolled-up carpet down. Then I scrambled out of the woods, went home, and waited for the news to come out.

All through high school, whenever I walked along that edge of the park, I'd look for the carpet. You couldn't see it when the leaves were out, but in the fall, it was easy to spot if you knew where to look. Every year, the carpet unraveled a little more, and its red fiber got duller. I couldn't help thinking of it as an open mouth, panting at the passage of time.

Remember how it was when everyone found out what the Judge did? People were stunned. My dad refused to believe it. He kept saying there must be more to the story. He grilled me. Did I ever see the Judge that drunk? Could I picture him doing such a thing? Did he ever mention his wife and child? I couldn't hide the fact that I was upset, but it wasn't hard to lie. I was protecting myself as much as sparing him. In some ways, I felt guilty myself for what had happened. If I had told somebody about Jack, how much he was drinking, how bad he was hurting, maybe he would've gotten help, and wouldn't have plowed into those boys.

When I got out of high school, the summer before I went off to Penn State, I told myself I'd go visit him. He was in a state prison outside Somerset. But I never got around to it. I thought about it again a couple years out of college, even made a call to find out if he was still there. But I couldn't do it that time either. Finally, a few years back, after my divorce, I looked up his name in the state's online inmate database. By then, the whole thing was really nagging at me. I felt like I'd let him down, broken a promise. His name didn't turn up. He'd gotten out. I tried to find him, searched the internet, checked obituaries, called a few longshots. Then after a while, I gave up.

He was 25 years older than me in 1992. He'd be about 65 today—and I'm almost the age he was back then. I still think about him. I wish I knew he was alright. I hope, after all these years, he managed to forgive himself, that he rediscovered even a little of the goodness I know was inside him. I wonder if he ever thinks of me. And I pray he doesn't misunderstand why I never came to see him, that it wasn't because I gave up believing.

But I guess I'll never know that, will I?

No. No, I never will.

SAVIOR

THE SANTONIS, 1994-2001
Told by Grace Carlson, St. Clair Hospital, Mt. Lebanon, PA

Relax Mom. You don't have to write any more. I know what you're asking. Let me take the pen. Just lie back and let the nurse tighten the straps. I know you don't mean to, but you keep pulling at the tubes. Every time you do it, your numbers go bad, and they have to keep you on the ventilator that much longer. If you can get through the night without any more episodes, they'll ease off the oxygen in the morning, see how you're breathing on your own, then take the tube out. But you've got to cooperate.

There. Good. First off, I don't want to call you Ilsa anymore. I want to start calling you Mom again, okay?

Thank you. Now: you want to know how I am. Really. And you're sure? We haven't talked in, what, four years? Nope. No more writing. You don't need the pad. Just listen. Lie back, and I'll tell you everything. If you fall asleep, don't worry. I'm recording this; you can always replay it.

I've been working on a surprise for you. That's the one thing I can't tell you about. Not just yet. No, Mom. I know what you're going to write. There's plenty of time. The cancer's in remission. This is just a complication. Your lungs are already clearing up. By your birthday, you'll know. This will be my gift to you. So just let me talk, okay? I shouldn't have even brought up the surprise. The only reason I did is because it got me back in contact with Mary Santoni. Nope. I'm *not* giving you the pen. *Will you just listen?* I know you blame her, but you shouldn't. I need you to understand that. I never told you everything that happened back then. You asked how I was. You wanted to know how I'm feeling. I'll tell you. But it starts with Mary. And ends. Sorry.

If it puts your mind at rest, Mary was married when I saw her. To a man. And they had two young kids. She lived in a big colonial in Connecticut. Hard to believe, right? Who would've thought Mary would grow up to be the model suburban housewife? She'd become exactly what we used to make fun of in high school. When I drove out to surprise her last fall, part of me thought it was some sort of joke. The other part wanted to turn around and come home. Imagine me in my rusty old Jeep clattering down some quiet lane. If anyone saw me getting out of my car, they were probably thinking about calling the cops. I actually had this fleeting notion as I pressed her doorbell that I'd be setting off alarms, triggering the wrath of attack dogs.

The look on Mary's face when she opened the door was unwelcoming enough. She seemed offended. I'm sure the smirk I gave her didn't help. You know how openly I wear my emotions. I couldn't hide my contempt. There was Mary, standing in the doorway, with a fancy dress, her hair done up, and her necklace and earrings all gold and glittering. And here I was, with this butch haircut and the silver coloring you hate and all my piercings and tattoos. I even did my eyes up for the occasion, laying on the black mascara thicker than usual. So you can imagine.

Neither of us bothered to greet one and other. I said, "Well look at you," and she answered with, "What are you doing here?" That's how touching our reunion was. After 20 odd years. "I came to surprise you," I said with a grin. Honestly, I enjoyed shocking her. I mean, I didn't know what she'd be like in person, but once I Googlemapped the address in Darien, it was pretty clear she wasn't going to be some militant feminist. I give her credit, though. As sickeningly transparent as it was, she did recover. It almost breaks my heart to remember how polite she became, how mannered.

What did she say? "And surprise me you did!" Just like that, putting her hand under her throat and giving out a practiced little giggle.

Then Mary's daughter showed up at her side. "Who is it?" she asked. The blank stare she gave me, I might as well have been the UPS driver. And what does Mary say? "Nobody dear. Just an old friend." *Nobody*. She must've realized how it came out. But she recovered again, shooed her daughter away, stepped out onto the landing with me, and eased the door shut. She smiled and said my name. "Grace Page. I've wondered about you for years."

I couldn't help but smile back. "And I've thought of you."

Then she took control. It happened so fast I didn't realize it until later that night. And I thought about what you used to say: how she manipulated me. *Wait*. Just wait. Hear me out. She tells me they're running late for some school function. then asks how long I'll be in town. She really wants to catch up. I tell her I'm driving back to Pittsburgh the next day. She says, perfect, we can get together that night. Then she asks for my phone number. I say why don't I just call her, then she'll have it. You know what she says to that? "I don't have a cell phone." I should've figured something was up right there. Who doesn't have a cell phone? But you know what? I bought it. So I take a pen out of the front pocket of my leather jacket and I start checking for a scrap of paper. She holds her palm out for me to write on, just like this, and gives me a wink. That wink. It won me over. It was like she was saying, *this is all a façade. You're the only one who knows.*

You know where this is going, right? She didn't call. I checked into this crummy motel, found a Wendy's, and watched my phone while I ate. At first, I chalked it up to being overanxious: how should I know how long a school function takes? On my way back to the hotel, I found a convenience store and picked up a bottle of wine. It didn't really sink in that she might be standing me up until I was back in my room and well into my second glass. I sat by the window, let the room get dark and drank, concocting reasons she might not have called yet, refusing to believe what I knew was happening. By the time I finished the bottle, it was around nine. What school lets little kids stay up that late?

You're not going to like this next part. I got in my Jeep. Christ, I shouldn't have done that. I'm always good about not drinking when I drive. Don't worry. Nothing happened. Except I got lost, even with GPS. Ever driven around Connecticut? It's a bowl of spaghetti. I'm amazed I found my way back to her house. When I eased to a stop in front of it, I didn't know what I was going to do. Part of me wanted to march up there, bang on the door, and start shouting. *What the hell? Is this how you treat an old friend…a lover? Are you this ashamed of me?*

Looking back, it's a wonder I didn't make a scene. You know how my brain switches off when I drink. There was a light on in the bay window. I got caught up with what was happening there. She was home, out of her dress, and into what looked like silk pajamas. She breezed by with her own glass of wine, then passed seconds later with the glass filled red. Then the man of the house sauntered into the window, stopped dead center and hung his head. He looked like he'd just come home from work, shirt open, tie yanked loose. There must've been a table in front of him, because he kept picking up envelopes and discarding them. At some point, not three minutes later, Mary came back and tried to sneak behind him. He turned before she was out of reach and grabbed at her. The way she jolted, it was probably a playful little goose. Mary didn't even turn around. Just went on her way. She didn't see her husband shake his head. It said it all. It was like, *what am I going to do with her?* That wasn't the thing that bothered me most, though. What really got me was watching Mary pass with that empty glass. I'm telling you, it hadn't been more than a few minutes, and she'd downed the whole heavy pour. That's one thing we had in common that night.

I didn't stick around too long after that. Mary's husband came closer to the window at one point and looked out into the night. He was all in silhouette. But it made me nervous. Minutes later, the light in the window went off. It wasn't totally dark. I waited to see if I'd catch a shadow crossing. I don't know what crazy hope I was clinging to. But Mary never came back from where she'd gone. I thought of her there in the dark, cornered on the short side of the house, far from the rest of her family. It wasn't a complete thought; I didn't put it together like that when I was there. The impression came later, after everything else.

When I drove away, when I flipped on my headlights, circled the cul-de-sac, and sped past Mary's house, I honked my horn. Not a tap either. I laid on it. A long, loud blare. I'll bet anything she heard it. And she knew it was me. It was a dumb thing to do, but it was the only thing I could come up with at the time to hurt her. I wanted it to sting. I wanted her to hear it like a wounded howl.

I was sure I'd never hear from Mary again. But next morning, when I was in the thick of New York traffic, my phone rang. It was her. She apologized for not calling, said she got in too late. Then she asked if I could meet her right then. "Sorry. Too late," I snapped. She started going on about what a shame it was, how the timing was bad, that maybe next time she could get a little warning. I cut her off. "Sure Mary. Next time. We'll get it on your social calendar." Then I hung up. A week later, she Facebook friended me. Can you believe that? Mary and I, everything we went through, reduced to Facebook posts. *Happy birthday, Mary. I like that you checked into Mommy Yoga, Mary. What a cute kitty, Mary.* I deleted the request.

You okay? Thumbs up? I can stop any time. We can turn on the TV or put it on that music channel you like. You sure? I'm still getting to what I want to say. That's one thing I've learned on this…this project. We want our lives to be stories, clear and complete. We want to make sense of them. But our memories are faulty, our judgments flawed. We never have time for the full truth. We don't know what we don't know. If I were to ask you, what was the story of me, what would you say? Nobody knows me better than you—and yet whatever you said would be incomplete. Filtered through the haze of *your* story.

I need to tell you something you don't know, Mom. Something I told myself I'd never tell you. I'm not even sure I should now… *Alright.* I will. But fair warning: it's not going to be easy. Part of it's about Mary, but not in the way you think. You know what we did in school, how angry everyone got, how defiant I was. You know what you saw us doing on Mary's porch. You know how hard it was for me when she left. What you don't know, what you never really asked, is *why*? Why did it all happen?

I have to go back to the beginning to answer that, back to that day you insisted I couldn't skip out on Mrs. Yancey's Welcome Wagon party for new students. Remember? That's the first time I met Mary. If it hadn't been for that afternoon of cookies, lemonade, and superficial chit-chat, I might've never thought twice about Mary Santoni. I was a cheerleader. I was popular. My boyfriend was the big quarterback. I didn't need another friend. I didn't want to have anything to do with those new kids. But from the instant I sat down next to Mary, told her we were neighbors, and asked where she was from, she grabbed me. "What the fuck do you care?" I'm just repeating what she said. And she glared straight into my eyes. I was stunned. Nobody had ever spoken to me like that. With that one question, she cut through all the pretense of that party. She pointed a finger at me. And she did it without any real hostility. She was hurting—I could tell that much—but beyond that, she simply wanted to know: what *did* I care? I sat next to her the rest of the party. I never did answer her question. I can't exactly remember how I got past it. But from that moment on, I felt I had something to prove to Mary.

A couple weeks later, a bunch of us were hanging out at the house—Jake and I, Kelly Clough and Paul, Drew and Tommy, a few more guys from the team. You and Granny Emma were gone somewhere. We were all drinking, and I started wondering about Mary. Here we were partying, there was a roomful of unattached guys, and she was right next door. I got her number from information and gave her a call. She acted like she didn't know me. "We met at that silly welcome party," I reminded her. "I'm the one who lives next door. The one you told to fuck off."

She laughed. "That's not what I said. What I suggested is you didn't give a fuck."

"Well now you know I do," I said. Then I asked if she wanted to come party with us.

"No," she said, "but you kids have fun."

"Alright," I swiped back. "I'll let you get back to your cozy night with the folks."

Mary told me they weren't there. I asked why she wouldn't come over then. She said, "I figure I'll have more fun painting my toenails." Then she hung up. I wasn't going to let things end like that. I found Jake and Drew and convinced them to go over to Mary's. Drew already knew who she was. He'd noticed her at school and wanted to meet her. Jake griped about going, but he never wanted to do anything that wasn't his idea. I know. You thought he was a saint. He wasn't. Just wait.

So we went over and knocked on the back door. Candles flickered in the kitchen. The doorways glowed. You could hear music playing, folky lo-fi stuff. It took a while, but Mary finally came and cracked open the door, looking all annoyed. "We decided we'd join your toenail party," I said. I was sure she'd send us away, but she just swung open the door and headed back into the glowing nook. We barged in. She was already sitting down, heel on the breakfast table, putting separators between her toes.

"You need a drink," Drew insisted, holding out a pint of rum.

"I don't drink," Mary told him. "Drunk people scare me."

We laughed, but she went on painting her nails in the flickering light. It was strange. The whole thing rattled Jake. He banged his bottle on the table. "Come on," he blustered, like she was any other kid he could bully. She stared at him calmly, her face lit up, sort of disembodied. What's that song you like so much? How's it go? *You know something's happening, but you don't know what it is?* That's how I felt that night. I was there to shake her up, to make her feel like the outsider, the one who needed our acceptance. But she turned it all upside down. I don't know. Maybe I was too drunk.

Drew said he couldn't believe a girl like Mary didn't party. She said what's that supposed to mean? He mumbled something about the way she looked. Finally, Mary said she wouldn't drink, but she'd smoke weed with us. Drew laughed, "Nobody has weed."

"I do," she said. Then she hobbled off into the darkness.

From then on, everything smears together. It was the first time I smoked pot. You may not believe that, but it's true. At some point, we went out on Mary's back patio. Jake spotted a motorcycle in the corner. Mary said it was hers. He didn't believe her. Next thing I knew, she was revving it up in the lane. I remember her straddling that machine in the moonlight, asking who wanted a ride. For some reason, I said I did. Jake got mad, said I was too wasted. Mary told him we'd just take a slow spin around the block.

Then we were cruising up Vernon. Mary told me to hang on, but I mustn't have been doing it tightly enough. Before we went down Virginia Way, she slowed the bike to a stop and turned back to me. "You have to squeeze tighter," she said. So I leaned in close, hugged her hard around the waist and put my cheek to her back. "There you go," she said. "We wouldn't want Jake to get mad."

I wasn't sure what she meant. But I agreed. No, we wouldn't. "I had a boyfriend like Jake once," Mary added. Then she turned away, steered the bike to the top of Virginia Way, and rumbled down the hill, over all those bricks. The rest of the way, that long hilly stretch on Mayfair, around the bend and back up from the other end of Vernon, went by in a blur; a dark dream where I was clinging for life at the same time I was floating free of it.

From that night on, we were friends. Not like you think, not at first. We walked to school together—and, yes, we got high a few times. Jake didn't like it. "Why are you hanging out with that loser druggie?" he said more than once. But Mary never was the outcast he made her out to be. A lot of guys liked her. She was the new girl. She looked tough, acted tough, talked tough. And at the same time, she was beautiful. I'm not the only one who saw that.

So homecoming rolled around. And all these guys were asking her to go, calling out of the blue. Every day, she'd ask me if I knew so and so, and wonder how she might know them. I gave her my yearbook, so she could put faces to voices on the phone. I was surprised she even cared. After the first guy asked her out, she told me she wouldn't be caught dead at our dance. So the more curious she got about all these boys, the more crap I gave her. "Why do you care who they are?" I said. "You don't even want to go."

Then one morning when we were walking to school, she told me she was going to the dance with Drew. I was floored. You

remember Drew. He just wasn't Mary's type; too much of a fol-
lower, not strong enough. And I told her that. She shrugged. "The
only reason I agreed," she said, "is because Drew told me we'd be
going with you and Jake."

That was news to Jake. "No way we're going with that crazy
witch," he said. I guess Drew had just told Mary that because he
thought it might get her to say yes. Well, it worked. And as adamant
as Jake was at first, he finally caved in. But he made it clear we
wouldn't be driving together or hanging out after the dance.

Last time I was over at your house, I found this old photo.
Take a look. Jake came by in his van to pick me up, and Drew had
his dad's Corvette for Mary. You insisted on getting a picture.
Remember? Look at us in those stupid dresses. And the guys with
the bad suits. It's strange to look at now with everything that happened from then on. It's like some cosmic clue. Look at me, head
thrown back with that big dreamy grin. Then Jake beside me on
the far left. See how his face blurs as he turns to look out of the
frame? It's like he started smiling but ended up snarling. Either
way, that blur gives him a spectral quality, like he isn't really there.
And Drew's all the way on the other side, glancing at Jake. See how
his eyes shift, as if he's watching him transform, but he's afraid to
draw attention to it? Then there's Mary between me and Drew, the
only one looking into the camera. No smile. No emotion. Just
staring at you, trapped in this fleeting unreal moment, but facing
it. Like she knows something isn't right, and there's nothing she
can do. But she's sending a signal to you with that dead glare.

I'm sure I told you we went over to Kelly Clough's before the
dance. Her mom put on a dinner for a bunch of us. It was quite a
production—fancy hors d'oeuvres, a guy in a chef hat slicing beef,
fine china. You know the Cloughs. They even had champagne,
never mind we were all under age. I probably didn't tell you that.
And I know I didn't tell you how much else we had to drink there.
At least Jake and I. Actually, I don't know how much he drank. All
I know is he had this flask he kept taking out of his coat and filling
my water glass with. Kelly's mom had no clue, not that she'd care.
And I didn't think anyone else noticed either.

I barely talked to Mary at that party. I'd see her now and then, out on the deck, over in a corner by herself, always on the fringe of things. I kept meaning to seek her out, bring her into the group. But things got away from me. Before I knew it, we were outside, heading down that steep driveway of the Cloughs. I must've stumbled or something, because I suddenly found myself flat on my back on the front lawn, laughing and struggling to get to my feet. Mary was the first one at my side. She helped me up, straightened my dress, fixed my hair. "You don't have to drink everything Jake pours you," she said. I thought of that later. I might not have noticed Mary at the party, but she'd been watching me.

We mustn't have stayed very long at the dance. I have a vague recollection of blue balloons, starry lights, and a big white castle. There was a fake carriage too, like what Cinderella rode, and people were getting pictures in it. The only reason I know that is because of the photo in our yearbook. I don't actually remember it.

Then I'm out in the parking lot. I can't stand up, and Jake is lifting me into the back of his van. He has a big mattress with a bunch of pillows and he sets me up there, lying on my stomach. There's a moment when I feel grateful. Everything's spinning, but I'm safe. God, to think of it now. "You're okay, you're okay," he keeps saying. Next thing I know, he's pulling at my waist and he's got my underwear down. I'm confused because he's telling me, "Just relax." Only I'm scared, and I know this is wrong and I keep saying no. But he won't stop. Then the walls are thumping. *Bang! Bang!* And I hear Mary yelling, "Let her go, Jake! Let her go!"

Then I hear Drew. "Come on, Jake," he's pleading. "Everyone's going to know."

Jake swears and yanks up my underwear. Then he pulls me off the mattress and suddenly lights are swirling and he's shoving me out of the van. "I don't need this crap!" he yells. "All I'm trying to do is help."

Mary puts an arm around my shoulder and props me up. "You're an asshole," she screams. Jake gets out and takes a step toward her. She's got a mace sprayer and she's pointing it at him. "Just try," she says. "Just try."

Drew starts begging Jake to back down. Suddenly, they're at each other's throats. "How the hell'd she know I was out here?" I hear Jake snap. "What did you tell her?" As if Drew knew what was going to happen, as if everything was planned.

Now you're upset. I'm sorry. I shouldn't have told you all of this now. Heck, I should've told you a long time ago. When it happened. I'm trying to make up for that. There's more, but I can tell you later. Keep going? You sure? Okay…

We didn't have a car, so we walked through the park. But I was still drunk, and it was just dawning on me what happened. So I was crying. We didn't get far up the hill before Mary sat me down under a tree. After I was settled beside her, she asked what Jake had done. I said I wasn't sure, that he touched me down there, but I didn't know what he stuck inside me. To this day, I don't. Not that it matters. Either way, it's a violation. Mary said we could go to the hospital and find out. I didn't want to. Then she said we should check. I was afraid and asked if she would. So Mary inspected me and was pretty sure I didn't need to worry about…you know…the worst. I started crying again, this time out of relief. And gratitude. I thanked Mary. For watching out for me. For getting me out of that van. For standing up to Jake. "You would've done the same for me," she said. I told her I wasn't that brave. She cupped my chin in her hand and turned my face to hers. "Don't you believe that for a second."

We talked into the night, well after all the car lights swept out of the parking lot across the valley. We talked about our lives and what we dreamed of doing with them. About our fears those dreams would never come true. About how everything already seemed planned for us. What we didn't talk about was what would happen that Monday when we walked down the halls at school and had to face Jake. That was the week I quit cheerleading, remember? You were shocked. You couldn't understand how I'd give up something I'd wanted so badly. And I wouldn't talk about it. I told you it was my business. Maybe if I'd said something then, things would've gone differently. At least for you and me. Nothing could have stopped what happened to me and Mary.

I never thought it would get as bad as it did—even after I saw Drew on Monday with a black eye. Then Mary got her locker spray painted: *FIND DRUGS HERE* scrawled in red paint with an arrow pointing to the lock. Finally, at cheerleading practice, Kelly Clough asked why I hadn't answered Jake's calls. She told me he couldn't figure out what he'd done wrong. I was steamed. If Kelly was defending Jake, it meant he'd fed her lies about what went on. I told her to screw off on the spot and left practice.

Things got worse. That night, I told Mary about my run-in with Kelly. She urged me to tell somebody about Jake. I'd already decided it was a bad idea. Remember the police chief? John Clayton? His son was on the team, Jake's favorite receiver. Mary suggested we stay away from each other, at least at school, and I agreed. It seemed like a good idea at the time. But when I saw her that next day, sitting alone in the corner of the lunch room, with all the seats empty around her, like she had the plague or something, it got my blood boiling. I went over and sat next to her. She was incredulous. "Screw it," I told her. I was standing by her, no matter what.

Within seconds, Jake came marching over. He pulled a chair around, wedged it between us and plopped down. "How we doing, ladies?" he said, with a big stupid grin. I got after him. How did Kelly Clough know about that night, I asked point blank. "How do *you* know?" he said. "You were passed out."

Mary accused Jake of plying me with booze. He said no one forced me to drink. She asked how Drew got his black eye. He brushed her off. "You lie about somebody," he said, "somebody's going to get upset."

"So should Mary be upset you accused her of selling drugs?" I said. He gave me that nasty grin and got up to go. "And you're the one telling everyone what happened. We haven't said a thing."

Mary caught my drift. "If it doesn't matter whether we talk or not," she said, "if you'll punish us either way, maybe we *should* say something." That flustered him. He said we shouldn't do that. I said then he shouldn't make threats.

You'd think that would've ended things. But that very night, Mary's motorcycle got stolen. Right off her patio. It didn't take a genius to figure out who took it. But when the cops asked Mary if she had any ideas, she kept her mouth shut. Mary told me she didn't name Jake for the same reason I wouldn't talk about the attack. What good would it do? Besides, she thought we should get him back ourselves, some way that would really hurt, more than a legal slap on the wrist.

The cops found the motorcycle later the next day. The tarp covering the public pool had been yanked up at a corner of the deep end, and they'd dumped the bike down there. It was pretty well broken up. Mary's dad wanted the police to dust for prints, like it was a murder investigation. They told him he was lucky to get the bike back. Mary and I didn't care. We were concocting plans for revenge. Mary's best idea was to stuff a bunch of dildos up his van's exhaust pipe when it was at school. A van exploding with dildos would be a fitting revenge. But we weren't sure what would happen when he started the car up. Today, I bet you could Google "dildos in exhaust pipe" and learn all you wanted to know about the procedure. Back then, we were operating in the dark. And, of course, there was the question of where to get dildos.

Before we could come up with anything, Jake struck again. It was Friday of the same week—can you believe that? All this happened in five days. I showed up at school, and there on my locker in big red letters was the word *LEZ*. We should've seen that coming, right? If you won't give it up to a guy, you must be a lesbian. And what could be worse? When Mary saw it, she laughed. I wasn't amused. I skipped out of third hour to find out when they could get the word off my locker. That's how embarrassed I was. Isn't that funny? Everything that went down, and that's what cut me the deepest. I went through the whole day like some grieving zombie; numb, angry, despondent. These were kids I'd gone to school with all my life—Markham, Mellon, Lebo—and suddenly I didn't know them. Sure, there were a few, Anne Kostich, Julie West, Eileen Brown, who offered me sympathy. But far more ignored me. I even heard a few insults muttered behind my back.

When the bell rang, I sleepwalked for the exit, forgetting my books and everything else. I was barely aware of people swirling around me. And I didn't care if they noticed how devastated I was. I got all the way outside, on the sidewalk behind the bleachers, when I realized someone was calling my name. I turned and saw Mary running toward me. In that instant, I jolted awake. I saw the bus behind her and the cheerleaders filing on, a line I would've been in if everything hadn't happened. I saw the football players nearby. And I saw Jake standing with a huddle of friends, all looking my way. But more than anything, I saw Mary's face. "What's wrong?" she said, when she was close enough to touch. I don't know what came over me. I kissed her. Right in front of everyone. I kissed her like I've never kissed anyone. I didn't want it to end. It was Mary who released us. She did it slowly, softening by degrees, and when we were finally apart, her eyes glittered, and she smiled. "Good for you, Grace," she said. "Good for you."

There was nothing spiteful in that moment. I hadn't planned it. It just happened. But there couldn't have been any sweeter revenge. From that moment on, everything changed. We were inseparable. In school, we walked the halls together hand in hand. We didn't care. We were strong and certain and brave. And it was thrilling. Have you ever laid yourself bare like that? Just came right out and shouted, *this is who I am. Too bad if you don't like it.* That fall was the only time I've ever done that.

Then there were the times we were alone, away from everyone. Mary's parents were never around. Sometimes they'd leave altogether on weekends. So we made our home in that big stone house next door. It's one thing to proclaim who you are to this terrible world. It's another to have complete freedom to be exactly who you want to be with your first love. I can't describe how I felt. Not because I don't have the words so much. I just can't remember. I can't feel it anymore.

It was dumb luck you saw us when you did. We never went out on the front porch. With all the windows, it felt too open. But late in November, it got warm. We went out there one afternoon when the porch was fluttering with sunlight and shadows. That's when you looked out my window. I didn't realize you could see down into that corner until you told me. I know you think Mary seduced me. But neither of us had done anything like that before. We were discovering together. I *am* sorry you saw it. But I hope you understand: I'm not ashamed of that moment. I was supremely happy. I wish I had more moments like that. Doesn't everybody?

That was the year we went to see Uncle Bobby in Arizona for Christmas. I told Mary weeks before we left. We knew it would be hard to be apart, but we kept ignoring it. Then it got darker. Then winter came. And before we were ready, it was the night before I had to leave. We were going to meet in the lane before bed to say goodbye. But when I called that night, Mary said she was tired, and couldn't we talk across the alley? So we opened our windows, even though it was snowing, and shouted our goodbyes over the howling wind. Then she shut her window, pulled the shades, and turned off her light. I did the same. But I couldn't sleep. I fought my blankets for a good hour. When I was just drifting off, headlights swung into my room. I waited for them to pass like always. But they stuck, and the engine kept rumbling. I went to the window. There was Drew's car, beside the Santoni's front walk. Mary ran out and got in. They backed out of the lane and drove away.

I was stunned. Why were Mary and Drew together? I'd been with her nearly all the time since our first kiss. They couldn't really be seeing each other. But clearly they'd been talking. And whatever it was about, Mary didn't want me to know. Why else lie and sneak out? I left my window shade open and got back in bed. I was determined not to fall asleep. I wanted to see when the headlights returned. A few times, when I thought I drifted off, I'd go and check for new tire marks in the snow. Before long, and sooner than I expected, the alarm was buzzing. They never did come back.

You were beside yourself that morning. Remember? There was half a foot of snow, you were afraid we wouldn't get to the airport on time, and I kept dragging my feet. The long shower. All the time getting my hair right. Finding new things to pack. Now you know why I did all that. Why I was so grouchy the first few days in Arizona. I feel bad for Uncle Bobby. He tried so hard to cheer me up. To this day, he tiptoes around me like I might break in a million pieces, and it's somehow his fault. You told me to shape up or we'd take the next flight home. I said fine. Then remember what you said? "Whatever's put you in this funk, find a way to get over it."

I took your advice. When you and Bobby went shopping, I called Mary. She must've heard something in my voice, because she asked right off what was wrong. I told her I'd seen her with Drew. "Oh." That was her reaction. *Oh.* After a silence, she added. "You can't possibly think there's something going on between Drew and me." But you lied, I told her. That's when she confessed. "It's a surprise," she said. "I needed someone to help me."

I asked if it was a good surprise. She had to mull it over for a second. "Yes. That will be a good surprise."

"*That?*" I repeated. Like there were more surprises.

Out of the blue, she said, "Grace, do you know how much I love you?" Talk about surprises. It took my breath away. "Here we are, hundreds of miles apart," she went on in a hushed voice, like someone might be listening, "and I can't stop thinking about you."

I told her I couldn't either. Then she said, "I'll love you forever, Grace. Don't you ever doubt that. When we're away from each other...like now...just know I'm still loving you."

I started to cry. It was exactly what I needed to hear. Then Mary whispered, "I have to go. My mom's sneaking around. Just remember. Please?"

Please. That was her last word. Just this quiet appeal to remember her love. She didn't need to do any more. I got off that call, alone in Uncle Bobby's condo, with those great red rocks of Sedona all around, and felt the keenest sensation of Mary's presence, buoying me. You noticed that very day. Remember? You said, "I'm glad you decided to be happy."

I wish it were that easy. Don't you? A simple decision. *I'll be happy now.* Maybe it is, like faith, and I just don't have that gift. You know what happened next. When we got home, I was so excited to see Mary I left you to unpack the car. Did I ever tell you what Mary's mom said when she answered the door? How she broke it to me? "I'm afraid Mary had to go to Connecticut and live with her grandparents," she said, with this disdainful little sneer. And when I asked why, she just ever so slowly shut the door in my face.

I don't know how they found out. I don't care anymore. Doesn't matter. Never did, really. I just needed something to be angry about. Because that's all I had after Mary left. Without anger, I was nothing. Anger sustained me, stirred up all the shards inside me, gave me something to feel. Who cared if the spectacle of my wounds repelled everyone? That was the whole point. The only person I wasn't mad at was Mary. I couldn't be mad at her, not just because I didn't think she'd have any part in her leaving, but because if I did turn on her, there truly would've been nothing to me. It would've been like lighting my soul on fire. I needed the hope Mary offered. That meager shred of hope.

The surprise she promised when I called from Arizona took on greater importance, I'm sure, than she anticipated. It gave me something to look forward to. I cornered Drew the first day back. He said he promised Mary he wouldn't tell, and I'd know soon enough. "When?" I demanded, "Today? Tomorrow? Next week?"

He looked past me at everyone in the hall. "It'll happen when it happens," he said. "But we can't be seen together, okay?"

I knew then that whatever they'd done was trouble. And Jake confirmed it at lunch that day, when he came up and said to me, "What you're doing is *not* cool." I told him I didn't know what he was talking about. Because I didn't.

A few days later, the weather warmed, and the snow started melting. I got a call from Drew. "Keep an eye on the football field tomorrow," was all he said. I got in early next morning. I wanted to be the first to see trouble coming. After every class, I found a window to look out on the field. At first, there was a bed of snow across the whole thing. Then there were just patches, with a mound in the center where the Lebo logo was. Finally, after lunch, enough of the mound had melted that I recognized what was underneath. You could only see a corner of it. But if you knew what you were looking at, it was unmistakable: a mattress. And if you knew who put it there, there wasn't any doubt where it came from.

After my next class, red letters started to appear, just on one side at first—a SHA on top of an ON. An hour later, the message was clearer. SHAM and ON J. *Shame on Jake.* I skipped out of last

hour and went to the park where I could look down into the stadium. I sat under the tree where Mary took me after the attack.
The snow melted off the mattress before school ended. The
message was complete, upside down and facing the school. I didn't
know how to feel. Did anyone understand what it meant, besides
me, Mary, Drew, and Jake—and whoever he'd told? Mary had put
herself in trouble's way to pull off this surprise. It meant something
to her. And she was sure it would to me as well. But the more I
thought about it, the emptier the gesture seemed. Nobody cared.
Except people who would get angry.

School got harder after that. Rumors swirled that I put the mattress on the field. The teasing was one thing. The anger was something else. I wish I could say I stood up to everyone who shouldered me in the hall, swore and spit at me, yanked at my clothes,
and threatened me. But I wasn't that brave. Without Mary there, I
couldn't muster any resistance. What we used to laugh at together
as petty ignorance took on a malignant power when I was alone.

I'm not telling you this for sympathy. The way I behaved—the
yelling, the things I said—I don't expect that from you. I won't
apologize for being gay. And I won't apologize for being too weak
to handle the hate. But maybe if I didn't shut you out, if I'd tried
to tell you what I was dealing with, you would've understood why
I had to leave. At least I wouldn't have left hating you, and you
wouldn't have worried so much.

You were right about one thing back then: I *was* planning to go
straight to Mary. My idea was to take the train to Connecticut after
school was over and sneak her away. We'd get an apartment in
New York with the money Grampa Wes gave me, find jobs, and
live our lives the way we did in Mary's house when no one was
there to judge us. Looking back, it was a good thing you told me
they'd already warned the police I might come. I know I said some
awful things to you about that. Sorry. I was just…shocked. That
you would warn Mrs. Santoni that I was threatening to leave. It
seemed like you'd gone over to the other side.

Don't get upset. I know you were hoping a threat like that
would keep me home. How were you to know it would have the

opposite effect? After that, I couldn't stay. Whether you meant to or not, you'd drawn a line. So I still went to New York, found a place with a couple roommates, and got a job waiting tables. I told myself I'd give it a month before reaching out to Mary, wait until late summer, long after everyone expected me to come. But August passed, and I started making excuses. Maybe Mary didn't want me to rescue her. After all, she hadn't put up much of a fight about leaving. Why didn't she?

So because I couldn't summon the courage to go to her, I put the blame on Mary. What had she done to hold on to me? So she snuck Jake's mattress onto the football field and called him out. Was that all she thought of us, that we were partners in revenge? If she really loved me, she would've stopped and considered all the blowback I'd get for her prank. I never did try to reach out to her that summer. Then the months started going by. Now and then, I'd circle back to the dream of rescuing her. But every time, it felt a little more painful, a little less hopeful. Every time, I beat myself up that much harder. So months became years, years became indifference, and Mary became nothing more than an old scar.

Then I started putting together this surprise for you. And I had see her. I say I *had* to. I didn't. I could've taken care of what I needed myself. That's how it's turning out anyway. I admit it. This whole idea sprung from selfish reasons. It was a good excuse, whether I knew it at the time or not. I wanted to see Mary. Simple as that. Sure, I dressed it up in loftier ambitions. But maybe I'd been wanting to see Mary from the moment she left. Maybe that desire was a tiny seed inside me I didn't realize was there, a seed I'd been nurturing for years—until the day I got this idea that popped it open.

Sorry to be so mysterious. You must be wondering why I'm telling you this now. Go ahead. Roll your eyes. Beats walking out of the room. That's our way of dealing with things we don't want to hear, isn't it? I'll have you know, I've become as good an escape artist as you, probably better. That's why I picked now to do this. You can't very well leave, can you? Imagine if we were at home and I started in about Mary. You never would've sat still to hear all this. How much I loved her. How she saved me. How devastated I was when she left. I never would've admitted how sorry I was to hurt you, how lonely I've been…how much I need you.

After I ignored Mary's Facebook request, she kept trying to connect with me. She friended some Lebo classmates I kept in touch with, and they accepted her. I was amazed they remembered her after four months so long ago. But that's Facebook for you. Hardly anyone's a real friend. They're just props in the fantasy we tell about ourselves. So she starts liking my posts. Then she starts commenting, cracking inside jokes, bringing up things only I know. I wouldn't take the bait. Finally, she drops the pretense and writes a few comments pleading with me to answer her. If you read them and didn't know the history, you'd think they were just friendly suggestions to get together. But I knew Mary, I could hear the edge in her voice. It was so unlike her, so vulnerable. I wish I could say I felt pity, that I extended her mercy and responded. But I didn't. I closed my account. That was about a month ago…

Just last week, I was out at the REI at Settler's Ridge to get some hiking boots for that Alaska trip I told you about. So I'm standing there, checking out the wall of boots, and someone behind me asks if they can help. I turn around and it's Drew. We haven't seen each other since high school. He shudders, literally twitches at my sight. His eyes dive all around for a place to hide. Then he gathers himself and asks, all serious, like he really wants to know, "How *are* you?"

I'm just as shocked to see him as he is me, but I'm in no mood to chat about old times. So I say, "I'm in need of boots." That seems to come as a big surprise. While he's mulling things over, I take the nearest sample, thrust it at him and say, "How's this one?" That snaps him out of it. He gets my shoe size and escapes to the back room.

I figure, that's that. He got the message and there won't be any mention of the past. But when he's kneeling in front of me, he says, with his head bowed, "I was so sad to hear about Mary." At first, I'm thinking he means something she said on Facebook.

"I don't talk to Mary anymore," I say. He looks up and he's confused. His mouth drops open and even before he says it, I can see it in his eyes. "Oh God, Grace. I'm so sorry. I thought for sure you'd know. Mary died a couple weeks ago. An overdose, I heard."

I don't know how to describe my reaction other than to say I switched off, went numb, vanished. I remember telling Drew I would take the boots, and him following me up the aisle to the register, saying how sorry he was, for everything, and me nodding and muttering, never mind, never mind. And somehow I got through buying those boots and getting in my car and driving home. And when I closed the door of my apartment, I took this huge gulp, this stab of air, and I fell to my knees and I wept, like I never have before, like all the tears I'd ever held in burst through all at once.

I still find myself crying. It comes on by surprise now. I can't control it. I don't think I'll ever empty of it. I'll always see her the way I imagined that night I spied on her—trapped in a corner of her beautiful house, with her family all the way on the other side of the darkness. I'll always blame myself for not seeing how wounded she was, not going back to her when she called me that next morning, not answering any of her notes to me, not recognizing the desperation in them. How could I have done that? How could I have abandoned the only person I ever loved?

Now, don't *you* cry. I'm sorry. I shouldn't have told you this right now. I know you said you wanted to hear it, but you didn't know where this was going. *No.* No, you can't write. I'm okay. Really. More than anything, I just—I wanted you to know. Because you've always worried about me finding someone. I wanted you to know that I did. I found my love. And it was pure, and it was over-powering, and it was…a miracle.

I don't want to have to hide that from you anymore. I don't want to have to be ashamed of it. No. You don't need the pen. You don't have to explain yourself. It's not your fault. I never opened up and trusted that you'd understand. I hate to say this, but I thought, how *could* she understand? She's never known a love like this herself. It's a horrible thing to think, I admit. And maybe it's wrong. Ever since I learned how young you were when you had me and how little _____ cared, I just held onto that. Warren and Drake and that guy you dated for about a month. Josh. I know you didn't love them. So I just assumed. I never bothered to ask.

Have you ever loved anyone, Mom? Not me. I know you love me. You know what I mean. Has anyone ever touched your soul? Have you looked into their eyes and known, with absolute clarity, this is what love is?

I didn't mean for this to be upsetting. It's just, if I could wish something for you...Never mind. I'll let you sleep.

Sorry. You closed your eyes. I thought that's what you wanted.

Come on. You don't need to write anything. We can talk later.

Alright! Don't shake so much. You'll pull the line out of your arm. I'll loosen the straps, but just enough. Just this much. Don't grab at the tube. Promise?

Here's the pad. Keep your hand still.

I'll get the pen.

ROGUE

OWEN MANLEY, 2001-02
Told by Josh Guffigan, The Green Weenie, Carson Street, Pittsburgh, PA

Told you it wouldn't be easy to find. I've been begging Butch ever since I got here: get a sign. We're a bar, for fuck's sake. You want people to know where the place is, put the name up in neon, carve it on the door, spray paint the window. Anything. Know why he doesn't do it? He hates the name. That's why. The Green Weenie. Sounds like an alien gay bar. Hell, I don't even like telling people where I work. But he owns the place. He should own the name. Fact is, it *does* means something. But you've got to be pushing 60 to know what it is. The Green Weenie was a charm for the Pirates in the Sixties. Their play-by-play guy, Bob Prince, used to waggle a real hot dog to jinx opposing teams or bring the Bucs good luck. It just so happened, those Forbes Field dogs had a sickly green cast. So someone got the idea to sell little plastic Green Weenies at the ballpark. Check out the top of the menu. That's a Green Weenie from 1967. Yep. Pretty much a Martian hard-on.

So you want to know about Owen Manley. The inside story, eh? Sorry to be such a prick on the phone. It's just, you caught me off guard. I was like, how's this chick know I roomed with Owen? I forgot about that article in the paper. That was my 15 minutes of fame. My Kato Kaelin moment. *Golly, I don't know anything. I just lived in the basement. Owen never said a word about the money or where he was going.* That's about the sum total of what I said. Now, you think you're going to come in here, turn on that recorder, and after 15 years of silence, I'll spill the beans. I hate to disappoint, but I don't know much more than what you read in that story. Sure, I lived in the basement of his house. And, yeah, I was as close to him as anyone. We hung out. We shot the shit. We partied. But Owen Manley never let anyone get to know him. The way things went down, I think that's pretty clear.

You don't believe me. Fine. I'm used to it. I'm a 45-year-old bartender. Everyone expects me to be full of shit. It's the currency of my trade. You come in here. You buy a drink. I listen to your bullshit. You give me a tip. And I let you fill me up with more bullshit. That's how it works. I'm coin operated. But sooner or later that bullshit's gotta come out. Who in their right mind would expect the truth out of a bartender?

I'll tell you what I *do* know about Owen. First time I saw him, he was sitting right there, at the front of the bar, that cramped wing under the window. I must've had my back turned because, all of a sudden, he was there. He and his girl. Casey. You know about her? I guess you wouldn't. Anyway, there they were, her with a sketch pad, sitting up straight, and him, slouching, wild-haired, wide-eyed, open-mouthed, head swiveling around to take in the scene. Like this was the hippest place he'd ever stumbled into. It wasn't, by the way. Not then. Not now. Carson Street has been happening for a long time, but this bar and the people who come here have always been the same—worn out, withdrawn, and uncompromising. Regulars. *Yinzers.* That's all we get here, and they wear their don't-give-a-fuckedness like a badge of honor. Maybe that's what Owen was mooning over. I don't know. How else do you explain a couple in their twenties digging on a place like this?

It just so happened they showed up on a Tuesday. That's when the most regular of regulars, the hard-core Weenies, get together. It's a wonder Owen and Casey found seats. I guess it was destiny for them to meet everyone that night. Werner showed them his old photos from his hometown in Belgium. Barry held court about Villanova basketball and tried to get them drinking bourbon, like he did with everyone else. Rhonda went on about all the movie roles she'd missed out on because she wouldn't blow casting directors. To hear her tell it, she lost out on the part in *Deer Hunter* that Meryl Streep got. Don't look. She's at the other end of the bar. Tim was there too, griping about how weak the pours were and badgering me to play Johnny Cash, no matter how many times I tell him we just play jazz. And Jesse doing crosswords. And Charles with his letters to senators about the drug experiments they did on him in Nam. And Rita. And Rusty. And Mike.

Like I say, everybody was there. And their special brand of crazy was on full display. I live it every day. Same old stories. It's a wonder I don't jump off the Tenth Street Bridge. But it was all new to Owen and Casey. They ate up the nostalgia. Then again, that could've been the whole appeal to Owen. Casey too. In their own way, they were throwbacks. Owen with the long blond hair and bushy red beard, a Viking hippie in that burlap hoodie he always wore. Thor incognito. And her all dressed up in tight black, with strawberry page-boy hair and round wire-rimmed glasses. Audrey Hepburn gone John Lennon. As small and wispy as she was, and as pure and untroubled a face as she had, you would've thought she was some innocent 13-year-old.

That's neither here nor there. Point is, they fit in right away. Part of it was, they actually bothered to listen to these loonies. They seemed to genuinely care. If you asked me then, I would've said it was all an act. Even now, I'm pretty sure that's how it started. Reason I think that, they were artists. She drew, he wrote. Every time they came in, Owen would take out his notebook and Casey her sketch pad. Then they'd get one of the regulars going. By the time they left, Casey would hand Owen a sketch of whoever they'd cornered, and he'd dash off a little poem.

See that picture on the wall? That's mine. I know. Who's that hopeful schmuck beaming out at the world? That was a long time ago. Trust me: it's pretty spot on. I'm not sure about what Owen wrote: *Brimming grin. Dancing eyes. What secret in you sweetly dies?* I don't know anything about a dying secret, but I was definitely happier back then. Hell, I was 30. We're all happier when we're younger.

Dumber too. After high school, all I wanted to do was be a trick rider. You know, one of those punks who twirls around on bikes and rides up and down ramps pulling off crazy stunts. I was pretty good too. Schwinn hired me one summer to go on a promotional tour across the country. I was stupid enough to let that go to my head, got dreaming too big, passed up on college, tore my knee up trying to push a stunt. Twenty-five years later, here I am, plying a bunch of incurable never-wasses with overpriced drinks.

Owen and Casey were dreamers too. But they weren't idiots. My dream was a dead-end from day one. Theirs were actually promising. Every sketch Casey did, even the ones from here, she tried to sell. And she knew how to do it too. She reached out to the right people, visited the right galleries, put up a website before most artists were even thinking about that. Owen was just as committed. He sent his poems all over the place—book publishers, magazine editors, snooty little journals you've never heard of. He'd be up in that corner folding letters and addressing envelopes a couple times a week. They lived up the hill somewhere. She was a receptionist at an ad agency and he was a writer for a software company. Crowdware. You know them if you read that article. But those jobs were a means to an end. As soon as one of them sold something big, they planned to move to New York. Like I say, they were invested. This was their lives. At least it was going to be.

One night, Owen and Casey came in later than usual, when things were winding down. They were celebrating. She'd just found out this gallery in New York wanted to show some of her sculptures and give her a job. It was a pretty big deal, and they seemed stoked about it. They elbowed their way into the crowd of regulars that take up this prime real estate in the middle here, where I can't get too far away. Casey passed around photos of the sculptures. I don't know shit about art, but I didn't think they were that special. She'd taken big colorful block letters, each one about two feet tall, and stacked them crooked on top of each other. Every stack was a different trendy acronym—LOL, OMG, WTF. Back then, people were just starting to use those on their phones. Then Casey decorated each stack with three or four crazy little sculpted scenes starting with the letters. So for WTF—that's the one I remember—she had white tigers fiddling, whores fishing for tacos, Andy Warhol tasting a bunch of feathers. The gallery thought they made a social statement. I thought they were gimmicky. The sketches she dashed off in here were a lot better, more from the heart.

Anyway, after everyone congratulates Casey, I buy her and Owen a few shots, and they retreat to their corner. Seems like the night's going to settle back to normal. Then comes the yelling. Owen smacks his hand on the bar and says, for everyone to hear, "I said I'd move for something real. Not this bullshit." By the time I get over to quiet them down, Casey's already calmed Owen. But I hang close just in case. And from what I gather, Owen doesn't think much of Casey's sculptures either. The guy who owned the gallery was the father of a friend from school, and Owen thinks he's just doing Casey a favor. She doesn't see why that matters. "But there's no money up front," Owen raises his voice again. "At least when I sell a story, I know there will be money."

Then I hear Casey mutter, "*When* you sell one." Ouch.

"What the fuck?" Owen snaps. Yeah, *WTF*. The whole bar gets hushed. I tell Owen to keep it quiet. Casey apologizes straight away. Casey; not Owen. Things settle back down. I take a few orders. Then I hear Owen going off again. "What you're saying is you don't believe in me." It isn't as bad as the last time. No swearing. No threatening edge. Still, I drift back that way.

That's when Casey says, "If we wait for something to happen, it never will. We need to go live the life we want."

"The life *we* want?!" Owen thunders. By the time I get there, he's ranting. "I'm not going to New York broke. I'm making money here. In the job you think is so demeaning."

I get my face down level with his. "Dude. You gotta chill. Right now. Seriously."

Owen ignores me. "The job that pays for our rent," he says to Casey, "so you can fuck around with these stupid-ass sculptures."

That sets *me* off. I lean down, nose to nose now with Owen. "Don't talk to her like that!" I growl it out, trying to keep it between him and me.

He gets up real quick, knocking over his stool, pulls out his wallet and throws three twenties at me, way more than enough. "Mind your own fucking business," he says.

"This *is* my business," I tell him. "Right here. This is where I work. Anyone else and I would've kicked your ass out already."

"Don't bother," he says. Then he turns to Casey. "You *hated* those sculptures. They were just a dumb school assignment. You're the one who told me they embarrassed you."

Casey sits there, head down, taking it. Since she isn't defending herself, I do. "At least she has the guts to put herself out there," I say as Owen's walking away. Then before he gets to the door, I rub it in a harder. "You don't want to go to New York because you're chicken shit." He stops with his back to me, the door half open. I'm sure he's going to wheel around and make it ugly. But after a couple seconds, he pushes the door the rest of the way and leaves.

I don't remember much more of that night. I know I was worried about Casey going home. She called a friend around the corner to stay there. I walked her outside and watched her head down the street. The last thing I said was things would get better. He'd come around and apologize. They'd end up going to New York.

Then they disappeared. I didn't think anything of it for a couple days. Then it was a week, and I wondered. Then two. Then a month. I told myself they were gone. Everything patched up. Off to the big city, like they'd planned.

About a year later, I'm waiting in the beer line at a Pirates game and I hear a guy talking behind me. I know the voice instantly. It's Owen, golden locks shorn off, beard shaved clean. He's with a bunch of Asian guys in suits and he's got one on too. Who wears a suit to a baseball game? He's explaining the difference between a Molson and a Yuengling. I butt in and say, "I'll take a Makers on the rocks." That was Owen's drink.

His head snaps around. For a second, he's got this stunned look, like I've caught him at something. Then he breaks into a wide smile and hails me, way too loud, so everyone in the line can hear. He seems relieved to see me, and I'm thinking maybe I'm rescuing him from something. We talk a minute or so. I find out he's still with Crowdware, only he's moved to sales. Then I ask about Casey. The energy drains from his face. His eyes wander off. "Aw, you know," he says. That's when the guy behind him, this stone-faced, slick-haired accountant sort, leans in and points me to the beer lady, like *hurry up*. I take my turn, tell Owen not to be a stranger, and that's that. A chance encounter. That's all I figure it is.

A week later, he walks in here with a group of businessmen. Americans this time. It's late. The kitchen is closed, and my cook's cleaning up. "My main man, Josh," Owen calls out, and he makes this idiotic show of throwing me a fist pump. All to impress his guests, I suppose. I just nod. I don't do fist pumps. Didn't think Owen did either. He asks if he can get a few orders of quesadillas. I tell him the kitchen's closed. He acts all disappointed, then slaps a 20 on the bar. I glance at the bill, then look up at him with this blank face. He knows what I'm thinking: *what the fuck is this?* He leans in, so his little delegation can't hear and he's begging now. "Come on. Can't you just ask the cook?"

"So this is his," I say, patting the 20. I don't mean anything by it, only that I've got to give it to the cook if I have a prayer of getting him to fire the grill back up. He takes out another 20 without thinking twice. I wave him off. Best decision I ever made; I never got less than 30 percent from Owen after that. Anyway, we get the quesadillas out, and his gang gets busy gobbling them up and guzzling beers. Meanwhile, Owen's circulating, wedging in between people, making sure everyone's happy. I'm standing there, filling up pilsners, watching him, thinking this isn't the Owen I know. He's got this smooth, back-slapping patter going on, and I can tell he's working these guys to bite on some big deal. Gotta say, it was a pretty masterful job.

From what I gathered, Crowdware sold software to manage crowd control, wherever a crush of people could be a problem—subways, airports, stadiums. The guys he was with were talking about sailors on submarines. But that night was just the start of it. Owen was here every week after that, either entertaining prospects or celebrating with work buddies. And it was pretty much always the same deal: he'd take over this prime area, ask for special favors, throw money around, and generally act like he owned the place. Butch, the owner, started kissing Owen's ass like no other customer I've known. He set up a deal where Owen only had to pay his bill monthly. He told me to make sure there were seats at the bar whenever Owen came in, no matter who I had to move out. At first, the regulars hated Owen. But after a while, they started warming up to all the action. Barry suddenly had a fresh audience for his bourbon tales. And Rhonda got to spin out a new line of B.S. about her brushes with acting fame.

Every once in a while, the night would end with me locking the door and counting the day's take while Owen nursed a Makers for the road. On the house. Figured that's how Butch would've wanted it. One time I got going on about my landlord. I lived around the corner back then. It was a dump, but the price was right. That is, until this jackhole decided he wanted to sell the place. I was on a month to month. Big mistake. He started raising the rent. Anyway, I'm griping about this to Owen and he says, "You should move into my basement." Then he proceeds to tell me how things have been going so well he's bought a house in Mt. Lebanon. "Strictly an investment," he says. "Only a fat, happy family man would think of this place as a dream home." But there he was, five miles south of here, with all these empty rooms and a big lawn, watching moms push strollers up and down the street. Why didn't I move out there with him and shake up that sleepy little neighborhood?

So I did. Hell, the price was right. He charged me 200 bucks, and I got the whole basement to myself—a bedroom, my own bathroom, a living room, even a pot belly stove. No kitchen, but you can't have everything. All in all, it was a big step up. Getting out of the Carson Street scene and mixing in with Owen's entourage was just what I needed. Put it this way: when all you are to people is a thirty-something bartender in a shitty little dive on the river, you're not exactly a popular guest at the in-crowd's parties. Unless you've been hired to work them. Almost everyone I know met me as a bartender and can't think of me as anything but, even when I walk out that door. That wasn't the case when I lived with Owen. To his work pals, I was Josh, his roommate. And to all the other people whirling around Owen's crazy orbit—the clients he entertained, the ladies who entertained them, the hangers-on who crashed our parties—I was anyone I wanted to be. An X-Games star. A dotcom millionaire. The guy who drives the Zamboni at Pens games. Sometimes Owen took advantage of my talent for bullshittery. Once I was a music promoter who couldn't say enough about how smoothly Coachella went, thanks to Crowdware. Another time, I was an executive with the Charlotte Airport, talking up the software. The shit we pulled. Just to see if we could. And you know what? We got away with it. Every time.

That was one insane summer. Best my life, now that I think of it. Then 9-11 happened—and things got even better. Sounds heart-less, but remember what Owen did. Suddenly, anyone in charge of crowd control was anxious to keep it safe. And Owen was right there to help. When he closed Major League Baseball for $20 mil-lion, everything changed. And not all in the way you'd expect. Yeah, he got a bundle of money; eight percent, he told me. And they brought him into the inner circle at work, treated him like a savant. He even got a nickname: Winman. But the big change to Owen was what happened inside. The parties got smaller. Then they got fewer. He stopped being the guy with nothing to lose and started acting like someone with something to keep. It got a lot quieter at the house. And that was fine with me. I was starting to enjoy getting out of control a little too much, if you know what I mean. So we settled down. Grew up. That's the best way to put it. I even started going out with a nice lady across the lane, for more than one night too. Ilsa. She was older than me. Imagine that. And she didn't buy into my bullshit. So, of course, it didn't last.

I didn't see much of Owen at that time. He was traveling a lot. He wasn't coming up to the Weenie much either. That didn't sit well with Butch. Anyway, one night, I come home after closing and all the lights are off. Nothing strange there; it's pushing three AM. So I'm in the dark, feeling my way to the basement, and out of nowhere, I hear, "Hey." I nearly leap out of my skin. I flick on the hall light and Owen's sitting off in the corner of the living room. That late, that odd a circumstance, you'd think he'd have a Makers in hand. But no. He's just sitting there in a t-shirt and shorts. And it's cold. Damn cold. "Turn it off," he tells me. I make it dark again, but before I can leave, he says, "Do you think she would've liked living here?" I ask him who. I know who he means. But he ought to say her name. Fact is, I thought he'd given up on Casey ages ago. "I don't think she would," he decides with a finality that made me wonder why he even asked.

"You're probably right," I say, turning again to go. I'm tired. I don't want to get into it.

"You know that gallery where she worked?" he goes on. "It's three blocks from the towers. I called a week ago to see if she was there. When I asked for Casey, they wanted my name. Then the phone got passed around to two more people before this guy with a snooty, lock-jaw accent like the rich dude on *Gilligan's Island* tells me she's been gone for months, and, no, he doesn't know where she went. So why didn't the first person who answered tell me that? Why did I need to give my name before I got the story?"

At this point, I'm not even responding. Owen's just going on. Somehow, he gets around to his company's software. "We can simulate the Twin Tower collapse," he says. "Show people trying to escape. You can actually watch it, like you're God, looking down on these tiny humans you created, scattering like ants." He stops for so long, I'm sure he's done. But he off goes again. "The software takes so much into account, it's scary. We know when these disasters happen, people don't react the same. Some move immediately; others wait and process things. There's a distribution curve for reaction time. And not everyone moves at the same speed, so there's that variable. Then, not everyone makes the same decisions, whether to go down the stairs, turn down this hall, hide behind that post. If you watch the simulations closely, they're anything but orderly. There's a general flow, but it's like quantum physics, a jumble of uncertainties. Occasionally, an ant or two will go against the tide, actually head toward the danger. Then there's this swarming knot of congestion and a cluster of ants go red."

I have no idea where he's going with this. I'm just making little noises. *Hmm. Ah.* Then he says, "Crowdware's incredible at showing the big picture. But it can't zoom in on one person, get inside *their* head. If they wait a minute later than everyone else before leaving their desk, if they freeze in the hall or go toward the danger, why? Do they have a death wish? Is it something about their past that makes them care less about the present?"

I know this is coming around to Casey, so I say, "Casey's fine. She wasn't on the list."

"I know," he answers. "It's just funny. I can see the mechanics of disaster on a grand scale, watch forces at play on thousands of lives. But I can't see what Casey did. Did she flinch when she heard that boom? Did she jolt out of her chair, go to the window, and see smoke billowing above her? Was she one of the orderly ones, part of the cluster in the distribution curves that made the right moves? Or was she an outlier? Did she pause before leaving? Did she go out on the street, turn against the crowd and head toward the towers? What did she do? I don't know, much as I try to imagine. There isn't a simulation powerful enough." I'm at a loss. Part of me's thinking, poor Owen, I didn't realize he missed Casey so much. Another's wondering, what brought this on? And the biggest part just wants to sleep. "Knowing Casey," he says, "knowing her rogue spirit, she did something different. Zigged when everyone zagged." Then Owen laughs, one of those laughs that keeps going, until you wonder if it's going to turn to crying. "Hell," he says finally, "isn't that why she isn't here now?"

He has a point. She did zig off a path anyone else would've taken if they'd seen it from a thousand feet above. "Yeah," I agree. "It probably is."

He slaps both hands on the arms of the chair like he's done. And he stands up, but instead of coming toward me, he turns and looks out the bay window. "When I bought this house," he says, "people wondered what *I* was thinking. They said it was too much money. They told me keeping it up would crimp my style. *Why settle in Mt. Lebanon, when you're not ready to settle?* It must've looked like a dumb move. An outlier. I never told anyone I had my own reason for buying the house." Owen turns away from the window, out of profile, fading back into shadows. He holds his head cocked that way for a while. I begin to wonder if he's expecting me to guess the reason. Of course, it's Casey. But I don't say it. He starts coming my way, gets right up in front of me, drops a hand on my shoulder. "Will you call the gallery and ask for Casey?" he says.

I'm confused. Didn't he just say he called? "Here's how I'm thinking about it," Owen explains. "They'll ask for your name, like they did with me. After you tell them who you are, if they pass the phone around and you get some pretentious bastard, I know there was nothing personal to how I was treated. But if they tell you straight away Casey isn't there, or by some miracle call her to the phone, then that tells me all I need to know." He doesn't give me time to think about it. Just asks if I'll do it. I say sure. Then he heads up the stairs. But before he's too far up, I ask what it'll tell him. He looks down and says, "That it's okay to move on."

The next morning, Owen was already gone to the airport when I got up. He left a note with the number of the gallery and the word CALL in all caps. And underlined. I put the note in my wallet. By the time Owen got back, I still hadn't called. He didn't say anything. A week went by. Another. Still, no mention of the call. I figured he'd forgotten about it. Then he got swamped with work. Owen was one of those people who usually thrived on action, rode it like a wave. Not that winter. He looked harried, weighed down. I wouldn't see him for days. Then when I did, he'd be hiding behind his laptop in some corner of the house. He wasn't angry or anything; he just couldn't be bothered with me. If I talked to him, the most I'd get is a glance and a few distracted grunts.

He stopped coming into the bar altogether. Butch pulled me aside one night and told me it was time for Owen to pay his tab. Like it was my job to squeeze him for the money. What did he want me to do? "He's your roommate," he said. So I had that hanging over my head around this same time.

Then, out of the blue, on one of those days that couldn't decide if it was winter or spring, Owen walks into the bar. It's the dead time; three, four in the afternoon. No one's around. He's got this grim look on his face, but I pretend not to notice. "Look what the cat dragged in," I kid.

He shuts me down. "Some guys are coming to meet me," he says. "I'll be in the back booth. Can you keep people away?"

He might as well have been talking to a stranger. No, *Hey Josh*. No, *Sorry I've been a prick*. Just these cold demands. I let it roll off. "Sure, anything to drink?" I'm just talking about him. I figure I'll get the other orders when the others show.

But Owen says, "Get me a bottle of Makers and three glasses."

It's on the tip of my tongue to bring up his tab, but the way Owen's acting, I think better. You're not supposed to bring bottles to the table, but the place is empty, it's Owen, and he obviously needs privacy. I'm up on the ladder getting the bottle when the door opens. Two guys are standing there, still on the sidewalk. They're dressed to the nines, and not in an everyday business sort of way. More like heavy hitters showing up to some Mafia pow-wow. They step inside like it's a pig sty. The first guy looks around with a smug air of disgust. The guy behind him stares straight ahead, dead-eyed, stone-faced. I've seen him before but can't place where. When our eyes connect, he turns away slowly. No reaction. I may as well be invisible. I figure since it's so hard to acknowledge me, I'll spare the chit-chat. "He's in the back," I say.

"Got any music?" mutters the disgusted one. I tell him sure, and it's on the tip of my tongue to ask for a request. "Then play it," he says before I can speak.

What a jackhole. I bring them their booze and turn on the music. I know the reason they want it is so I can't hear them. But fuck that. I turn the volume down on the speaker by the bar and leave it up on the one near them. I can't catch very much, just the big shots mumbling and a few of Owen's reactions when he gets worked up. The first time he raises his voice, all I hear is, "I got it. Okay?" A minute goes by. Then Owen has another outburst. "I said I'll do it, damnit!" Then there's all this hushing and whispering.

I'm worried things might get out of hand. So I start back there. The big shots are standing now. The one with the stone face is holding out his hand to shake. Owen laughs. Then they realize I'm watching. There's this creepy pause where they stare at me. That hand is still hanging there, and the way the guy's glaring, I'm thinking he's going to point it at me and there'll be a gun. Owen laughs again. That unsticks everything. The big shots walk right past me, without a glance.

Owen's still laughing after they leave, a laugh that's souring by the time I get to him. "He expects me to shake hands. You believe that?" he says, like I knew what went down. The big shots' drinks look like they weren't touched. Owen pours one into his glass and downs the other. I ask if everything's okay. "Oh yeah, fucking great," he sneers. "Just lost my job. For something I had nothing to do with. Winman's on top of the world!"

He leans back and puts his legs up on the opposite bench in the booth. That's when I spot the briefcase in the corner. "One of your buddies forgot something," I say, pointing it out.

Owen barely glances at it. "I should throw it out in the street," he says. I tell him I'll keep it behind the bar. That gets him laughing again, quieter this time, more to himself. "Nah," he decides. "I better take it to 'em. The fuckers."

He straightens up and takes another big swallow of Makers. I'm not down with where things are going at this point. "If you're done with that bottle…" I say, and let it hang.

He looks it over for a good five seconds, like it magically appeared on the table. "No," he says finally. "I'll be needing it."

"That's a pricey bottle," I point out. "You're talking 15 drinks at 10 a pop." He just says put it on his tab, with a big hand wave. That pisses me off. "About that—" I start to say.

"Don't fuck with me, Josh. Alright? Not now."

If I keep pushing, things'll get ugly. So I leave him be. Before long, a few people wander in and I get busy. Then someone calls out goodbye to Owen and the door's swinging shut. I can't concentrate after that. I call the house three times. All I get is voicemail. I start kicking myself for not chasing after him. I'm supposed to work a double, but I call Butch and tell him I've been throwing up the last few hours. He gets Sid to cover and I rush home. At least I try. That night, we got half a foot of snow. In the middle of April. It's a blizzard all the way home. White knuckle driving. I don't remember breathing until I see Owen's car in the lane. It's cock-eyed and blocking part of the road. But he's home.

I figure Owen's gone to bed. But he isn't there. I check the living room. Not there either. When I get to the kitchen, it's cold. There's a low whistling, and I see the back door cracked open. I go to shut it, glance outside, and see Owen, slouched in a lawn chair on the patio, turned to face the driving snow. I go out to him. He doesn't realize I'm there until I get in the way of the pelting snow. "What the hell," he grouses, like he's tanning, and I just blocked his sun. He's got his coat open and there's a crust of snow on his shirt. His neck and cheeks and ears are flaming red. I tell him he's going to freeze to death. He rolls his eyes up to me and breaks into a clumsy grin. "Got a warmer," he says, pulling up the bottle of Makers. I tell him I'm not going to let him sit out there and die.

"Ah, yer jus' bad's zay are," he slurs out. That's my Owen drunk voice. Imagine that all the way through this. "You could've told me you had no intention of calling about her," he says then. Casey again. I tell him I already *did* call, that I was waiting for a good time to tell him. He throws his hands up. The Makers splashes out. "Liar!" he yells. "Such a liar."

"I'm not lying," I say. "I know what happened to her." And that part's true. "I called. They told me she'd left a month after she got there. No idea where she went."

"Just like that?" he perks up. "Didn't even ask your name?"

I say no without thinking. I forgot that meant something to Owen, that if they weren't screening calls, Casey wasn't trying to hide from him. I forgot that gave Owen hope. He sets the bottle down, leans up, brushes snow off his shirt. Then he starts grilling me. Did they say anything else? Why she left? What her plans were? I fend him off. Then he starts in with the speculating. Maybe she needed help. Maybe she was too proud to reach out to him.

I snap. "What do you give a damn? She left you over a year ago, and she's never tried to talk to you since. What more do you need to know? Wasn't it you who said if they told me right off she was gone, you'd know to move on?"

For a second, Owen's befuddled by his own logic. He gets all cross-eyed and slack-jawed. I'm sure it's over at this point. But he rallies. "That's only if they asked for your name," he says. "But they didn't. You could've been anybody. You could've been me."

I backpedal. Maybe they did ask for my name. I couldn't remember. Owen stares me down. "What the fuck is with you?" His eyes are suddenly clear and hard.

What I say next is true. I say, "I'm worried about you, Owen. That's all. You're making yourself miserable thinking about her."

"You're not telling me something," Owen says. "You're just like them, staring me in the eye—and screwing me."

I can't take it anymore. "Awright. Fine. Fuck you, Owen," I yell. "I wasn't going to tell you for your own good, but you won't let it go. Casey got married, okay? Two months after she went to New York. She met some stockbroker, they had a kid, and moved to the suburbs. Happy?" The news hits Owen like I knew it would. He rocks back in the lawn chair as if the driving snow's finally worn away his resistance. His feet go in the air, but he catches himself before tipping over. He claws for the bottle in the snow, like that's going to keep him anchored. Then he takes a swig, blinks his swimming eyes, and drops his chin into his chest. "This is why I didn't tell you," I say. "I knew how hard it would be on you."

Owen huffs. "Looking out for me," he says quietly. "Like everyone else. Tweaking the algorithm of Owen."

He's lost me. I figure it's got something to do with his work troubles, so I say, "If those guys are trying to force you into something, they can't do it unless you let them."

He laughs. "Sure they can."

"Not here," I say, tapping my chest. I don't even know what we're talking about. I just want him out of the snow. "You get to decide that. It's like you said, they can't control what one person does. It's like those outlier ants. You can always zig."

He snorts and wobbles his head. "I wish," he says, "I wish."

I take the lull to distract him. I ask if I can have a pull on the Makers. He checks the level. "For a buck off my tab," he jokes. I laugh along, and when he holds out the fifth, I pull him up by the arm. Then I take the bottle and help him inside. I walk him up the stairs, watch him career down the hall, and hear the whoosh when he hits the bed. Then I go to the basement and crash myself.

Next thing I know, lights are blaring. My shoulder's getting driven into my mattress. Owen's yelling at me. I go from dead to panic like that. I'm thinking the house is on fire. "How'd you know that?" he barks. Before I can form a thought, he's on me. "How'd you know she was married?" *Oh shit.* "All those details. Married after three months. A stockbroker. Having a baby. They didn't tell you all that when you called." I put my hands up, beg him to calm down. "Calm down?!" he roars. "*You're* telling *me* to calm down? You've been living under my roof and lying to me all this time. How long, Josh? How long have you been talking to her?"

"She calls every few months," I admit. "Ever since she left."

"She's—called you?" He restates it slowly, like I didn't hear what I said. I tell him she was lonely. She needed someone to talk to. "Were you fucking her?" he says, just like that.

I've had it. I get why he's angry, but he seems to be enjoying himself. He has this odd smirk on his face. "You know what, Owen. Fuck you. Believe whatever you want. Your whole life's a lie anyway. Go on. Keep pretending Casey gives a shit about you."

Owen's face gets all red. He keeps opening his mouth with nothing coming out. He shakes his finger at me. Then he stomps away. I think we're done. But when he gets to the door, he wheels around. "Get out of my house," he says with a trembling calm. "Now." I laugh in his face. Four AM with a crazy snowstorm raging. It's absurd. But Owen's dead serious. "Pack your shit and leave. If you're still here in an hour, I'm calling the cops."

"Great," I say. "And ask them for a U-Haul while you're at it. Because how the fuck else am I supposed to move my furniture?" He says I can back come Sunday for the big stuff. But he wants me out now. I shout after him as he's leaving, "Thanks Owen! Don't worry about me. I'll just build a fucking igloo in the fucking park."

Looking back, I wonder what he would've done if held my ground. I guess Owen could've started breaking up my shit. Whatever. At that moment, I was just tired of it all. Tired of Owen, tired of fighting, tired of secrets. Yeah, and maybe feeling bad about my part in things. So I got a hold of the Motel 6 on Banksville and left.

When I call Owen on Saturday to find out when to pick up my shit, he doesn't answer. I don't think much of it. He had caller ID. I wasn't exactly his favorite person at that point. But he doesn't answer Sunday morning either. I get worried. I'd borrowed Butch's pick-up, but he needed it back by dinner. I decide, screw it, I've got the keys. He can't lock me out. I get to the house around noon. Owen's nowhere to be found, but the garage door is open, and the house is unlocked. I should've suspected something right then. But I'm in too big a hurry. It's really gusty and warm at this point. I'm glad the snow's melted off, but the wind's a bigger pain in the ass than a few inches of slush would've been. I reverse the pickup into the garage, close the door, and shut myself in.

It takes about an hour to pack everything. I would've been out of there before the shit hit the fan if I hadn't gone looking for a shirt Owen borrowed. As I'm going up the stairs, I see kids out the front window, but I think they're playing in the yard next door. I see more out Owen's window when I'm looking for the shirt. And now I can tell they're in our yard, leaping around, snatching at the air, throwing themselves on the ground. I forget all about them, though, when I open Owen's closet door. It looks ransacked. There are big gaps on the clothes rod and hangers strewn across the floor. The shelves where he kept his kick-around clothes are all cleared off. I check his dresser: underwear and socks gone; t-shirts rifled through. In the bathroom, all the drawers are pulled out and picked over.

I know then that he's left. My first thought is New York and that crazy dream of Casey. It hits me he might've left a note. I'm on my way downstairs when I hear voices outside the front door. I yank it open and there they are, right on the stoop, a half a dozen kids huddled around like I'd caught them with a *Playboy*. Their eyes shoot up to me in horror. Then they scatter. One tosses a handful of paper in the air and it bursts open, a cloud of big confetti. Only it isn't confetti. I realize as it's raining down and fluttering away that it's money, strewn across the lawn and cartwheeling down the road. I look at my feet. There's a briefcase, the same one that stone-faced creep brought into the bar and supposedly forgot. It's nearly full of fifties. They're jittering in the wind. A few take flight as I stare down at them in disbelief.

There's nothing I can do about the bills that have blown away. It wouldn't look too good running through yards, chasing down that kind of dough. I straighten up what's left in the briefcase, snap it shut, and go inside. I have no idea what to do next. Part of me thinks: not my problem. Get in the truck and go. Then I remember those kids. If the cops get a hold of them, I'll get mixed up in things for sure. I take the briefcase into the kitchen, set it on the counter, and look around for a note. All I find is 10 fifties with a sticky on top of them. "Weenie tab," it says. I call Owen. Straight to voicemail. I decide the best thing is to call the cops myself.

They show up pretty quick, two in a patrol car. After I tell them what happened, they seem confused. Of course, I don't go into everything, only that I'd lived there but was moving out, that Owen seemed to have left, and that I heard some kids by the front door and discovered the briefcase. I don't tell them where it came from or why I was moving out. And they don't ask. They just keep glancing at each other, waiting for the other to take control of the situation. Finally, the old one says, "Well, there's no law against leaving a pile of money on your front steps."

It puts me in a weird position. I'm the one trying to make them see this isn't right. "Yeah, but that's a lot of money just to let blow away," I say. "And by the looks of his room, he seems to have taken off."

"Maybe he went on a trip," the old guy's partner offers. I argue with him. Why would he take half his clothes on a trip? "Maybe it was a long trip," he suggests, glancing at his partner and grinning.

They make a show of mulling it over, just to humor me. And they check out the house. They even look though my stuff in the pickup. Probably spent more time with that than anything. Then they go out front and search the bushes for fifties. At some point, I tell them I have to get the pickup back to my boss, and they say okay, like what was I telling them for? So I leave. And that's that.

Only it wasn't. Next day there's a story in the paper about Crowdware, how they'd agreed to be acquired by—who was it? Not Microsoft. You know… About how they were in the midst of a scandal because they'd sold software to the Chinese against federal laws. About this rogue salesman who'd set up a phony LLC the Chinese has funneled millions into. About their beleaguered president Julian Peters, local boy made good, who was heartbroken over the betrayal and working to salvage the deal for the 200-plus employees who didn't deserve to have their dreams crushed because one bad apple got greedy.

And there on the front page of the business section is Owen, standing behind Peters, grinning as his boss shakes hands with some executive; a PR photo after that big baseball sale. And Peters is staring into the camera with those same dead eyes that looked through me the day he stepped into the Weenie. The first time I saw the photo, it didn't click. But it nagged at me. How did I know that guy? It hit me a day later, when I was working. Somebody asked what a Green Weenie was. I started in on my spiel about Bob Prince and, all of a sudden, I knew. That game in the spring when I was in front of Owen in the beer line. He was there with those Asians, probably Chinese now that I think of it. And so was Peters, standing over his shoulder, watching me the whole time. That's where I'd seen the son of a bitch. He was the one who stuck his nose in and prodded me to order my beer.

If the police had talked me then, I would've buried that asshole. With what I saw, him out with Asians, him leaving the briefcase at the bar, he'd have some serious explaining to do. He's lucky I had a night to sleep on it. I kept coming back to Owen. He was getting paid to take a bullet; that much was clear. And he took it right between the eyes. They killed him in that story. He'd never get another job in high tech. Hell, if they found him, he'd be in jail. But then not to take the payoff, to leave it scattering in the wind on our front steps. Why? My first thought was, he decided not to go through with the deal. He'd taken to heart what I'd said on the patio, in the driving snow: nobody could reduce him to an ant in the software. He wanted to keep his conscience clean. Then why not leave a confession note with the money? Why let Peters and whoever else off the hook and still take the blame? All I can think is he figured if the truth came out, Crowdware wouldn't have been bought, there'd have been an Enron-like scandal, and lots of people he cared about would lose their jobs. So he kept the secret, left the money, and disappeared. A sacrifice all the way around. I'm not sure that's right either. Only Owen knows why he did what he did. And he was my friend, so all I could do was protect him. That's where I wound up after lying awake half the night.

The police came to the bar the next day and took me for questioning. After trying to convince them two days before there was something worth investigating, I found myself playing dumb and wondering what there was to talk about. They didn't buy it. They worked all sorts of angles to crack me. Asking how I met Owen, why I lived with him. Questioning how such a good friend could know nothing about his roommate's business dealings. Threatening to take my phone, check my messages. In the end, it came down to the same question I wrestled with the night before: why did Owen leave that money on his door step? By then, they'd counted, and it was just shy of $420,000. Who knows how much those kids took, how many fifties are still lost in the bushes down Vernon, or what Owen took as his fair share. Let's call it a half million for the sake of argument. Who walks away from that? And why? That's what they kept drilling me on. I just said I didn't know. And they finally let me go. What else could they do?

I don't know why I'm telling you this. I should respect Owen's secret. But it's been 15 years. Anyone he cared about has long since made their money off Crowdware. And if this story happens to blow back on a snake like Peters, oh well. He should answer for what he did, and Owen should have his good name restored. Hell, even around the Weenie, the regulars started cracking jokes about Owen. Instead of Winman, Owen Manley became Owing Money. Losing Badly. Scamming Many. No. Telling the truth now isn't going to hurt anything. Owen's long gone. They lost him in that ferry town near Detroit, where he ditched his car and went across to Canada. If Owen doesn't want to be found, they won't find him.

That's what bothers me though. Look at these. I got a bunch more at home: postcards from Canada: Kincardine, Parry Sound, Magnetawan. No return addresses. No signatures. Just these little poems: *Boats in the harbor. Bagpipes in the air. You could be anywhere. You're just not here.* Always written to some nameless *you.* I started getting these a month after Owen left. They haven't stopped for 15 years. Every six months or so, I'll get one. Of course, it's Casey he's writing to, pining after, praying for. Casey he cherishes and comforts, begs and laments, muses over and charms. I'm just someone who has a snowball's chance of connecting with her.

I think what Owen decided the night I told him about Casey, and the reason he kicked me out and bought himself time to pack and leave, was that if he couldn't live with her, he could at least live for her, honor that spirit they once had. He couldn't undo his decision not to go with Casey to New York or the mess he'd gotten into at work, but he could decide how to live with it. He could zig, like I told him on the patio, when everyone else would've zagged.

I'm going to tell you something I never thought I'd tell anyone. You have to keep it to yourself, though. Owen was right: I *am* a liar. Shocker, eh? Casey never got married. Never had a kid. I made all that up on the spot. Here's the truth. She went to New York, barely got a chance to show her art, started hanging with people she shouldn't have, and found herself hooked on heroin. She was back home in rehab for months before Owen left. She wanted to see him too, but I convinced her to wait until she'd cleaned up. She looked like hell; hollow eyes, bony, pock-marked, pale. It was good advice. But I didn't give it for her sake. Owen was just starting to make a name for himself then. I couldn't see him giving it all up to deal with a junkie. It would've been one thing if she'd been a few months down the road to recovery. But she was still raw, full of crazy dreams and crippling delusions. As it turned out, I was right to keep her away. She snuck out of the safe house and OD'd in some dump in Clairmont. Her parents took over then, got her into a program in Ohio. She called me once before she left, then I didn't hear from her, all through the winter and well after Owen left. It felt bad losing touch. But her disappearing *did* make things easier.

I didn't have to worry so much. The two of them weren't going to ruin each other. Don't get me wrong, I care about Casey—more than care, I guess. Owen was right about that too. That last night he left her in the Green Weenie, she came back to my place.

One dead night, long after Owen left, in walks Casey. I recognize her right away, but I don't say anything. She has this tight-mouthed determination, like it's taking everything she has just to walk over to her old seat in the corner. And she looks so different from the last time I'd seen her. Better, sure. Just not…her. She's had work done, not much, just enough to throw everything off—teeth too bright, skin too tan, smile wrinkles gone. She's trying too hard, when what had made her so beautiful in the first place was how effortlessly she carried that beauty, how unaware of it she was. She takes off her coat, still without making eye contact, and reveals a bright green, skin-tight dress. Then she scoots up onto the stool, lifts her eyes to me, and smiles, like we'd been whispering all night long. The whole entrance shook me. It all seemed so rehearsed. I lie and tell her it's good to see her.

"You too, Josh," she replies, and I think she means it, but it doesn't make her any happier.

"Chardonnay?" I ask. It was the only drink she ever ordered.

"I'm being good," she says. "Ginger ale is fine. In a champagne flute if you have one." I tell her I think that can be arranged.

She smiles, a brittle smile, as if stretching too much might strain old cracks. I make her the drink and we chat about nothing for a minute, I wait on a couple at the other end of the bar, then I start back her way. Before I can get close, she blurts out, "Does he ever come in anymore?" It stops me cold, first because I don't know what she means, then because I do. She hadn't heard about Owen. As big a story as it had been in town, it hadn't even made it to Ohio. So I tell her. Enough to make her understand that they'd tried to pay him off to take the blame for something and he wouldn't do it, so he had to disappear. I don't tell her how much Owen was thinking about her those last days. And there's no way I'm bringing up how I'd lied to keep him away from her. She listens to it all very quietly, gazing into her undrunk flute, and when I'm done, the first thing she wants to know is if I'd ever told Owen what she'd been through. I don't have to lie about that. She seems relieved. Then she asks if I have any idea where he went.

I thought about lying, but I figure what the hell. I reach under the bar where I kept the postcards and fan them out in front of her "These come every few weeks," I say. She turns over the one from Burks Falls. This one here, with the drawing under the poem. Read that: *Riverbend. World unwinding. Heart unwound. Hardly minding.* Now look at the drawing of Owen, with the river swirling around his face. See how the trees blend into his hair? That's all Casey's work. She did it that night. I didn't even notice when. I leave the postcards with her, help a few customers, come back to see how she's doing, then get another rush. Next time I turn to Casey, she's gone. And there's this postcard on the bar, turned so I can see the drawing straight on. Look at it. Look at the detail in the eyes, how realistically the river bends to the horizon. It's not just some hasty sketch; it's a vision, like it was already in her head.

It wasn't until later, after I'd collected up the postcards and put them back that I thought, *didn't I have five?* I recounted and realized the most recent one, a shot of the back waters of Lake Nipigon, was missing. I'd like to think Casey used it to go after Owen. Who knows? Maybe one time, I'll get a postcard with a poem *and* a drawing on it. A simple code: we found each other—and we forgive you. I have to admit, every time one of these comes now, there's that spark of hope in me before I turn it over. It all depends on Casey, her finding Owen, then convincing him what I did was for the right reasons. I'm hanging on to that last time I saw her, when she asked if I told Owen what had happened to her and was relieved that I hadn't. In her eyes, I did something good. I know Owen wouldn't see if that way. Truth is, I don't either. Unless...

Unless...

You can't put that last part in your book. I'm okay coming clean about how Owen took the fall for Crowdware but refused to be bought. But I don't want him finding out how much I kept from him about Casey. Until they find each other, that's our secret. And you'll have to keep it for as long as I live. Deal?

MONSTER

DALE MULDER AND ALICE BAILEY, 2002-2008
Told by Alice Bailey, State Correctional Facility, Cambridge Springs, PA

I still can't fathom what possessed Grant to enlist. How did such a bright boy, such a kind soul, decide that joining the army was the best move for his future? I blame the divorce. My ex says I blame everything on the divorce. Losing touch with friends, letting so much get me down, winding up here. Ask him if the blame's deserved. See what he says then. All I know is this: when we lived on Ashland, right across Washington, we were happy. Then, when the boys were in high school, Dale decided he *wasn't* happy. With anything. He didn't come right out and say that. It got voiced over time, in a series of dissatisfactions. First, he didn't like his job, so he started his sign company. Then, he was suddenly embarrassed by how shabby our house looked. His words. So we moved to Vernon. Lastly, there was the affair, with the quote-unquote intern, a 20-year-old party girl who could've been the boys' sister. An affair he never apologized for and somehow became my fault, because— again, his words—I'd lost my youthful outlook on life. I was 47. He was 49. I was a little past snorting coke and giving him blowjobs in his convertible. Just being real.

Whatever Dale thinks, it won't change my mind about Grant. How could watching your family dissolve *not* have an impact? If Dale could hear me now, he'd say, look at Scott, our older son. He went through the same thing as Grant and came out fine. Depends on your definition of fine. If you mean he went to college, found a job, and got married, okay. Beyond that, I wouldn't know. He doesn't talk to me, barely did after the divorce and stopped altogether after the troubles with Grant. What I suspect, though, is Scott's the same person he was when he also concluded it was my fault Dale ran off with his intern. Harder, more certain of himself, less thoughtful. He was the one who always talked about serving his country. He had his heart set on being a fighter pilot. Then he found out the Air Force didn't take six-foot-six pilots, and that was the end of all the military talk.

Until Grant just up and enlisted. Without so much as a word to anyone. Dale couldn't have been prouder. Scott too. Grant went from being slighted to admired, dismissed to worshipped. Maybe that was all he wanted. But what a big risk for such a flimsy reward. Neither Dale nor Scott said a word about the danger. That was left to me. Whenever I'd bring it up, Grant would stop me with a big hug and tell me it would be alright. Look where I am now. And look how much his dad's adulation was worth. After Grant came home, Dale saw him once in the hospital, called a few times, promised to visit over and over, then stopped reaching out altogether.

Don't get me wrong: I'm proud of Grant. It was a brave thing he did, going to Iraq, then coming home and enduring so much. If fate hadn't singled him out, I'm sure I'd feel differently. But once Grant left for Fort Benning, everything moved so fast. It was like he stepped onto this dark, steep slide, and I went hurtling down with him, blind, out of control, utterly helpless. Four months after training, Grant was in Baghdad. Days later, he was in his first battle. A week after that, a guy in his platoon was killed by a sniper. Then his convoy got hit by a roadside bomb, and he was pinned down in a ditch while two wounded men moaned for help, just out of reach. That was the last email I got from Grant—and the first time he questioned whether putting someone out of their misery was better than letting them suffer.

The next time I heard about Grant was the phone call. I knew everything that captain was going to say. I'd already played the call over and over in my mind. Of course, he had important information to share. Of course, there'd been an accident. And, yes, it was good news Grant was alive. But. A lost leg. A lost arm. Severe burns. On his face? Yes, his face. And, sure, Grant was a hero. And, sure, he was a fighter. And he'd pull through and he'd be home soon. And did I understand, Miss Bailey? Yes. I understood. And I would be okay. And thank you for calling. I hung up. And I said, "Well, it's done." Out loud, by myself in this big house. Then everything flooded over me. I fell to the floor. I was sobbing. I was angry. And from that moment until I left Mt. Lebanon, nothing was real. I could never seem to catch my breath.

I didn't find out what really happened until Grant came home. I knew the basics. It was in the paper. Grant and a few other soldiers were handing out candy to a group of kids when a car bomb exploded and killed 46 people, nearly all children. The fact alone was terrible enough, but to hear Grant tell it—what he saw, what he felt, how it smelled—made everything so much more horrifying. He'd finally managed to coax this one shy boy to step forward. He was holding the candy out, and the boy was closing his hand around it, looking into Grant's eyes. Then the bomb went off. Next thing he knew, he was heaped against a wall, staring at where his hand used to be. There were little bodies all around him, ripped apart. And there was screaming and moaning, and smoke and burning flesh. One paper said corpses were still clutching the candies the soldiers had given out. Grant was sure one of those belonged to the boy whose trust he'd worked so hard to gain. He talked about that constantly, from the first time I saw him in Aspinwall, all through rehab, and nearly every day when he was home. He kept adding to the story, remembering more details, seeing things he'd never noticed before out of the corner of his mind's eye. Then at some point, the story started changing.

I'm getting ahead of myself.

Grant came home just before Christmas. It was good timing. Scott was back from Arizona State, and he had a way of drawing Grant out. He wasn't depressed then so much as withdrawn. He was struggling to get his gait down with his leg. And the arm they gave him was more trouble than it was worth. It was just easier to use his left hand. But the limbs never were that big a deal to Grant. What kept him home was his face. One eye was almost melted shut and half his nose had burned nearly to the bone, so the nostril was open and raw. And that side of his lips had been smoothed away and didn't shut right. Plus, nearly all his hair was gone.

I don't blame him for not wanting to go out. Whenever we did, people stared. One girl wouldn't stop crying at Wendy's, no matter how much her dad tried to comfort her. Grant just got up and left, didn't even take his food. I never did get used to his face. Isn't that awful? They say beauty's skin deep, but I couldn't get past the image of my son as he was before and the monster skulking around our house. It's not like I displayed revulsion—that's the honest word for it. I made a point of looking right at Grant. Warmly. Showing my acceptance. Maybe I tried too hard. Maybe I'd never done that before, and it was so different he saw through me. For whatever reason, I could never help Grant come to terms with his looks, to accept that others would accept him.

That's what Scott was good at. He had a way of getting Grant not to worry about it. Whenever Grant used it as an excuse, Scott got after him. "Since when did you start caring what other people thought?" he'd say. Or, "If anybody shames you, I'll kick their ass." Once, when Grant was really in the dumps, Scott said, "You know how many people would kill to look like you? You see all these wannabes tatted up with gauges in their ears and piercings in their faces. Being a freak is cool, and you don't need anything to be one. You're the real deal." By the time Scott left in January, he'd pried Grant out of his shell. He was more dedicated in rehab, asked more questions about his upcoming face surgeries, went out a few nights with a couple local vets he'd met. We were settling into a routine. I even let myself think about going back to work part time.

I can't pinpoint when things started changing. It happened by degrees. He'd always complained of headaches, but the doctors said that was normal with traumatic brain injuries. He had a bunch of drugs for it: Ritalin, Zoloft, Oxycontin, you name it. And there were drugs for his burns and amputations. Tramadol and Lyrica and Ketamine. Grant was one big ad for the drug industry. We followed all the instructions, got on and off things when the doctors said, made sure not to take certain drugs with others. We weren't perfect, but we always erred on the side of caution. Still, how could that concoction of drugs *not* have an effect? So many were mood altering, with a list of scary side effects as long as your arm. Maybe they brought things to a head faster. Then again, maybe they forestalled the inevitable. All I know is Grant experienced what he experienced. He was a bombing victim, he suffered devastating injuries, and the images of those mangled kids were burned in his brain. No magic cocktail of pills could obliterate that.

So I guess it started with a bit more complaining about headaches. Then he was having trouble getting up in the morning, and his doctor worried about the deep sleep with his brain injury. But after he took drugs for that, he had the opposite problem: he'd wake up in the middle of the night and not be able to get back to sleep. There was nothing especially alarming about any of this. We'd been dealing with those kinds of changes in Grant's routine since the day he came home.

The first time I wondered, *is something different going on?* was the day I saw Grant sitting by our front window with his camo jacket on. I'd never seen him wear it inside before. I asked what he was looking at. "We have to keep watching," he said without taking his eye off the street. "Especially when the kids go to school." I thought, what did it hurt to stare out the window? It was a good sign. It showed he still had an interest in the world. But the next morning, I found him kneeling beside that window with the curtain drawn, peeking out a slit he'd made in the corner. I asked why he'd shut the curtains. He said, "He saw me yesterday." I asked who, and he answered, as matter-of-factly as could be, "That killer."

Nobody's going to kill anyone." I told him. "This is Mt. Lebanon. We don't see those things here."

"Because we never look," he said. "But it's here. It's everywhere. Hiding in plain sight. Waiting." I asked what he meant by *it*. Grant laughed. This sad, world-weary laugh. Then he said, "Evil, Mom. *Evil*."

I'm not a religious person. Our family never went to church. So hearing Grant talk like this came completely out of the blue. "It's just the world," I argued. "There's nothing out there more than that. And if there is, isn't it better just to trust in God?"

He took a deep breath, like he'd already run this around in his head. "Why is it," he turned to me, exposing both sides of his face, the pure and disfigured, "that we believe in God without any evidence, yet refuse to admit evil when the signs are all around us?"

I pointed out the window. "It's all in what you choose to see," I said. "Good. Evil. Nothing. Why not decide on good?"

"I've tried that already," Grant said. "If I hadn't been so trusting in the kindness of the world, I would've seen the fear in that boy's eyes. I would've seen his father off to the side, pushing him toward me, forcing his son to blow himself up."

The story from Iraq. It was twisting in his mind. "But that's not what happened," I reasoned with him. "They traced the bomb to an SUV across the street."

Grant looked confused. Then his mouth dropped open and he clapped his hand over it, like he'd been struck with a great revelation. "Now it makes sense," he said. "There were two bombs."

No, it didn't make sense. Not at all. Nowhere in the report had they mentioned two bombs. As I watched him nodding, eyes darting around, I decided not to argue anymore. This wasn't Grant. It was the drugs talking. The insomnia. The reliving of that horror. We'd been warned there might be side effects from everything he was taking, told to look for signs of PTSD. As soon as he went back to bed, I called his doctor. We got him in that day for what I passed off as a check-up. Dr. Solomon pressed him about his sleeping, his moods, whether he'd had any flashbacks. Grant did say he wasn't sleeping well, and his headaches were worse. He even admitted to feeling more downhearted. But he didn't say a word about the thoughts he'd been having. I tried, gently as I could, to bring up all the talk from the morning. I didn't say *evil*. I thought he'd take that as a betrayal. Grant wouldn't go into it, but Dr. Solomon convinced him he wasn't himself. So we switched his meds, dialed back on a few drugs with side effects of depression.

When we left the doctor's office, Grant seemed relieved, open in a way I wished he would've been at the meeting. "If I can only get some sleep," he said. "If I could just not think of anything for a while." I agreed and, driving home, allowed myself to be hopeful. But stop and think about what Grant said. How do you *not* think about anything? What would happen if you made that the condition for your wellbeing? If I tell you, don't think of a rhinoceros, what's the first thing you think of?

When we turned on Mayfair and started gliding down the hill, Grant gasped and started shaking a finger in front of us. "That's *him*," he cried out. At the base of the hill, coming toward us, was a gloomy teen, head down, fidgeting with his collar. I thought he was adjusting his backpack. But as we drifted closer, I saw his contorted face, his gnarled fingers, the way he twisted at his shirt. It was obvious he had some sort of disorder. Grant sank in his seat. "He's the killer," he whispered as if we could be heard outside the car.

I sped past the poor child. "That boy has mental problems," I said to Grant. "That's all. Just look at his face and hands."

Grant popped back up and watched the kid recede in the rear window. "He's the kind they'll take advantage of," he said. "The helpless, the innocent." Then he went on about the boy's backpack, how every time he saw him, it was heavier, and wasn't that odd? I told him again, there was nothing bad about that child; he was just damaged. Grant went quiet the whole ride up Virginia Way. Then I heard him mutter to himself, "Like me."

I couldn't get Grant on his new meds fast enough. Thank God they worked. He started sleeping in, stopped all the scary talk. We got through the summer without incident. Part of the reason things went so well is Grant had something to look forward to. Scott was due back in August and that was all Grant talked about. He was pushing himself in rehab, getting his gait down, working out, even giving his arm prosthetic another try. And they'd done a couple surgeries on Grant's face, so his nose and mouth looked better. He had a picture of Scott and himself on his nightstand, back from when the burns were bad. He pointed to it once and said, "Scott's going to be floored when he sees me. I'm almost normal again."

Then Scott didn't come. He called the week before and said he couldn't get off work. I asked why he couldn't get someone to cover for him. This trip had been planned for months. He said it was really a money issue. When I told him I'd pay, he finally came out with it. There was a girl. She'd invited him to some resort for that same week. He liked her and was worried he'd miss his big chance. I told him, "*You* tell Grant why you can't come." Scott said, no problem. Grant would understand, even if I didn't. That's exactly how he said it too, with that nasty dig. He was right, though. Grant took the news calmly. After he hung up, he just gave a spasm of a shrug, left the kitchen, and went back to exercising. For days, I watched for signs of anger, disappointment. But he never acted out. Finally, I decided it was my issue. I blamed myself for thinking the worst. After all, maybe he wasn't let down. Maybe all the rehab and therapy and drugs were working, and he was getting better. If you had seen Grant then, you would've thought so. He was sleeping. He was working hard. His spirits were up. Who was I to doubt the powers of healing?

We were weeks past the problem, into September, when the kids were back in school. I woke early one morning and couldn't get back to sleep. I was downstairs, heating up some tea, when I heard the front door open. I went to check it out and found Grant on the staircase landing. He wasn't coming down; he was going up. I mentioned that he was awake early, and he just said, "You know me. Keeping the kids safe." If it hadn't been for the mud print that the blade of his prosthetic made on the carpet, I never would've questioned him further. When I pointed out the dirt he'd tracked in and asked where he'd been, he said, "I found the perfect place." Then he smiled. It was a smile I'd never seen before, melted face or not. More of a crooked sneer than the vulnerable half-smile he'd always given. It wasn't him. I don't know how else to say it. I asked what he meant, and he said something about a tree across from Markham. That if you climbed high enough, you could see every path in the woods, along the sidewalk on Beadling, and up the driveway into the school. "You can see everything," he told me. "If they try to do anything, you can stop them."

It was coming at me so fast, I couldn't make sense of it. "Hang on. Are you saying you walked all the way to Markham? This early? And you climbed a tree?" He grinned again. Proudly. And he said it wasn't as hard as he thought it would be. Sometimes, like Grant used to say, you catch the truth out of the corner of your eye. I saw the camo shirt and the green ski mask around his neck. Then I noticed what looked like a mini-flashlight in his hand. I was feeling that sense of dread, but I hadn't put things together. And Grant seemed so pleased with himself. So I praised him. Then I pressed one more time. He went all that way, that early, to do what again?

"To see," was all he said, like that explained everything. And he jiggled the flashlight. That's when I realized what it was. My ex was a deer hunter. It was a rifle scope. I asked what on earth he needed that for. Grant huffed and cocked his head. "Trouble," he snapped. I tried to get through to him. He couldn't be climbing up in trees near a school with a rifle scope. He just cocked his head, almost like he was amused. Then, in a voice that under any other circumstance I'd call comforting, he said, "Yes, I can. No one will ever be able to see me." I told him it wasn't a question of being seen. It was about doing it at all. For a moment, he was still, mulling it over. Then he seethed out with angry finality, "Somebody has to." And with that, he stomped the rest of the way up the stairs, turned into his room, and slammed the door.

I couldn't let it go. I bounded up the stairs after him, pounded on his door, and called out his name. He didn't respond. I tried again. "If you get caught spying on a school with a rifle scope, nobody's going to care what you've been through."

"What *I've* been through?" he said finally. "What does that have to do with it?"

I'm sure there were words that could have redirected where things were headed. But I didn't find them. "You've been through a lot," I said. "People realize that—"

He cut me off. "Because they can see. Because I don't have an arm and a leg, and my face is mangled." I told him that had nothing to do with it. It was about what he was *doing*, how he was thinking. It wasn't right. I gave him a hypothetical: What if he saw someone up in a tree, aiming a rifle down on kids? What would he think? There was a pause. Then he muttered, "I wasn't aiming a rifle."

I seized on the hesitation. "Still. Think about it. You saw that boy with the backpack and you were suspicious. Imagine something…" It was on the tip of my tongue to say *worse*. But I caught myself: "Something more."

It didn't matter. There was a thump on the door, then a scraping. Grant had slid down to the floor. "So what you're saying," he whispered, like he was telling me a secret, "is that *I'm* the one I've been watching for. *I'm* the evil."

"What do you mean?" I cried out, not demanding an explanation so much as emphasizing, *you're making no sense.*

Grant ignored me. "Maybe that's how it works," he went on. "If you look hard enough for it, it finds you, like looking in a mirror. Then, if you let it, it takes hold."

I had to shut him down. So I played along. "Good thing you're not letting it then," I declared. Then I tapped on the door, like I would've patted his shoulder if there were nothing between us.

Thank God he accepted the logic. "Good thing," he agreed.

So. That prompted another round of doctors and therapy and drug tinkering. And things settled back to normal again. Normal; strange to call it that. We both knew our lives would never be normal again. We were just waiting for the next thing to happen. I delayed going back to work. He got more and more anxious to be left alone. Sometimes he'd ask me to stay with him and just be quiet for a while. Sometimes I'd tell him I didn't have to leave. It was like we were tensing together. Waiting for the release.

It happened on what I thought was a hopeful morning. Grant was in better spirits. He'd taken more time to make himself look presentable; showered, shaved, used his face lotion. When I told him I needed to go to the store, he said he didn't want to come. I asked if he was sure. He nodded and smiled, like it felt good to cross that hurdle, to not be afraid for me to leave him. So I went. And I felt fine about it. Right up until I got into the checkout line. I don't know if it was a premonition or just the course of an idle mind. But I started to worry—first that something could happen, then that it was about to, and finally, when the woman in front of me was counting change so slowly, that it already had.

I've never driven through town so fast in my life. I slowed to a crawl, though, when I saw Grant hobbling around in our street. It felt like the moment was floating toward me, like it had dislodged from some dark depth and was rising to clarity. Even after I saw that poor afflicted boy, red-faced and raging, flailing at our neighbor Mr. York, I eased to a stop. You know that sensation when you think your car's moving, but it's the world shifting around you? That's how disoriented I felt, even as I got out and walked into the trouble. Mr. York was straining to comfort the boy, but he was grunting and slobbering, lurching away and pointing all around the street, where his comic books scrambled in the breeze. And there was Grant, scurrying after them and stuffing them into the backpack. When he saw me, he smiled and rolled his eyes, like *there I go again*. "At least now we know," he said with a sheepish shrug.

After Grant rounded up the comics and gave the boy his bag back, he calmed down. And I managed to get Grant to go inside before the mother got there. It was left to Mr. York to explain what happened. He made it sound like nothing more than a misunderstanding. Grant had asked what was in the bag. Byron—that was his name—seemed like he wanted to show Grant, then had second thoughts, and things spiraled from there. The mother bought the story. She even conceded it might've been her fault for letting her son walk the streets by himself. "It's just that he sees all these kids going to school with their backpacks," she said, "and he wants so badly to be part of it."

It broke my heart. And made me furious. Mr. York was kind enough to whitewash the story, but I knew better. After they drove off, I asked what really happened. He hemmed and hawed, then finally told me. He was mowing his lawn when Grant came bounding across our yard. Byron didn't see him coming. Grant yanked at the backpack. There was a struggle. Comic books went everywhere, and the boy wound up on the ground, terrified and howling.

I could barely stand to listen to it. Mr. York is quite the talker. So it took some doing to break away. But once I did, I marched straight upstairs, banged open the door to Grant's room, and let him have it. He was lying on the floor, doing leg exercises. "What the hell is with you?" I shouted. "Are you out of your mind? What has that poor child done to you?"

Grant sat up slowly, open-mouthed and perplexed. Like he couldn't fathom what the problem was. He explained very slowly, as if I were a four-year old, that it wasn't what the boy had done to him; it was what he *could've* done to everyone else. I snapped back at him. I said everyone could see that boy for who he was, that no one else had a problem with him. "And no one else had a problem with the kid who blew me up either!" Grant bawled, going from calm to frantic like that.

"Oh for God's sake!" I yelled. "Are you on that again? Give it up! It never happened. It's another thing that's only in your head!"

"I can't help what I see," he said, on the verge of tears.

I knew where he was going. I wasn't going to let him go there. I wasn't going to let him say the word. I roared at him, "What you think you see is *bullshit*."

He shook his head. "It isn't," he declared with chilling certainty. "It's evil."

"No it's not!" I shouted. "You're talking yourself into it—and it's destroying you!"

Something broke in Grant then. His head slumped against his good knee and he nearly toppled over at my feet. He started moaning. "You're right," he said, in a thick, tortured voice. "You're dead right. This is why. This is why I need you to—I need you to kill me." And he looked up at me. Miserable. Expectant. I slapped him across the face. Hard. The force knocked him onto his crippled side. He shriveled into a fetal heap. "I can't fight it!" he yowled. "It's crushing me." Then he was sobbing uncontrollably, begging me, shrill and hysterical. *Please. Please. Please.*

I didn't say a word. Didn't apologize. Didn't comfort him. Just walked out. Down the stairs, out the door, through the lane, and into the park. A zombie. Is there anything more painful that a child could say to a mother? I collapsed under a tree on the hill overlooking the public pool, the same pool where my boys splashed and laughed when they were young and didn't know any better than to be happy. And I lied there face down in the leaves, trembling.

I didn't come back home until well after I usually made dinner. The house was quiet. I figured Grant was in his room. I got a glass of water and headed for the den. I was almost there when Grant spoke up. "Sorry," he said. I seized and sloshed water on the front of my blouse. I wasn't going to turn around. Part of me still wanted to inflict punishment on him. And silence was the only weapon I had. But he waited me out, didn't say another word—no excuses, no appeal for sympathy. Just that simple apology. Finally, I faced him. He was sitting in shadows at the end of our dining room table, like he was presiding over some long-abandoned family meal.

"You can't ask me that," I said.

"I know," he answered, "but—"

"Don't," I cut him off. And turned to go.

"I want to stop," he went on. "With all the drugs. I don't know what will happen, but I have to find out. I want to be myself again."

I couldn't make out his face in the dark, but the way his shoulders heaved, it softened me. "Okay," I said. "We'll start tapering off." And I pulled out the chair at the other end of the table and sat with him. And we let the night come on in peace without any other words.

I wish I could say everything got better. Some things did. Sure. Grant got more open about his demons. He'd tell me what he was thinking, no matter how crazy it sounded. And he was more receptive when I tried to talk him out of his delusions. But he was more volatile than he'd ever been on meds. The emotional turmoil was exhausting. I came to feel like he was trying to draw me in, make me an accomplice in his disorder. In my most vulnerable moments, I even suspected him of plotting all of it, from the moment I'd sat down in the dining room. Still, for weeks, he didn't act out. There was no hiding in trees or spying on neighbors. And when he saw that troubled boy again, Grant was astounded he'd suspected someone so benign. And he was ashamed

Then came West Nickel Mines. Remember that? The Amish massacre? I know. Hard to keep all these shootings straight. That was the one where the milkman, a father of three, broke into an Amish schoolhouse, took a group of little girls hostage, and shot five dead before killing himself. Horrible. Hard for the most stable of us to stomach. But for Grant, it was unbearable. Within seconds of hearing the news, he wailed as if those girls had been the very kids he was trying to protect. And when they showed the killer's face, and all the talking heads acted mystified that such a seemingly contented man would do what he did, Grant made me turn off the TV. "Evil! That's why!" he yelled at the black screen. I couldn't argue. Or I should say, I didn't want to. I was still of the opinion that there was no absolute evil outside of people's heads. I still thought it was the outcome of a mind gone bad. But the last thing I wanted to do was have that debate. I took it as a sign of progress that Grant wanted to shut off the story, that his revulsion for the deed was stronger than his obsession with the motive.

If only the media didn't talk about the story for days, showing the killer's face, dissecting the note to his wife, pondering the reason. I forced Grant to change channels whenever it came on, got after him if he holed up with his computer. But you can only keep the outside from coming in so long. Days after the killings, Grant bounded into the kitchen, stopped in front of me, and wagged a finger. "Whenever this happens," he started; *this*—like we'd just been talking about it, "people are shocked. Nobody the killer knew can believe it. *He seemed so normal. He was so mild-mannered. Nobody could've seen this coming.* They say these things. And we accept them. Over and over. It reinforces itself. Evil is unfathomable. You can't detect it. Yet nobody takes the time to look, to really look." Then he hurried away before I could react.

Next day, I was in the laundry room when Grant burst in. "Look at these," he demanded. On top of the dryer, he spread out three grainy images of the killer he'd printed off the internet. Then he took his hands to each image, one after the other, covering all but a strip across the killer's eyes. By itself, there was nothing too ominous about it. We'd been through worse moments. Maybe it was because he caught me with my defenses down. Whatever the case, I suddenly felt small. And sad. "Look at his wedding photo," he went on, pointing out the tilt of killer's eyes and the light in them. He compared it to the middle picture. There, the eyes were more settled, with barely a flicker, or so Grant said. Then he framed the third set of eyes. "Now. See this?" he asked. "Nothing. Just black. And flat. That was his last photo." He nodded, more convinced now than when he'd barged in. "See what I mean," he added. "You can tell. It's not that hard. You just have to look."

I covered my face and burst into tears. That made him angry. He pounded the top of the dryer. "This isn't about me, goddamnit! I'm not the bad one here." He grabbed my wrist and pried one hand free of my face. "Look in my eyes," he demanded. "See all the light? Even the ruined one shines." I nodded, just to make him stop. With that, he left. And there I was, alone in the laundry room, tears still coming, with those grainy pictures of the Amish killer gazing up at me.

A few days later, I walked into his room and there he was, crouched beside his dormer window, peering into that sight he had. Only this time it was attached to a rifle aimed down on the street. He didn't hear me come in. I marched over and shook his shoulder, the way I would if I were waking him up. The gun jolted and was swinging my way before Grant snapped out of his trance. "You scared me," he said flatly, like he wasn't scared at all.

I should've been horrified, hysterical. Wouldn't you have been? Wouldn't anyone? I held out my hand to guard the barrel from swinging closer and said, in a tone that matched Grant's understatement. "I scared *you?*" He assured me the gun wasn't loaded, like that made it okay. I asked where he'd gotten it, and he reminded me that Dale had bought it for him in middle school. It had been hidden away in his closet since then. I remember nodding and saying, "Ah yes," like you might if you weren't really listening. It was strange. The whole exchange was this contest of tranquilized indifference. "What are you doing with it?" I asked.

"I might as well be ready," he said.

"Oh," I wondered aloud. "What for?"

Grant pointed up Vernon at the Jansen's house. You know where that is. They've been here longer than your mom. An old man was sleeping in a wheelchair at one end of their front porch. And at the other end, there were three boys, teenage or older, maybe as old as Grant. They were drinking beer and lobbing something at the old man. Grant said they were trying to throw pretzels into his open mouth. Okay, so it was mean. But isn't it the sort of numbskull thing boys that age do? At least ones who don't decide to take on the harsh truth of the world so young?

I asked Grant if that was why he was aiming a rifle at them. He just said something wasn't right. That's when I told him, "You can't have a gun up here." I said it without any of the force you might expect, as if the moment hardly merited emotion. He answered that it was just to stabilize the sight. But he kept his head cocked. And his finger on the trigger. "Grant?" I prodded. Gently. Finally, he sighed, lifted his head, and held out the rifle, stock end toward me. When I took it, he swung the barrel into his chest and there was the slightest tug of resistance as I pulled. Our eyes met. Then he let it go. I gave him a little nod of gratitude. I was going to leave it at that—and wish now that I had. Instead I said, "What are we going to do, Grant? How are we going to stop this?"

"You know what I want," he replied. And he had that same miserable look as when he first begged me. I didn't get angry this time. I just repeated: I wasn't going to talk about that. Grant looked out his window, this time up into the morning sky. "Don't worry," he said, in a voice at once absent and consumed. "I'll figure it out."

I went to the kitchen, set the rifle on the counter, and stood there, staring at it. Then my knees buckled. Everything flushed out of me at once; blood from my head, pressure on my heart, any strength I had. Good thing the counter was there. It held me up when I collapsed, arms bracing across the gun, forehead smacking the granite. That should've put me out, but oddly, it knocked me awake. Suddenly, the implications of what Grant said, and how I'd reacted to it, came flooding over me. *I'll figure it out.* When he said those words, I could've protested, tried to talk him out of it. But I just walked out of the room. It was as good as giving permission. And now it was there between us. A bargain: *I won't kill you, but it's okay to kill yourself.* That's what I'd agreed to with my silence.

I took the rifle to the garage. There was a big plywood sheet we'd laid across the rafters for extra storage when we'd moved in. As it turned out, we didn't need it, so nothing was up there, and it had long since been forgotten. Where better to hide the rifle? I got the ladder and set it up under the sheet. Then, just before I climbed it—I don't know why, maybe out of an excess of caution—I checked the chamber for bullets. Dale had shown me how to do it once. When I pulled the bolt back, a live bullet fell onto the cement. I did it again. Another jumped out. Then one more. Three altogether. Three rowdy boys on Jansen's porch. I doubled over and threw up, covering the live rounds.

That was the turning point. After that, I never gave another thought to talking Grant out of planning his death. He was unstable, dangerous. And he was convinced there was no hope he'd get better, whether I believed it or not. What I started worrying about, given how deeply his mind was betraying him, was the solution he'd come up with. I never confronted him about the bullets. Maybe it was an honest mistake. Then again, maybe he'd tried to fool me into shooting him. He wasn't himself. Who knows what kinds of violent ends were roiling in that brain? I couldn't wait to find out. You understand what I mean, right? Whether I wanted to or not, I had to come up with the answer.

I'm not going to talk about the Seconal. I promised myself I wouldn't drag others into this. What's the point 10 years later? I'm opening up because I need to. If someone else wants to tell his story, that's up to him. Here's what I told my lawyer: Grant had a prescription for Seconal to help him sleep. What I didn't tell him was we needed a lot more. I got away with refilling the prescription once. Then, I got help with the rest. That's all you need to know.

The night I decided to do it, I brought Grant a glass of water and set it on his nightstand. Grant straightened up in bed and thanked me. Then I showed him the vial. I told him the pills helped with sleeping. He screwed his face up. He'd been sleeping fine for weeks. I pointed out that if he *did* take them, he shouldn't take too many; they could be very harmful. Then I stared at him. Waiting. He rubbed his jaw with his good hand, pinched at his melted lip, and finally asked how many was too many. I said all of them. He shook the vial. There were 60 pills. What would happen, he asked, if he *did* make a "mistake"? I told him he'd fall asleep—and not wake up. Then I said he shouldn't take the pills too fast. He could get sick. But not too slow either. I suggested taking 10, waiting 30 seconds, taking 10 more, waiting again, and so on. All that time, Grant's good eye shifted back and forth like he was doing math in his head. Finally, I told him I had to get changed. I was going out for the night, meeting an old friend downtown. His chest lifted like something had inflated him. He nodded slowly at me and whispered, "Okay."

When I came back 15 minutes later, he was slouched over, rubbing the back of his neck. He didn't hear me come in, so I had a chance to watch him thinking. It was hard. After a moment, I said, "You don't have to do it." He gave a start and straightened up in a way I'd never seen before, probably how he snapped to attention in the army.

First he said, "It wouldn't look like much of an accident, would it?" I told him I didn't think he cared. Then he said, "I don't want people thinking I killed myself. I don't want Dad to think that." I was stunned. His father? What did Dale have to do with it? "It would hurt him to live with," he explained. "Just the shame of it. Not because he cared." It was sad. Here was a boy—yes, he was still a boy—disfigured, broken, haunted, who through it all, loved his dad, even knowing his dad didn't love him.

I didn't have the same sympathy. "So you wanted this to be an accident?" I asked.

"I guess," he said, like it was the first time he'd given it thought. "I don't know. This way, it's either going to look like I did it—" His eyes flashed to me. "Or you."

I was incredulous. Did he want me to make it look like *I* did it? I told him I'd go to jail. He said he didn't mean it that way. What he meant was he didn't want to hurt *anyone*. That's why he was thinking of an accident. "This is the best I could come up with," I snapped. "No, it's not an accident. And people are going to be hurt. But we'll all be hurt no matter how it happens."

Grant stared at me, thinking it over. "And if it doesn't happen," he added, "a lot more people could get hurt." I didn't say anything to that. Then he hit me with this: "What do you think God would say?" Now he was wondering about *God*? This late? "He doesn't want us to take anyone's life," he went on, "even our own. But what if taking our life spares others?" I told him I didn't know. Frankly, I was losing patience. But Grant kept at it. "Do you think God will love me even if I sin against him?" Like I say, we weren't religious. Grant may have believed in evil. But he never talked about God being real. Until then.

I didn't have the energy to argue. So I asked, "Do *you* love him?" He closed his eyes and shrugged. I thought he was going to cry. I had to console him somehow. "If there is a God," I said, "one who truly cares about us, he has to be forgiving." It was the best I could do. Thankfully, it was enough. Grant exhaled and put on a brave smile. Then he told me I should be going. We stared at each other. His smile started crumpling. I leaned down fast before it fell, hugged him hard, whispered I loved him, and hurried away.

I wheeled onto Washington like an escaped convict. I cracked the windows, turned the radio up, and sang to it. I weaved in and out of cars. That feeling of breaking free lasted all the way to the tunnel. Something about passing under the hills brought me back to Grant. I felt the pull of his anguish, the chain tightening. What was he doing? Was he taking the pills? Had I been clear enough that he could pass out if he wasn't quick about it? As the lights of the tunnel streamed by, I got this crazy pang of remorse. How could I turn around? I'd made a mistake. The whole thing was a terrible, unpardonable mistake.

By the time I popped out the other side, crossed the bridge, and found myself in the snarl of downtown traffic, I came to my senses. Going back so soon was the worst thing I could do. If he'd already started taking pills, would I stop him and call the hospital, or would I let it go on, sitting there, waiting for him to die? And when the police asked why I didn't do anything, I couldn't say I wasn't there. There wouldn't be anyone to back me up. No, I had to go through with this. The time for reconsidering was long past.

So I drove to the restaurant and met my friend. And we talked and laughed about our time in high school, when the world was so much simpler. And I told her about Grant and the accident and said he was getting better. And I proclaimed my hope for the future without a hint of doubt. Then I got drunk. Not falling-down drunk. Four-glasses-of-wine drunk, enough to worry about driving. After we said our goodbyes, I found a coffee shop and sat there, drinking cup after cup until they closed. At midnight, I started for home.

When I turned onto Parkridge, I saw the light on in Grant's window. At the foot of the stairs, I called out his name. No answer. I climbed the steps, paused outside his door, then poked my head in. He wasn't in bed. I checked the room. Nowhere. I checked all the upstairs. Not there either. I went downstairs and circled the living room, dining room, den, and kitchen. I was heading for the basement when out of the corner of my eye, I noticed Grant's leg prosthetic. It was leaning against the wall beside the back door. I turned on the outdoor lights and looked out into the yard. He would've been easy to miss if I hadn't known what I was looking for. Flat on his back in the grass, one foot cockeyed, he could've been a pile of leaves, forgotten lawn tools, a heap of clothes.

I turned the light off and went out to him. Spread-eagled in the grass, without either prosthetic, Grant was gazing at the sky, mouth open, with this expression of sudden wonder, stuck forever in ep-iphany. I looked up at what he was gazing into. I'd never seen our sky so big, the stars so bright and crowded. I kneeled beside him. I didn't need to check to know he was dead. I was going to close his eyes, but he looked so peaceful, his gaze glinting with stars, welcoming the void. I left them open. I thought about covering him from the neck down, running inside and getting a blanket. But there was something about the way Grant was splayed out. It was a cold night, yet here he was in a t-shirt and pajama bottoms. And he'd come all this way without his prosthetic, hopping, I suppose. He knew he was going to die and decided to lay down and face it, without any defense. He died this way for a reason.

In the end, all I did was kiss his forehead. Then I called 911. When the police showed up, they turned on the floodlights. I waited on the patio while they searched around Grant. I saw them pick up the empty glass, and one of the officers called out that he found a vial. I didn't think anything of it until he added, with a hushed voice I wasn't meant to hear, "This guy really worked for it, hopping all the way out here on one leg and his one hand full."

I don't know what happened then. Call it a mother's instinct. Suddenly, I forgot about all the plotting I'd done to hide my guilt. Seeing my boy there, flat on the ground, so naked in his brokenness, and those officers traipsing around and throwing out easy judgments, it got to me. I stormed across the yard. "He didn't kill himself," I shouted. "I did." And the instant I said it, I fell to my knees and burst out weeping. My whole being was given over to this unearthly wailing. Imagine a dam of thin glass suddenly giving way. It wasn't the force that overwhelmed me so much as the surprise. Amazing as it sounds, until that moment, I hadn't really confronted the magnitude of what I'd done. Of course, I'd killed Grant. It might've been for worthy reasons; putting him out of his misery, sparing others the threat. And, no, I hadn't forced him to take the pills. But I'd given them to him. I'd come up with the solution. And the astonishing thing about it all—the miracle, if you want to call it that—was the relief I felt, the serenity that flooded into me after I said the words: *I poisoned my son.*

That's how I felt in the early hours after Grant died. That's what the police have me admitting on record. But it wasn't that simple, not after my lawyer got involved. He wanted to know if Grant asked me to help him die. I said no. He didn't come right out and say, "I don't believe you," but I could see it in his face. What he said instead was that there was a big difference between Grant asking me, and me convincing him to die. The sentence could be years instead of months. If there was anything, any shred of evidence at all, that Grant had put me up to this, it would help. I wouldn't budge. I wasn't about to stand up in court and tell the world my son begged me to take his life. If people believed that, they'd think the worst of Grant. In the end, the only evidence we offered was medical testimony about PTSD and Grant's discussions with his psychotherapist. We played it as a mercy killing, a mother lifting a burden from her tortured son. The jury found me guilty of manslaughter. That's why, after 10 years, I'm still in here. Probably will be for another four.

I'm not telling you this to absolve myself. I accept the blame for Grant's death. What I've been wrestling with is whether it was right to keep his story a secret. It's not dishonoring Grant to tell the truth about his struggles. They shouldn't be hidden. Whatever happened to Grant after that bombing, he felt the force of evil more intensely. You can say it was a delusion. You can call it the product of a damaged mind. Psychosis. Schizophrenia. Whatever. But it had a grip on him. There's no denying that. It filled him with the most horrific obsessions. Yet rather than succumb to them, he chose to destroy them. He fought evil and defeated it. And in those final moments, out in our backyard, in the depths of his anguish, God came to him. And he forgave him, filled him with light, and took him away. I believe that. I really do.

I know a lot of people won't see Grant as a hero for this. Or they flat out won't believe me. I know I'll be accused of trying to deflect my guilt. The truth is, I'm still not sure whether telling you all this is right. I wish I could be more certain. I wish I had the peace that faith brings. But I don't. Even after all this, I'm still not that close to God. That's a gift I haven't gotten. At least not yet. So I could be wrong telling you all this. I don't know.

What do *you* think?

PROPERTY

GARY BRONSON AND KUMI, 2008-09
Told by Rick York, Granny Barnes Road, Nashville IN

I haven't lived next door to that house since I was a kid. The only reason I knew the people you're asking about is because after my dad died, I spent the summer cleaning up our house to get it ready to sell. Go figure that one. I'm the youngest of six kids, the farthest away, and Dad makes *me* his executor. It's just lucky I got laid off and had time to fix up the house. Otherwise I would've sold it as is—and way below what it's worth—leaky roof, bad septic, basement mold, and all.

Anyway. One thing you should know right off the bat: I'm a happily married man. So yeah, my job situation hasn't been the best for marital harmony, but we get along. For the most part. That spring was a little more tense than usual. The kids were sowing a few too many wild oats. When you live in these backwoods, there's a lot of ways to get in trouble. Let's just leave it at that. So I was yelling at them, maybe too much, and they were yelling back. Nothing out of the ordinary. But Eileen, my wife, said, "Enough. You've been griping about all the work your dad's house needs, and you've got all this time on your hands, why not just go over there, spend a couple weeks, and fix it up?" When she put it that way, it made a lot of sense. See? I'm not one of these crazy, wives-should-besubmissive husbands. She had good advice and I took it. That's what I mean: happily married.

What was I talking about? Oh yeah. Point is, it's not like I went to Lebo looking for trouble. Things just happened. Damned if I know why. I met Gary first. He was in the front yard, spraying dandelions with Round-Up. Not exactly the most environmentally conscious thing. But I get it. Weeds are weeds. I went over, shook his hand, introduced myself. He seemed like an average Joe. I would've pegged him for mid-thirties. The only thing that looked old were his eyes. He was really pale, and he had two layers of bags under these teeny slits, a thin one that was bone white and a puffier purple one that went below the socket in a succession of darker ripples. Really more like five bags. My first thought was, dang, he looks like a raccoon. If that doesn't draw a picture, imagine some- one recovering from a bad hangover. I can look that way after a few too many. I chalked it up to him being an indoor guy, one of those nerds who stared at computers all day. I don't know. I never did find out what he did for a living. That's what I mean: a flat-out mystery through and through.

Anyway. Like I said, he seemed normal enough, except for the eyes. And maybe his voice. I forgot about his voice. Definitely the voice. He had this deep, grating—what would you call it?—not quite pompous, but overdone; this stagy, overdone voice. And he just boomed words at you. Some people are like that. They can't hear themselves. Maybe it's an inner ear thing. So, yeah, I noticed that day one, too. But I didn't hold it against him.

Even when he warned me about his woman, it didn't change my opinion. Actually, he came across like such a thoughtful guy, I felt bad about myself. I remember thinking, *man, I'd never get this personal about Eileen with a stranger*. I understand now why he thought he had to tell people, though. It was the only time he lowered his voice. He quit spritzing the Round-Up and said, real hushed and all confiding-like, "Just so you know, my wife's only been in the country a few weeks. She speaks English okay, but it's hard to understand. And she's just getting used to the customs. No big deal, but I didn't want you to be surprised."

Now that I hear myself talking, I guess it wasn't such a low-key heads-up. But I'm lousy at reading body language. Maybe if he'd mentioned, "By the way, she's such a teeny wisp of a thing, she could pass for my child," or "I'm putting her to work on lawn chores," or "Did I tell you she's Asian?" that may have grabbed my attention. Not saying there's anything wrong with *any* of that. No discrimination here. If it was my dad, that might've been a different story. But he fought in the Pacific during World War II, so you can understand. All I'm saying is, a little more information would've been nice. Fact is, I *was* surprised when I first met her. You would be, too. Imagine coming home and there's this—how else to put it?—oriental fairy pushing a lawn mower across your neighbor's yard. And I say fairy not just because she was small, but also because, well, she was dressed like Tinkerbell, if Tinkerbell was going to war. She had on this wispy flowered dress, white knee-high socks, and—no shit—black lace-up boots. To mow the lawn. Dead serious. So that was weird. And a touch unsettling.

Actually, walking over to introduce myself, the feeling I had for her was pity. There she was, leaning into that old clunker, trudging behind it in those boots, barely making headway. My mood changed, though, when I got to the line between our lawns. Only calling it a line is an insult to geometry. You know how going between properties, you mow along the line first? That way, when you turn the mower, you're not making a bunch of jagged teeth in your neighbor's lawn? Yeah, she didn't know that. So, some rows went a few feet into my yard, some were close to the mark, others fell short. It wouldn't have been a problem if she hadn't set the mower so low. I'm talking fairway-for-the-Masters low. Low. So I had these tongues jabbing into my lawn all down the front yard.

My pity for her? Gone. As she slogged toward me, I waved my arms like she was headed off a cliff. When she was steps away, I shouted. Her head was hung as low as you could go, below her hands. That's how much she had to lean into that beast. If I hadn't moved, she would've run over my feet and stalled on my shins. So I moved. Like a bullfighter. And I got next to her and gave her shoulder a tap. I may as well have lit off a firecracker. She didn't just flinch. She pogo-sticked away like some frightened wingless bird. The mower went dead, so I knew she could hear me. I wanted to tell her what she was doing wrong, explain the little trick about cutting the boundary first, educate her on the proper height to mow a lawn. Maybe she didn't fully understand me, being new to the country and all. And maybe I came off kind of scary. Eileen always thinks I'm mad when I'm really just thinking. Whatever. You would've thought I was the Devil incarnate. She backed away with the widest eyes I'd ever seen. I raised up my hands. *Whoa-whoa-whoa. Hang on. Just trying to talk here.* But she wasn't having it. She backpedaled like I had a bomb strapped to my waist, bolted into the house, and slammed the door.

So. That first encounter didn't go well. And I was just trying to help. That and protect my lawn. I felt kind of bad about it and wanted to make amends. So I went out and bought these kindling sticks, a little longer than a pencil, maybe twice as fat. And I hammered them in along the property line, from Vernon all the way to the back hedges. Spaced around 10 feet apart. Just to say, "Hey, here's the line between the yards. Not trying to threaten anybody, just offering some neighborly guidance."

That didn't work either. I don't know where I was the next time she mowed. She must've snuck it in while I was sleeping. Whatever the case, I woke one morning to a lawn that looked like a slalom course. The good news was, she mowed along the line first, so my lawn wasn't gouged by a bunch of ugly turns. The bad news: she couldn't hold a straight line from one peg to the other. And we're talking no further than a car length. So there was this super short ridge meandering between our houses. Oh, and as a bonus, she went out of her way to run the pegs over. Every single one. That's one thing she was incredibly accurate about. Standing there, looking at that curvy line, I could barely hold my temper. And I wanted to. In the grand scheme of things, this was no big deal. I counted to 20, out loud, like all the anger management classes tell you. And it worked. Sort of. What I decided as I simmered down was that, as neighbor conflicts go, this barely rated. Heck, the guy down that hill has a dog that ate my chickens. And my boy broke a window in his house shooting off his BB gun. You want to talk about potentially explosive situations. Difference is: I can reason with that guy. And Eileen's pretty sure he's cooking meth down there. So you wouldn't expect reasonable out of him.

Anyway. I couldn't have that kind of talk with this lady. She wouldn't let me get near her. And Gary seemed to have dropped off the face of the earth. I hadn't seen him since our first meeting. As the week wore on and we were coming up to the next mystery mowing, I decided to adjust my peg strategy. Since she was having trouble following a straight path—and why wouldn't she with the way she hung her head to shove that mower?—I figured a line of string might do the trick. And in case she didn't get the point that she shouldn't run over the pegs, I got bigger stakes and hammered them in, so the string hung about two feet off the ground.

Oh, and the last thing I did—very important—was stay home Friday and set my alarm for eight. No late-night trips to The Saloon. No hangover to sleep off. Even at that, I nearly missed her. It was just after six when I started flopping around in bed. I drifted in and out a while before it registered; that was the sound of a mower I was fighting to muffle. I bounded out of bed and hurried downstairs in my t-shirt and jammy bottoms. By the time I got outside, the mower had stopped. I was glad at first to see a straight line separating our backyards, but when I came around the corner, my heart sank. There she was, two feet into my lawn, just past a crooked stake, sitting Indian-style, untangling the string from the mower. The whole run of string from that stake to the road had gotten gobbled up in the blades. I give her credit. She was trying to fix it. But she was going about it all wrong. She had the mower on its side, propped against the handle bars. Big no-no with those old machines. The gas can easily leak out, which is exactly what it was doing, only she couldn't tell because she was on the other side of the mower. At least this time she was dressed for the part; no fairy outfit and army boots. She had on a Steelers t-shirt, a pair of Levis, and white Converse high tops. Everything was new.

So she'd been doing okay until something went haywire. Maybe she bumped the stake and didn't notice the string popped free.

But then she'd drifted into my yard and was compounding the problem by spilling gas everywhere. I didn't want to startle her again, so I kept my distance. And I spoke with the friendliest voice I could manage. "Looks like someone could use a hand." Not the smoothest thing to say, but it seemed to work. She still shot me those wide eyes, even made a few crab-walk scuttles away from me. The difference this time, though, was she didn't look terrified.

"I follow string," she said. More or less. I mean, her English was much more broken than that. I'm not going to try to imitate her. Just imagine the usual troubles with L's and R's, and jumbled word order. It did take me a while to get past that. But what captivated me immediately, what made me stop and listen to her, was the sound her voice made, the music of it. It was quiet but dignified, fragile yet still somehow forceful.

Can you tell I've been thinking about this? I said we got off on a bad foot, and it's true. And things got worse. But I don't want you thinking I was a slave to circumstance, that I had no feelings in the matter. It comes back to that voice, the first time she spoke, cowering beside that mower. I can't help but think she got to me then. Anyway. She said she'd tried to follow the string, and I made a point of praising her. Then somehow the string got caught in the mower. I said accidents happen. She apologized and started to say she'd fix it, when I interrupted. "By the way, my name's Rick." I held my hand out. She just bowed her head. "And you are?"

Her eyes cast down. She gave the quickest flash of a smile. You might wonder if it even happened. "Kumi," she answered at last.

Kumi. That's what she said. I pronounced it just like that, right after she told me. I'm terrible with names, so I use that technique to remember. "Well, Kumi," I said. "This probably isn't the best way to fix things. You're leaking gas." She went into this spasm of bows and waggling prayer hands and mumbled apologies. I calmed her down. Then I crouched beside her. I was trying to figure out how to tilt the mower to stop the leaking when things got weird.

"Hey!" came this angry bark behind us. It was Gary. He was stomping our way with this pissed-off frown. "What's the problem?" he boomed in that over-important voice of his.

I tried to smooth things over. "No worries. Just got this string caught in the mower. Probably my fault. I put it there to help Kumi tell the boundary."

"Kim," he corrected me. I glanced back at Kumi—I knew for certain that's what she said her name was because I did the repetition thing. But she wasn't sitting next to me anymore. She was standing now, over in their yard, head down, facing Gary. "Why does she need help with the boundary?" he asked.

Hell. I knew right then I'd dug myself too deep. "Oh, well, you know," I stumbled along in an aw-shucks kind of way. "She just strayed a bit too far the first couple times. No biggie."

Gary stared me down for a good long second. Then he started jabbering at Kumi. I don't care what Gary said; that's what I'm calling her. I say jabbering because it was in some Asian language, so I couldn't understand a word. But I got the gist: he was demanding to know what happened. She whispered some pained confession. And he wasn't pleased.

"Hey, it's fine," I said, standing up for her. "All good, really."

He came toward me and, for an instant, I wondered *is he going to take a swing?* But he brushed past, grabbed the handle of the mower, and wheeled it over into his yard. "I'll take care of this," he said with that cold air of his. He clamped his other hand onto Kumi's elbow. Then he marched away, practically dragging her beside him, she having to double-time it to keep up. I noticed then how baggy her clothes were. The jeans kept slipping off her hip and she kept hitching them up. Her Steelers shirt had fallen too, but she didn't bother with that. These weren't clothes she'd taken part in buying. That much was clear. And for some reason, that morning, that was the most disturbing thing of all.

Next day, I discovered a perfect white line painted between our houses. I'm talking baseball-foul-line perfect, straight and clean, wide and white, from the curb all the way back to the hedges. I would've rather had a jagged lawn. Maybe that was Gary's point. Maybe it was his way of saying, "If you're going to get bent out of shape about the property line, fine. How's this for marking our territory?" Then again, maybe the line was just foolproof guidance for a young wife lost in a strange world. If it were me, I would have cut the lawn myself. But I wouldn't have snapped at her either. Who am I kidding? My wife would've carved me a brand-new asshole if I got after her like that in front of someone. No. We were in two different situations, Gary and I. Who was I to judge what I barely understood?

So I let the whole foul line thing go. Gave him the benefit of the doubt. And I have to say, next time Kumi mowed, she stayed right on that line. But it wasn't long before we had another flare-up. It was early one night. I was sitting in the den, having a beer, watching the Bucs, and slowly it dawned on me that there was this fluttering. *Dut-dut-dut-dut.* Then it went away. Then—*dut-dut-dut-dut*—it came back. Sounded like a woodpecker. I went to check it out. It was Kumi. She was struggling to aim one of those rapid-fire sprinklers at the strip of lawn between our houses. My first thought was, here we go again. But watching her soaking herself, it was clear she had no idea how the sprinkler worked. Against my better judgment, I went to help. Kumi seemed relieved. I showed her how you could adjust the rings to shoot water in any wedge you wanted, pegged it into the ground, and stood back with her to watch the results. As the arc climbed the stone on the side of their house, I caught a glimpse of Gary spying down from the shadows of an upstairs window. I didn't think he saw me spot him, at least he didn't duck away. But looking back on it, maybe he knew I saw him and stayed where he was to make a point. Anyway, I pretended not to notice him, made a few tweaks to the sprinkler rings, and hustled back inside.

Who needs to get messed up in that crap, right? Well, apparently, giving Kumi even that much help wasn't appreciated. Next morning, having coffee on the deck, I heard this weird fizzing. When I went to find it, I saw a puddle curling around the corner of my house. Right away, I thought, *damn, she left the sprinkler on.* Sure enough, the whole side of the lawn was flooded. And because of how Vernon slopes, all the water was on my side. Both my basement window wells were filled to the brim. I figured the sprinkler had just keeled over in the grass. But no. It had been stomped down, so the top was flush with the ground. The whole thing was fizzing and crackling like a live wire. This wasn't an oversight. Someone had done it on purpose. And no way it was Kumi. So I got a little mad. I clawed the sprinkler out of the mud and whipped it against the side of Gary's house. I say "whipped." That's too strong. More like a slow lasso. I *wish* I could've whipped it, but the hose was too stiff with water. So the sprinkler barely clanked against the stone. It definitely didn't smash.

That became a point of contention an hour or so later. I was busy bailing water out of my basement wells when Gary bellowed right behind me, "What happened?" It was like he was trying to put on a bad show of false innocence. I just glared at him. I didn't notice Kumi at first. The son of a bitch had brought her along to witness his charade. Gary cocked his head, exaggerating his confusion. Then he turned to Kumi. "Did you leave the water on?" She was busy gaping at the flood and didn't seem to hear him. "Kim," Gary barked. "Look at this mess. Look what you've done."

"No, no," she protested. "I turn off!"

I'd had just about enough. "Who are you kidding?" I snapped. "I suppose you're going to say she's also the one who stomped the sprinkler into the ground."

He gave me this incredulous look, this mock disbelief. "What's going on here?" he said to Kumi, with a sort of gritting menace.

She cowered, like she'd heard that tone before and knew where it led. "I didn't do," she mumbled, bleak and downcast. His left arm shot across his body and froze in the start of a back hand. Kumi flinched. He let his hand drop, turned to me, and grinned. Actually grinned. It was sickening. He ordered her inside. I just stood there, silent. To this day, I don't know why. He accused me then of breaking the sprinkler. I said it probably broke when he stomped on it. But there was no fire in my words. Again, no excuse. He claimed he didn't know what I was talking about, then vowed if Kumi had done something wrong, he'd get to the bottom of it.

"I saw you last night," I said finally, as an afterthought. "Up in the window." That rattled him. I wish I'd thought of saying it before he threatened Kumi. He went silent, and we faced off, both knowing the truth, but neither sure of how to use it. Finally, he marched away, broken sprinkler choked in his hand, hose following like a captive snake. It was all so…ominous. And I felt miserable; for his open threat to Kumi. And my silent complicity.

Talking to you now, I can call it what it was: shame. Pure and simple. But at the time, that was a hard pill to swallow. I didn't want to admit I'd stood by while a man all but announced that he beat his wife. For days, I couldn't get any work done. I kept looking for a sign that Kumi was okay. When I finally saw her mowing the lawn, a weight lifted off me. Thank God it's over, I remember thinking. Now, how can I avoid that sort of trouble again? I'd been considering a fence even before I'd gotten to town. My dad always wanted one, ever since that girl who hung around the Judge started cutting through our yard. So I went to Rollier's, bought a bunch of fence panels and posts, rented an auger, and got busy. I fenced in the whole backyard, so Gary wouldn't think it was personal. And I made sure to keep the fence a good six inches inside my property and not extend it past the back corner of my house. Those are the neighborhood rules.

Still, when Gary saw the fence, he griped about it. He asked if I was sure the whole thing was on my side, said he'd hate to make me tear it down. Then he told me I'd put the panels up wrong, that with all the boards in a row aimed his way, and all the back-side cross boards facing me, people would think it was his fence. I had to explain that wasn't how it worked, as if I was talking to a child. Who doesn't know how to put up a fence? If you own the fence, you have the good side facing out, so that's what people see.

"If this were my fence," he said, "I'd put it up exactly as you have it: good side facing in, so I can enjoy it."

"Well, then," I said, "I'm happy you're happy."

"I'm sure you are," he boomed and laughed. "Thanks Rick. You just built me a fence."

The son of a bitch. I can't tell you how badly I wanted to hurt him. So as he was walking away, I said, "How's Kumi?"

He stopped, turned his head slowly and glared over his shoulder. That creepy grin spread across his face again, and for what seemed like forever, it was his only answer. Finally he said, "*Kim* is more of a homebody now." Then he disappeared behind the new fence. I remember wondering right then whether I'd made a mistake. A fence might block out what was happening next door, but it wasn't going to keep me from thinking about it.

Sure enough, the fence only made things worse. Gary got a surveyor out to stake off the property line, and—wouldn't you know it?—his lot was more pie-shaped than anyone had ever treated it. The back two panels strayed into his yard. Before I had a chance to reason with him, Gary had painted his run white, even my side, because technically, it wasn't my fence back there. So I had a beautiful run of natural red cedar extending nearly all the way to my back hedge—then 16 feet of milky, half-assed crap.

Next time I saw Gary, he was on a ladder, propped against the fence, cutting a branch from a tree in my yard that hung over the new property line. This wasn't any tree. It was my dad's favorite, a redbud that had sprawled across our yard since I was a kid. And this prick was taking a chainsaw to it. It was a hot night, and, okay, so I had a couple of beers in me. But I wasn't in the bag, nowhere near. My blood would've been boiling, alcohol or not. As soon as I heard that chainsaw and saw him going at our redbud, I was out the door. At the last second, I thought, I need to protect myself. There was nothing around but an old push broom. That was a mistake, not just because, you know, chainsaw versus broomstick, but also because I may have come off a tad confrontational. Gary had his back to me, sawing away at the lowest branch hanging over his yard. I had to get his attention somehow. It might've been smarter to nudge the ladder instead of his leg with the butt end of the broom. Still, it wasn't any harder than poking him with a finger.

He scowled down at me, eased off the throttle, and yelled over the rumbling two-stroke. "What the hell? I could've cut myself!"

"I'll tell you what the hell. You're cutting down my tree."

"I'm not cutting down *your* tree," he said. "I'm cutting down *my* branches. Read your by-laws." With that, he revved up the saw and finished off the branch. I took the brush end of the broom and shoved the ladder. Gary lost his balance for a second and gave a spastic wave with the whirring saw. Then he caught himself. And he looked at me. And there was murder in his eyes. I don't know how else to describe it. I stared right back with the same menace. I wasn't going to back down this time.

"If I fall," Gary said, "who knows where this chainsaw might go." He revved the saw and slashed the air between us, in case I didn't get the point. Then, he turned and lined up the next branch. I shoved the ladder again, and this time, I kept the pressure on. Gary swept the chainsaw down and lopped off the brush end. I fell to my knees, the saw snarling above my head. When I looked up, he was grinning at me. Then the shrieking started. I thought something was wrong with the chainsaw. But after Gary shut it off, the shrieking was behind us. I turned around.

There was Kumi, kneeling in the yard, her hands together in prayer. She called out to us: "Please stop! Please!"

"Go back inside," Gary ordered, with a threatening calm.

Kumi dropped her hands and sat back on her haunches, upright and unguarded, like she was offering herself in sacrifice. She was wearing the same Steelers shirt she had on when she was wrestling with the mower, only it was ripped at the collar now. And it hadn't been washed. From halfway across the yard, I could see the dark blotches. Blood stains. And I could see her face, the dull purple around her half-closed left eye.

"Jesus." That's what I said then. It just came out.

"Get in the house. Now!" Gary commanded. He might as well have been talking to a dog. I looked up at him. He was already looking down at me. The rage had drained out of his eyes. In its place, I detected a glint of weakness, the smallest crack where his shame was exposed. "I'm within my rights," he told me, starting the chainsaw rumbling again.

"Why don't we call the police?" I shouted over the saw's stuttering growl. "Let them sort this out." I cocked my head, just a twitch, over my shoulder, and added, "All of it."

Gary's face went red. Kumi started screaming again. But this time it was at me. "Please Rick! No. Don't call!" She had her hands together like before, in prayer, imploring me not to bring the police into it. Everyone was quiet for this long awful moment. Kumi was staring at me, tears shining on her face, that one swollen eye. I stood up. When I turned, Gary was a couple rungs lower on the ladder. He gave me this sad sort of half grin, like it was all out of his hands, like he was the one at her mercy.

I couldn't let it go. "If there's any more…damage here," and I paused just like that to get that word right, "I'm going to make that call. Understand?"

Gary's jaw jutted out. His mouth puckered. "You don't want to do that," he hissed. "That would be bad."

I picked up the pieces of my ruined broom and walked away, all the while looking to Kumi. When I got to the end of the fence, I gave her a nod. I could've done it on my side, shielded from Gary. But I wanted him to see me do it, to know that I'd do what I could for her. When I got inside, though, I had second thoughts. So I had the police to hold over Gary. But what would they do? I hadn't actually seen him hit Kumi; it's not like they'd take him away. And as long as he was alone with her, who knows what sort of abuse he'd inflict? He'd made it clear that getting the police involved was a bad idea. Did I really want to force that issue?

I called Eileen. "You've got two more weeks," she said. "Then you can stop worrying. If you see anything else, wait and phone the police from here." It sounded sensible enough, but even as I listened to her, I wondered. How was it helping to wait? What if Kumi got hurt in those last days? How would I live with myself? Just because I called from Indiana, would Gary be less inclined to punish her, or would I worry about her less? I didn't raise any objections to Eileen. Even with the little I'd told her, she seemed annoyed I was so preoccupied with the issue. Part of it was how we treat our neighbors. But there was also the Kumi thing, the fact that I cared about her. You could hear it in the way she called her *this Kumi girl*. Don't get me wrong, Eileen cared—and she wanted me to care too. She just didn't want it to get personal.

I couldn't help it. Not that I didn't try to care less. In fact, after the redbud standoff, there were reasons to think things would get better. For one, Gary didn't break out the chainsaw again. Then he let Kumi mow the lawn. She smiled and waved, and I didn't spot Gary spying anywhere. Then he came into my yard one day, said he was sorry for being such an asshole and offered to repaint the fence. Had colors picked out too, slate grey for the panels, white for the posts. They looked nice together. And he foot the bill for everything; paint, brushes, fancy mitered post-tops. He wanted to paint the whole fence himself too, but I didn't feel right about that. So one day, we got after it together. There wasn't much talk, but no tension either. Halfway through, Kumi brought us glasses of water. When she came close, she looked me straight in the eye. Two things struck me: she didn't bow like she'd always done, and the bruising around her eye was gone. I took those as good signs. Then. Now, I think they were all part of a show.

Gary probably would've gotten away with it too. Seeing Kumi like that, free to hold her head up, smiling, even wearing something other than that ratty Steelers shirt, it all made me feel better. And when we were done painting, the fence looked great. If it weren't for an exchange I had with Gary while admiring our handiwork, I wouldn't have started worrying again. "This ought to boost the curb appeal," he said. I agreed. He waited, then went a step further. "You must be getting pretty close to putting it up for sale." I told him it would be up that week. "Then you're gone. For good, eh?" I nodded. "Well…we'll miss you," Gary said. Then he smiled. There was a slight quiver as he tried to hold it. He slapped me on the back and walked away. And I watched him go, trying to figure out what it was that suddenly bothered me.

For a few days, I got consumed in the details of listing the house, working with my real estate agent Donny Dale. But after everything was settled, I found myself coming back to that trembling grin. The hand hitting my back. Kumi. What was going on next door? Were things really better? Or was this all an act to keep me quiet until I left? I needed to talk to Kumi, get her alone, ask if she needed help. Time was running out.

One day, Kumi was out in the yard, back where the hedge runs along Parkridge behind our houses. She was kneeling with her back to me, working in the garden. If I wanted to talk to her, I'd have to walk all the way across Gary's lawn. I pictured him up in a window, shielded by curtains, eyes trained on Kumi, like she was bait. If I could get onto Parkridge, behind the hedge, I could crouch in front of Kumi, talk through the branches, and Gary would never see. But I couldn't just walk down the lane. You know all the windows facing that way. Then I had an idea; why not go along the far side of my other neighbor's house? I snuck out my garage door, ran across his yard, and hurried down his driveway. There was a path alongside his backyard. It was choked with brush. I doubt anyone had taken it in years. I fought through the overgrowth and got into the lane. As soon as I saw Gary's rooftop, I bent down and duck-walked behind the hedge. It hurt like hell. As you can see, I'm not in the best shape. I probably didn't need to squat so low. But I'd come that far. I didn't want to blow it right at the end.

I started whispering Kumi's name a good 20 feet before I got in front of her. I didn't want her to be surprised and make a sudden move. Still, when she saw me in front of her through the tangled branches, she gave a jolt. "It's okay," I said to calm her. "It's Rick." She whispered back that Gary could be watching. "I figured. But he can't tell I'm here. Not if you keep working." She gave a slight bow. Even at that, I winced. "Don't. Just do what you've been doing and listen. I'm leaving next Monday. For good. If you're in trouble and need a way out, I'll drive you somewhere. But it's got to be in the next four days, before Saturday." She stopped digging then. Her eyes lifted to find mine between the branches. She didn't say anything. She didn't have to. The look said it all—how much she hurt, how afraid she was, how desperate things had gotten. "Remember," I said. "Before Saturday." She buried her head and went back to work.

I didn't think she'd pull it off that day, but I kept an eye out just in case. On Wednesday, it rained, from morning to night. Next day, Donny called. Someone wanted to come through the house. He said the light was best in the afternoon, when the sun slanted into the kitchen. But I made him get it over with by noon. I also refused to leave, told him I'd hang out on the back deck. He begged me to go, said it would be off-putting for people to come out and find me there. I didn't care. I wasn't going to miss the one chance Kumi might have to escape. Nothing ended up happening that day either, if you don't count pissing off Donny.

Friday was the last day I could do anything. I'd already arranged for movers to come Saturday and take the last of my father's stuff away. Sunday I'd agreed to go with an old buddy to the Pirates game. And Monday, I was driving home. I started watching out the window at six AM. Gary mowed the lawn around 10, then he went back inside. Later, I made myself busy in back, watering my dad's flower beds while I snuck glances next door, hoping for a sign.

Then it was night. I didn't stop watching for Kumi. But I did start drinking. I found a half-empty bottle of George Dickel in the back of the cupboard above the fridge. Not where we usually kept booze. That was my dad's whiskey—until Mom made him quit liquor. The sneaky bugger; he must've hidden one away. I resolved to kill it in Dad's honor those last few days, a finger at a time. But the Kumi thing rattled me. Had she wanted to escape, but couldn't find a time? Had she tried and gotten caught? Why did I tell her it had to be Friday? What if the only time she could do it was the weekend? Could I really not have left the movers or missed a lousy ball game? What a shit I was. The whiskey drained away with the night. I never made it to bed. Fell asleep on the couch in the den.

When I heard the doorbell, I knew I'd screwed up. The movers were supposed to be there at eight. As I staggered through the kitchen, I saw the clock at 8:20. I opened the front door, all ready to apologize. But there was Kumi, wild-eyed and skittish, clutching an old blue suitcase. It looked like a toy. I couldn't have fit two days' worth of clothes in it. She was wearing the same frilly dress she had on when I first saw her mowing the lawn. Same boots too. That's what registered first. I don't know why, because she also had a fresh shiner under her left eye. I should've reacted better. "What are you doing?" I demanded.

"You say Saturday," she said, her head jerking from me to the street and back. "Gary gone. I have place."

I was going to tell her I'd been clear about coming *before* Saturday. But what was the use? She was here now. I pulled her inside and grilled her. Where did Gary go? The store. How long would he be gone? Maybe half an hour. Which way did he go, up or down Vernon? Up. Where was I taking her? Downtown. She handed me a scrap of paper with an address. Everything was happening so fast. It didn't help that my head was pounding from the Dickel. I wrote the movers a note on the back of a pizza box. It was all I could find. Then I put it on the welcome mat. *Door open. Back soon.* I hustled Kumi into my car, had her duck down as I backed out, checked that Gary's truck wasn't coming, then raced away, down Vernon, down Mayfair, and along Cedar, past the park.

I didn't let Kumi sit up until we were near Dormont. That's how nervous I was. And I didn't punch the address on the scrap of paper into my phone until we were cruising through the tunnel. It was on the north side of the Allegheny, just off the 279. They call it Spring Hill. Not the worst place in the city, but nowhere I'd want to live. Once we got across the river and there was just the exit to wait for off 279, I started asking questions. Did Gary hit her again? Yes, she said. He hit her all the time. Were they married? He promised they would be, but no, he'd never kept that promise. Would he come looking for her? Probably. Was I taking her somewhere he'd been to before? No. Did *she* know the place we were going? No. We got off the highway and looped back toward town on this lonesome road. Suddenly I felt desperate, like I was dropping my daughter off at a stranger's house. I fired off more questions, cramming a month of wondering into these last minutes. Did she know the people at the address she gave me? Her mom knew them. How long had she been in the US? Not long. How did she and Gary meet? It was a mistake. Where was she from? Vietnam.

We passed a big limestone church and wound our way into the hills, on a web of crumbling roads with more empty lots than houses. The higher we went, the worse it got; more sparse, run-down, and overgrown. The road we wanted was the worst we'd taken. I'll never forget its name: Golden Way. It was a jumble of weeds, broken-down cars, and caved-in foundations filled with trash. Every third or fourth lot, there would be a house, either perched looking down the hill or teetering back on it, like it was getting shoved off. No sidewalks. No front yards. Just the road, a sloped strip of shrubs, then houses.

We came to where my phone said to stop. A rickety, three-story wreck stood between garbage-strewn lots. The siding was a sick faded green. Half the boards were gone, exposing black tar paper. The gutters were rusted out. The two top windows, which jutted out of a worn-down roof, were broken. The second-floor windows were all boarded up. And on the first floor, there was a sad little porch, covered by a sagging roof. The wall that framed the front door had been taped over with fake stone peel-and-stick paper that was charred on one side. I couldn't describe what my dad's house looks like as clearly as I can that dump where I drove Kumi. That's how hard it is in my head. I still dream about it.

We eased to a stop. The house loomed over us. "This can't be right," I said. A head-high thicket of weeds hid the way to the porch. Kumi opened her door. "*No-no-no!*" I grabbed her arm. "You're not going up there." I heard a screen door creak and clap shut. A frail Asian woman was waving from the porch. I rolled my window down. She chattered at me. Whatever she said was good enough for Kumi. Before I could catch her, she was out of the car, yammering back at the woman, who was coming down a little path toward us, pushing through the weeds. I jumped out and got between them as the woman was reaching to take Kumi's suitcase. "No," I barked, chopping my hand down in front of her. She lurched back, eyes blinking. "No!" I repeated louder.

Kumi tapped my shoulder. "Please, Rick," she said, as quietly as if we were in church. "Is okay." What could I do? Every instinct told me it was wrong to leave her in such squalor, maybe as harmful as leaving her with Gary. But she wanted to stay. I can't explain why, but at that moment, standing beneath that ruined house, with the skyline of Pittsburgh gleaming in the distance, I began to cry. Kumi dropped her suitcase and hugged me. I hugged back—and this magnetic current seized us. "Is okay," she repeated, comforting me. *Her*, comforting *me*.

I put my hands on her cheeks, holding her face like some precious vessel. And I was going to kiss her. I knew I was, felt it so powerfully that it was as if I'd been dreaming it forever. Then I didn't. I just ran my thumb, gently as I could, over that bruise above her cheek. And I closed my eyes, hard, then harder. And the tears stung. "I'm sorry," I sobbed out. "I'm so sorry."

When I opened my eyes, she was gazing back at me, tenderly. "You save me," she whispered. "You *save* me."

So I left her there. By the time I got home, the movers were nearly done. There wasn't much to take, just the antiques I wanted. Everything else had been sold. It was more than a U-Haul, but less than a Mayflower. Anyway, my dad's money was paying to get it to Indiana. While I was checking the house, one of the movers said, "Your neighbor asked if we knew where you went. Seems ticked off about something." I was going to ask what he told him, but decided what was the difference? I was going to have to deal with Gary no matter what. It was good, at least, to be forewarned.

Sure enough, soon as the truck pulled away, Gary came stomping across my lawn. "Where the hell did you take her?" he boomed. I gave him my best Indiana slack jaw. "Don't play dumb with me," he snapped. "Kim's gone. You're gone. And the movers you were supposed to meet don't know where the hell you are."

I screwed up my face and asked him who Kim was...then I acted like it just dawned on me. "Oh, you mean *Kumi*." I've never seen someone's face get so red. He tried three times to talk, the whole time brandishing a finger inches from my face. Finally, what came out through that big voice of his was: "You fucker. You fucking fucker. You want to go down this road? You want to fuck with a man's property? Okay."

I couldn't let that go. "Property?" I challenged him. He gave me those murderous eyes, hissed, and stomped away.

You can guess what happened next. I even went out on the deck and waited for it. It wasn't 10 minutes before Gary came out, ladder in one hand, chainsaw in the other. He cut off every branch and every twig of my father's redbud that so much as brushed the air on his side of the fence. When he was done and walking back to his garage, he stopped just beyond the fence and gave me the finger. I wasn't going to do anything until he did that. Then I drove uptown, rented a chainsaw of my own, and cut down the rest of my dad's redbud. Fuck Gary. He wasn't going to have the last word on my memory. Better that I destroyed it altogether than he got the satisfaction of knowing he ruined it for me. All the time I worked, I kept an eye out for him. I was sure he'd come out to gloat or somehow escalate things. But he never did.

The next day was Sunday. I was supposed to go with my friend to a Pirates game. But I was afraid to leave the house. I called him an hour before he was due to pick me up and begged off going. He wouldn't hear it. "If you don't want trouble," he said, "you're better off getting out of there." In the end, I let him talk me into going. It was a shitty farewell to the Bucs. They lost to the Brewers, 7-0. And I couldn't stop thinking about Kumi. If I were driving, I would've left early. I would've driven into those bleak hills, parked under that skeleton of a house, pounded on the door, and insisted on seeing that Kumi was safe. Instead, we stayed to the last lousy out. We forced our way through more warm beer and stupid banter than we had the heart for. And when my buddy dropped me off at my dad's house, neither of us was up to a proper goodbye.

I'll say one thing, though. He was right about getting away. I didn't think once about Gary at the game. But as soon as I punched in my garage code and the door starting lifting, all my suspicions came back. The light was on. Not the one from the automatic opener; the bare bulb by the house door. Had I left it on? I wasn't sure. I looked around. Nothing seemed out of place. There wasn't anything left to *be* out of place. Inside, the doors and windows were locked. No way Gary could've gotten in. I'd convinced myself I'd left the light on and was just being paranoid—until I saw my car keys next to the sink. Not on the side I always put them, but by the dishwasher. That's when it dawned on me. I went back into the garage and tested the side door. It was open. Damn. What did Gary do? I started my car and drove around the block. It worked fine. I checked the water main, the electrical box, the furnace. Hell, I even checked the stove for leaking gas. There wasn't much else to mess with—except my head. That's finally what I decided Gary was doing. Leaving the light on, not locking the side door, moving my keys; he wanted me to know he'd been in the house. He was counting on it eating at me.

I wasn't going to give him the satisfaction. I laid down on my blow-up mattress to take a nap. With all the sun and beer, it didn't take long before my mind was a jumble of swirling dreams. Then it hit me, jolted me so hard I was sitting upright before I even formed the thought. Gary was looking for where I'd taken Kumi. My stomach lurched. That scrap of paper with the address on it. In seconds, I was out in the garage, searching frantically though my car. I couldn't find it, not on my side or Kumi's, not in the cup-holders, not on the floor, not between the seats. Maybe Kumi had taken it with her. Maybe it had fallen on the street when I'd jumped out to confront that old woman. Maybe. But probably not.

Before I could think, I was pounding on Gary's door, scream-ing for him to show his face. I'd had it. I was going to punch his lights out right there and then, consequences be damned. Nobody answered. Screw it. He'd broken into my house. I could trespass around his. I spied in the windows, tried every door. His car was gone; I could see that much through the little windows on the garage door. And he must've left in a hurry. Dishes were out, lights were on, the TV was going. None of this was good. When I rounded the corner by the fence, I looked up at the window where he'd spied down on us. There, taped across the panes, was what anyone else might mistake for a Steelers pennant. You see Terrible Towels all over town. I knew better. It was that ratty yellow shirt Gary made Kumi wear, and it was splattered with her blood. Rather than hide it in shame, he was waving it in my face.

I don't know how to explain what I did next. I could say it was my way of exposing Gary, laying bare his savagery. But, honestly, that didn't even enter my mind. Had you seen me then, you would've just thought I'd gone mad. The chainsaw was the closest weapon I could find. And the fence was the first thing I thought of that would hurt him to lose. You can read more into it if you want. I'm sure deep down, severing my complicity had something to do with it. After all, I'd overlooked the reasons why he might fortify his privacy. So there's that. At the time, though, it was pure madness. I slashed and kicked at that fence, roaring over the growl of the chainsaw. I was mindless, primal. There was no purpose, no restraint to my rampage. It was all fury and hate. Wood chips flew everywhere. Boards keeled over at my feet. By the time I came to my senses, not from any pang of conscience, but out of sheer exhaustion, I was five panels in, a good forty feet of ragged gashes. I turned the chainsaw off, surveyed the damage, then made my decision. The whole thing was going to go, all the way to the two last panels, the ones Gary said were his. Take them. Try to hide your hate behind that.

I started the chainsaw again and got busy, this time with cold, concentrated tenacity. All that I left was a line of three-inch high stumps, the exposed parts of the posts I'd sunk into the ground. Standing there, sweaty and covered in saw dust, heaving to catch my breath, I thought of the twigs I'd put along the property line weeks earlier, the ones Kumi had accidently mowed over to start all this. Maybe that mistake, the fact that she got my attention, wound up saving her. Anyway, those stumps seemed fitting.

So did leaving. What was there to stay for? Just waiting in that empty house to see if Gary brought Kumi back? If he did, it would break my heart. I'd call the cops, but what would they do? Then when they left, we'd have to have it out. Was I ready for that? Did this really matter that much to me? My family, the people who counted on me and loved me most, were 400 miles away. Why hadn't I gone already? There was nothing left to do. What was I hoping for? What had I been hoping for all summer? That was the real question. I could've taken care of my dad's house in two weeks; there wasn't that much to do. Fact is, I wanted to get away. I wanted to be alone. Why? What sort of man was I becoming? I took a shower, packed what little I had left, wrote a note to Donny apologizing for the fence and asking him to take back the chainsaw, then left. I should've headed south and picked up 70 west toward Columbus. That was the way I came. But, I couldn't. I had to go north. I had to go back to Pittsburgh, back up that blighted hill and down that desolate street. One more time. One more chance to do what was right and have it matter.

By the time I turned on Golden Way, the sun was going down. It was still light enough to see the vaulting silhouettes of those ramshackle houses. I stopped across from where I'd dropped off Kumi, thought twice, then eased around the corner. Gary's car was nowhere in sight. Either he'd already come, hadn't come at all, or would be coming. If it was the last of these, I didn't want my car giving me away. The house was quiet. I pushed through the bushes that choked the walkway and knocked on the door. Nobody came. I pounded and shouted out, "Anybody home?" My voice echoed down the street. I checked the grimy windows on the porch. One had a fist-sized piece of glass broken out. Through it, I saw the scattered shadows of a stark room. I cupped my hands around the hole in the glass and called out again. No one answered. Who knew how long they'd been gone? Maybe the old woman never lived there in the first place, and the house was just somewhere to drop Kumi off. Maybe they were gone for the night and coming back soon. Maybe Gary had already gotten Kumi, and the woman left to tell someone. There was nothing for me to do. I'd done all I could, far more than most would've done. You see that, right?

So I left. I got back in my car and set Googlemaps for home. For here. Nashville, Indiana. It said to go south, back the way I'd come, out the Fort Pitt Tunnel, and along 376, a couple miles from Mt. Lebanon. I had a fleeting notion of going down Vernon again, checking one last time to see if Gary had recaptured Kumi. I thought of it—and let it go. I say I let it go, but every time I passed an exit that could take me to Mt. Lebanon, I'd think of going back. It wasn't until I crossed into West Virginia that the idea left me altogether. And that's exactly how it felt, like the grip it had on me, right here at the base of my neck just…let go. I exhaled as though I'd been holding my breath the whole ride, shut my eyes, and shuddered. After that, I just drove. No radio. No looking back. Nothing but the game of getting Googlemaps to take one minute, then another, then the next off the time I'd be home.

When I turned into these woods, rumbled up the dirt road you took to get here, came to a stop, and turned off the car, it was four in the morning. I didn't bother unpacking. I came inside, felt my way through the dark and up those stairs there, tiptoed into our room, took off my clothes, and slid into bed beside Eileen. She didn't wake up until I reached out, rubbed her shoulder, and nuzzled into her back. Then she turned over and pulled me toward her. "What's wrong?" she asked in a drowsy fog.

"Nothing," I whispered. "Just came home early."

"Hmm," she hummed distantly, still half asleep. Then she squeezed me, harder than she would if it were any other night. Something about that made me well up. A shiver passed through me. I squeezed back, feeling for that electricity between us. Her hold softened, and she let herself go weak in my arms. "Not so hard," she said. So I went weak with her, and we fell asleep like that, facing one and other for the first time in years.

The next thing I knew, I was alone, sunlight slanting across the bed. I came downstairs. No one was around, like any other day that summer. The pot of coffee on the burner was still warm. I poured myself a cup and, while I was sipping it, Eileen walked in holding a clothes basket. "Are those mine?" I asked, noticing the sleeve of a shirt I'd taken to Mt. Lebanon.

"I unpacked for you," she said. "Figured I'd let you sleep." She started up the stairs. Then she stopped, hitched the basket on her hip, and reached for something in the clothes. "Oh, I found this." And she held out a scrap of paper. I crossed the kitchen and took it from her without a word. There it was: the address Kumi had scrawled. Eileen couldn't have helped but notice my wonderment. "I'm glad I didn't throw it out," she said, setting the basket down. I looked up at her, open-mouthed, stunned. "Why does it matter so much?"

"It's a long story," I said.

"Does it end well?"

"I don't know," I told her. I shook the scrap of paper. "But it might. Want to hear it?"

Her eyes found mine then and held them. She stepped close, put her arms around me, and whispered, "Can it wait?"

NONBELIEVER

THE ROHANS, 2009-16
Told by Joyce Rohan, Avalon at Newton Highlands, Needham MA

I take part of the blame. After all, I'm the one who kept telling Harold how worried I was for the state of his soul, how much it pained me to know he was doomed to eternal damnation. But I'd been telling him that for years, ever since I found the Lord. You could argue I wore him down, caught him when he was at his weakest. I'd always said he'd need a little adversity to come to Christ. Now, I'm sorry I did. Still, that doesn't explain it all.

If you're looking for me to wax sentimental about our time in Pittsburgh, forget it. Nothing against the house. As houses go, it was fine, at least while we were living in it. Trying to sell it has been another story. We had a cash offer for $625,000. Then the inspector found wood rot in the kitchen wall. Now it's going on two years, and I haven't had a single serious call. Know anyone who wants a half-million-dollar house?

If I could do it over, I would've objected to moving more strongly. I barely said a word to Harold. Told the kids not to complain either. Never mind it was an awful time to uproot them. Jake was a freshman at Brown; he didn't care. But Brady was a junior in high school. He'd just made the basketball team and started going out with his first girlfriend. And poor May was an eighth grader with a mouthful of braces. Flat, skinny, shorter than everyone, she made up for it with bossiness and spunk. Of course, she got away with that in Boston, around kids who'd known her all their lives. But in Mt. Lebanon, miles from everything she knew, pluck wouldn't go very far. Kids would judge her on what they saw— and the best she could hope for was to get ignored.

She told me as much when Harold said he was taking a job in Pittsburgh. "Too good an offer" is how he put it. A move he'd never make unless he was sure it was in the family's best interests. I knew better. One thing you have to understand about Harold: work was everything to him. All his self-worth was invested in his career. You already know he didn't have God. As for family, he was glad to have one, but he didn't exactly nurture or take comfort from it. The same could be said for our marriage. It was different when we first met. I was all-consuming to him. But over time, his attention shifted to work.

I blame the genes. The Rohwedder genes. That's his real name. Not Rohan. Harold's grandpa changed the name in the Forties. You can imagine why he'd change a German name then. But it had nothing to do with the war. Ever heard of Otto Rohwedder? I'm not surprised. Nobody I've quizzed ever has. Otto Rohwedder is the world's least-famous famous person. He was an inventor. Like every inventor, he was obsessed with making something great. You might say the greatest thing since sliced bread. But Otto wouldn't have put it that way. That's because he *was* the person who made sliced bread. That's right: in 1928, Harold's great grandpa Otto invented the first machine to cut bread slices.

So Otto cleaned up, right? Not exactly. He sold his patent to a company in Iowa and became their head of sales. A cog in the machine. Meanwhile, another company swooped in, perfected the slicer for industrial use, and made the real killing. Everyone knows Wonder Bread. No one knows Otto Rohwedder. The way Harold's father told it, his dad Walt, Otto's son, never forgave the old man for not capitalizing on his big idea. Otto was still alive when Walt changed the family name. Legend goes he told Otto, "You didn't care enough to put the name on your slicer. Why do you care if I don't use it for my family?" I don't know if that's true. But just that a story like that would get passed down, repeated as a Rohan point of pride, that gives you some idea what Harold was saddled with.

Of course, he didn't see it that way. To him, the Rohan's Type-A ambition just made for a funny story to tell at parties. *My ancestors were so driven, they kicked the inventor of sliced bread out of the family. Not great enough, Otto!* He didn't mention Walt went broke speculating on real estate. And he never brought up his dad. That was too sore a subject. Harold's father Max was every bit the innovator Otto was. But he specialized in quieter inventions. He was an efficiency expert. His life was devoted to optimizing time. When you go to an amusement park, you can thank Max Rohan for the layout. You may think it takes long now to get around, but before Max came up with Disneyland's hub-and-spoke design in 1950, parks were one big chaotic country carnival.

Max made life better for a lot of people. Too bad Harold wasn't one of them. Imagine being raised by a man who thought about nothing else but squeezing time out of the day. To say Harold had a regimented childhood is to suggest a Navy Seal's training is a touch strenuous. Everything about his home life was boiled down to the essence of efficiency. What they ate, when they ate, how, and where. How much of his free time—and I use that term loosely—should be devoted to homework versus extra-curriculars, and what the balance should be there between sports and music and academic clubs. Because Harold had to be well-rounded. He had to keep his options open. That was the efficient thing to do.

Here's how crazy things were at the Rohans. Harold had a younger brother and two younger sisters, spaced two years apart, all September babies, alternating boy-girl-boy-girl. Then Max got the snip, because four children was the optimal number to have while still handling parental duties free of bottlenecks. Anyway, you know how normal families take turns opening Christmas gifts, then spend time thanking each other for their thoughtfulness or marveling at the clairvoyance of Santa Claus? Not the Rohans. When Harold was a kid, everyone opened all their presents at once. There was even a time limit. Ten minutes. Then there was another ten-minute period of gratitude. Then clean-up time. And done.

Why? Because doing it the normal way was a protracted waste of time. Max's method accomplished the same thing five times faster, or so he claimed. Statistically speaking.

Statistically speaking. I've never heard anyone use those words more than Max. It was a verbal tic with the man. No matter what you talked about, he had to statistically speak. Once I mentioned what a bad heat wave we were having. "Well," Max said, "statistically speaking, it's not really an official heat wave until we exceed norms by x percent of degrees for y number of days. And, of course, we've been z degrees short of that threshold for the past two days. So…statistically speaking."

It goes without saying Max was divorced. He had no use for the sloppiness of love. Besides, as a single man, he could use the passenger seat of his car to stack papers with the *Times* crossword puzzle. Then, whenever someone was late to meet him, he'd do a crossword. No lie. I can't tell you how tickled that made him, how often he said he never wasted time on crosswords. They were done on the thousands of precious minutes inefficient people squandered. Love. Pleasure. Loyalty. None of these sentiments were useful to Max. Especially hope—and the more abstract that hope, the more pointless in his mind. So you can imagine his take on faith. He had no time for it. Literally. And he wouldn't let his kids waste a second on it either. That became a sore point between Max and Harold's mother, Jeannie. By the time his parents divorced, when Harold was 15, the damage had been done. Jeannie started going to Catholic church, and she got her three younger kids to come along, but not Harold. He refused to go near the place.

Harold portrays himself as the rebel child, the one who broke from his father. In many ways, he was. As the oldest, he had the closest relationship with his mom. And her moony artistic bent—Max called it flightiness—rubbed off on him. She was a garage saler, a craft show junkie, a lover of knick-knacks. Even Harold admitted she was a hoarder. You could barely walk through the halls of her condo, they were so crammed with junk. When Harold was a boy, he thought his mom was magical. She took him on garage sale hunts, despite Max's objections. She taught him to value the old, forgotten, and unusual. She invented stories about the objects she found, surrounded them with outlandish, romantic characters. Fifty years later, Harold could still name them—and tell you exactly how they fit into his mom's imaginary cosmos: Ivan Hornschmeyer, Suzie Snollygoster, Lothar Shagnasty, Sappy Sam the Salami Man…and those are only the ones I remember.

When Harold dropped out of Columbia business school and switched to English, he only told Jeannie. They kept it a secret from Max until the semester was over. When Harold announced he was going to marry me in his junior year, Max said if we went through with it, he'd stop paying for college. Harold called his bluff. His dad *did* refuse to pay our rent, but kept paying tuition. And when we were dead broke, down to our last 25 dollars, and Max arranged a job for Harold doing motion studies on factory workers, Harold refused it. We got by living in New York on two six-dollar-an-hour bookstore jobs.

So, yes, on the face of it, Harold *was* his dad's renegade offspring. The others went into careers revolving around productivity—supply chain logistics, lean management, business process consulting. You should hear them together. It's an efficiencyfest. Each tries to outdo the other with some arcane statistic that illustrates how they're nudging the world ever closer to perfect running order. Meanwhile, Harold committed the sin of going into advertising, Max's idea of the most useless profession, where zero effort is expended on improvement and the entire goal is to pretend things are better than they really are.

Harold had one big thing in common with his dad, though: a claim to fame. Like Max with his park layouts and Otto with his bread slicer, Harold had something that made him an advertising legend. When you think of fish sticks, what comes to mind? *Come on!* The Gorton's fisherman! You've seen him, right? That ruddy looking bearded hunk with the yellow slicker and rain hat? *No?* Ah, you're too young. Well, Harold created him back in 1975, at his first job out of college. It was a very big deal. It launched his career. He was suddenly the young hotshot. All the best New York agencies wanted him. Before he turned 22, he was head of creative at

Crave, and they won a bunch of food accounts on the promise that Harold would invent for them the next Gorton's guy.

Harold thought coming up with great mascots would be as easy as that first iconic fisherman. He didn't appreciate what inspired the Gorton's breakthrough. It was really an homage to his mom, who at that point was losing touch with reality, retreating into her crowded fantasyland of knick-knacks. She'd given him six Royal Doulton figurines when he graduated from high school. Pricey mementos to lay on a teenager and expect him to keep intact. But he did. There they are, on the top shelf of that display case. See the two on either end? *Sea Harvest* and *The Boatman*. Those are where the Gorton's fisherman came from. He took the yellow slicker and hat from *The Boatman* and put it on that strapping young sailor yanking up the fishing net. Sure, it was an invention of his own mind. But the source for it, the heart of that creativity, was his love for his mother and the fascination he had with her powers for bringing life to the quietest, most neglected things in our world.

He didn't see his mom's influence back then, got caught up in his own hype, and lost his muse. Not to say his career didn't go well. It did. The teams he managed did good work, and he earned a reputation as a director who could get the most out of talent. Still, what he wanted most was to catch lightning in a bottle again. The closest he ever came was in the mid-eighties. Crave landed the Domino's account, and his writers were struggling to come up with concepts. So he shut himself up in our apartment, pulled an all-weekender, and came up with this oddball idea the account team didn't even want to pitch. But when Domino's hated everything else, they gave it a shot. That's how the Noid was born.

You know the Noid, don't you? Everyone knows the Noid. Most people hated him. Google "worst mascots ever." You'll find him, right there with the plastic Burger King and the Quizno's Spongemonkeys. Harold said the Noid was misunderstood. People thought he was annoying, but that was the whole point. He was the villain; a chattering, buck-toothed, crazy-eyed goofball in a red rabbit suit whose sole aim was to foil Domino's perfect pizza delivery process. Yes, he grated on your nerves, and his antics were silly and pathetic. But that's exactly the reaction Harold wanted. The more you hated the Noid's plots to delay your pizza, the more you loved the efficiency of Dominos' process.

It didn't take a psychotherapist to ferret out the inspiration for the Noid. Let's see: a rebellious, gibbering man-child raging against the efforts of a higher authority to bring order to the world. The Noid was an exaggeration of how Max viewed his son. A caricature of Harold. Look on the middle shelf. That's a photo of my husband as a young man. How can you deny a resemblance to the Noid? Harold would never admit it. I saw it as a positive—Harold's way, however back-handed, of showing his dad how much he admired him. It's strange. His greatest career success came from paying homage to his mom, and his biggest failure from coming to terms with his dad.

Really, though, the Noid wasn't the failure people make him out to be. At least the character wasn't. What doomed the Noid to infamy was a tragedy Harold never could've foreseen. A couple years after the Noid went big, a man walked into a Domino's, pulled out a .357, and took the employees hostage. He was convinced Domino's had created the little gremlin to mock him. His name was Kenneth Noid. The police got him to give himself up after a five-hour standoff, so no one was hurt. But the damage had been done. Across the country, newspapers reported the story with the same variation on the headline: "Domino's can't avoid this Noid." And that was the end of the Noid—not just Harold's creation, but that poor man as well. He went into a mental institution, certain he was some kind of Uber Noid, an evil scourge to society. Ultimately, he killed himself.

A horrible story. Not the sort of achievement you highlight on your résumé. At first, Harold shrugged off the episode. And his agency sold it as an unfortunate incident that derailed a great campaign. That's at least what they told Domino's. But within Crave, the leadership started questioning Harold's instincts. And that's when he began losing confidence in himself. His downfall, if you want to call it that, was barely perceptible. They appointed a co-creative director, ostensibly because of increased business. Then his team's ideas stopped getting picked. Finally, the board suggested he'd be more valuable as the senior copywriter in the Boston office. It was a huge blow to his ego, but over time he came to accept it. After all, he was pushing 50 in a business that's a young person's game. In a way, he said back then, stepping off the corporate treadmill was a blessing in disguise. Less pressure would mean more family time. And he still had his share of small career victories. Cheese-filled Combos cheese your hunger away. Crispix is crispy times two. Cheesasaurus Rex and his dino-mite appetite for Kraft Mac and Cheese. See that toy up there next to the Noid doll? That's C-Rex. Fitting that Harold's last mascot at Crave was a dinosaur. And sad, really. He never saw the irony.

Another thing he never did was spend more time with family. If anything, he worked longer hours. He was still too wrapped up in preserving his reputation. The final straw came when the agency assigned him to refresh the identities of old mascots he never had a hand in creating to begin with. They sold it to Harold as a vital role, but this time, he wasn't buying. How much creative horsepower did it take to turn a baseball cap backwards on the Trix rabbit's head, put him in saggy shorts, and give him a skateboard?

So around 10 years ago, when other men his age were content to hang on and ride out their careers, Harold started looking for a new challenge. A chance to reinvent himself, as he described it. He targeted seafood companies from the get-go, figuring his status as father of the Gorton's man would impress them most. Seafare Tuna was the first company to bite. And that's why Harold suddenly wanted to uproot the family. I say "wanted." Really, it was a need. Not going would be conceding defeat, admitting his dad had been right all along, that he'd wasted his career producing frivolous novelties, a heap of knick-knacks like his mother collected. That's why after he broke the news to the kids, I took them aside and said no complaining. Moving to Pittsburgh, I told them, wasn't just important to their dad; it was vital to the family.

Oddly, that turned out to be true, but not because it resurrected Harold's career. The job itself was doomed before it began. There was a misunderstanding in the interview. Harold told a roomful of

Seafare execs that the age of cartoon mascots shilling products was over. In the era of social media, people could smell marketing a mile away, and they'd scroll past in a heartbeat. People didn't want to be sold to anymore; they didn't want to hear fake characters exaggerating claims they knew were lies, no matter how entertaining those characters were. They wanted to have dialogues with real people telling real stories about what the product really was. That's what Harold thought Seafare should do; use social media to tell the actual story of a day in the life of a Seafare tuna, and how it touched the lives of so many people, starting from the catch, all the way to the consumer. It was music to those executives' ears. They'd been wanting to move out from under their Tommy the Tuna mascot for years. Harold seemed to have the answer.

There was just one problem: the Seafare CEO hadn't been in the room. When Harold's big idea for reality-driven advertising got translated to him, all he heard was that the Gorton's guy had a great idea for replacing Tommy the Tuna with a fisherman and telling the story of how he caught the world's best tunas. Nothing radically different than what they were already doing, just a real mascot on the other end of the fishing line. In other words, he got it all wrong. When the two men finally had a face to face, and Harold clarified his idea, the CEO laughed it off. "Do you know what an ugly business commercial fishing is?" he said. "How disgusting the processing plants are? How the workers get treated? We can't tell those stories. No one would buy another can of our tuna. Make us a hero like you did for Gorton's. I want *Old Man and the Sea*."

Clearly, he hadn't read the book. Whatever. Harold got the message. He didn't like it, but he sucked it up. He had to. He'd painted himself into a corner. We were stuck in Pittsburgh. At his age, no agency was going to hire him. Besides, the kids were nearly done with high school by then. We couldn't tear up their world again. So he did what they wanted: killed Tommy and gave birth to Captain Steve Seafarian. It took Harold about two years to roll out the new campaign. But it turned out to be a decent success. Two million people saw the YouTube video. It starts in the cartoon undersea world of Tommy the Tuna. The camera moves slowly up the fishing line, out of the water and onto a real ship, where Captain Steve leans over the deck, jaw set, peering down like he's watching Tommy. Then the tagline: "The best tasting tunas get caught by the hardest working captain."

The ad industry showered it with awards. The Facebook site blew up. Everyone was happy. Except Harold. In his mind, the campaign wasn't close to what he'd envisioned. It was nothing more than a pale imitation of the first thing he'd done in his career. Gorton's warmed over. He hadn't made advertising purposeful like he'd wanted, like his father might be proud of. All he'd done was blow the dust off a relic from his bag of novelties. Don't get me wrong: Harold wasn't despondent about his success. Disillusioned is more like it. He just didn't care anymore.

For the first time in his career, he had trouble getting up and going to work in the morning. He started working from home on Fridays, then made it Mondays too. Sometimes, I'd come into the den when he was on a conference call and catch him watching YouTube. He was a sucker for laughing baby videos. Forget about TED talks. Harold just wanted to be distracted by sweet, innocent babies. Even the kids noticed Harold's penchant for babies laughing uncontrollably. How could they not? Whenever he found one he liked, he'd show it to whoever was around. It could be the middle of the work day, and he'd come charging out like a deadline was on top of him, only to thrust his iPhone in our faces and gawp at some giggling baby. Once May asked, "Why are you so obsessed with baby videos?" He didn't deny it. "They're just so happy," he told her. "So pure and happy." Sad, really. He never took the time to appreciate when his own children were young. Maybe those videos were making up for what he missed.

Around then, Max went to the ER complaining of back pain. At first, they thought he blew a disc. Then they thought it was a kidney. By the time they found the mucus clot and diagnosed pneumonia, it was too late. They put a tube down his throat twice to get him oxygen. It didn't work. When his breathing failed again, the doctor told Harold and his siblings the odds of survival were 10 percent, and even then, he'd be hooked to machines for the rest of his life. Harold thought they should let Max go. The others, stat wonks that they were, argued whether 10 percent was a decent survival rate. Harold lost his temper. Were they really going to put their dad through an ordeal they wouldn't let a dog suffer, all for the slim chance of living a few months in misery? They took a vote: Harold's sister Jane changed her mind. She lived closest to their dad and would've been on the hook to care for him. The other siblings relented, but not before Harold's brother Randy told him, "This was your decision. It's on your head."

When they brought him out of anesthesia, shut off the breathing machine, and gave him morphine, Max was lucid for about 10 minutes. Harold explained what was happening and asked if he wanted to keep trying. Max's eyes rolled to the ceiling. He shook his head. Then Jane asked if he wanted a priest. He shook his head again. "I wish I deserved that," Max rasped. Harold started sobbing and left the room. His father died the next morning.

To see Harold get so emotional about his dad's wish for faith broke my heart. But it gave me hope, too. I decided I'd bring it up after the funeral, so he didn't think I was taking advantage of a weak moment. I didn't have to wait. On the drive from the hospital to our hotel, Harold said, "I want to start going to church. Every Sunday. If I tell you I don't want to go, remind me of this. Don't let me talk my way out of it."

So Harold started coming to St. Paul's on Sunday mornings. You know the church at the top of Mayfair. It was so close, we usually walked there. Harold didn't like to stand through so many gathering songs, so we'd get there 15 minutes later than I would've wanted. And he wouldn't stay after the sermon, not even for the snacks. When we were alone on our way home, he wouldn't say much. There was one priest he liked, Father Bob, and sometimes I could get him talking about his sermon. I told Harold once that Bob met with people exploring their faith for lunch. "You mean, one on one?" he said. "I couldn't do that. Bob knows too much. What would I say to him?" I let it go. It was enough that Harold was attending church, at least for the time being.

I always thought it would take a personal trauma, some existential crisis, to get Harold to embrace the Lord completely. Is it horrible to say part of me hoped for it? I have to admit, as his work problems mounted, I did feel this perverse sense of anticipation. I saw it as the will of God. For a long time, his situation was merely disheartening. Sure, he was frustrated. But they were paying him well, and he'd been smart enough to get an eight-year contract. He just had to persevere for four more years and it would be over. This was his rock-solid line of thinking all through the kids' high school years and even when we were empty-nesters. But it changed in a hurry, literally over the space of two months.

They brought in a new head of sales. He started squawking to the CEO about Harold from the get-go. Didn't like how he worked from home. Didn't like how safe the advertising was. Basically, didn't like Harold. So the CEO decided to try a little experiment. That's how he pitched it to Harold. He put him under the new guy. That was the first issue. Issue number two was messing with Steve Seafarian. Remember: Captain Steve was never what Harold envisioned. But where the CEO saw him as Gorton's 2.0, the sales VP wanted the tuna equivalent of Dos Equis' most interesting man in the world. Minus humor. He started jamming Steve for silly blog posts on the over-the-top exploits of the captain. Steve saves a shark caught in his net. Steve outsmarts the big, bad corporate tuna boat. Steve pulls a drowning crewman out of rough waters. Harold pushed back, pointing out the web traffic they were getting. He insisted they meet with the CEO to talk about the fate of Steve. His new boss shut him down. "I'm in charge now," Harold said he told him. "If you won't do it, I'll find someone who will."

Then came the Thanksgiving incident. A day before the holiday, the CEO emailed Harold and his boss asking for a Facebook promotion to boost followers. He wanted ideas by the next Tuesday. Harold responded, "We'll have something for you then." No big deal. Seconds later, he got this snippy email from his boss: it wasn't Harold's place to say when they'd deliver work. Then out came a second email from this jerk to the CEO, with Harold blind copied: they'd have three new promos ready Friday morning. Can you believe that? Black Friday. And, of course, he expected Harold to do the work, never mind all the kids were back for the holiday. Suffice to say, it wasn't our best Thanksgiving. Harold was grouchy and distant, wouldn't help with preparations and left the table before people were even done eating. Plus, he drank too much—and took a bottle of whiskey upstairs with him when he left to get his work done. So while the rest of us tried to make the best of the occasion, Harold was locked away in his office, pulling a good old-fashioned drunken all-nighter.

When I came down next morning, he was at the breakfast table with his laptop, a pile of papers, and an empty bottle. He looked like hell. But there was a manic glint in his dark eyes. He thrust out a page and asked what I thought. I read through three entries from the annals of Steve. In the first, he'd rescued a mermaid and was nursing her to health. She had amnesia and couldn't remember her name. Steve was asking Facebook friends for advice. Whoever came up with the best name would get 100 cans of tuna personally delivered by Steve. A little hokey, but okay. The second promo was called, "Where's Seafare?" Steve wanted followers to send photos of themselves enjoying Seafare tuna in unexpected places. Again, the winner would get 100 cans of tuna. Then came the last promo. In this one, Steve waxed poetic about Seafare tuna's aroma. The CEO always thought that was a big selling point. To me, it smells like any other tuna. Anyway, Steve was asking followers to send their best description of what Seafare smelled like for a 100 more cans of tuna. I told him I wasn't sure about that one.

"What's wrong with it?" he asked, with this overcurious look on his face. I said it was just weird. Tuna was tuna. Who wanted to think about how it smelled? He smiled and started typing on his laptop. "The CEO will eat that one up," he said. "And my boss is going to serve it to him." I remember thinking, so much for my opinion. It wasn't until everything blew up that I connected why Harold asked me to read over the entries.

Within an hour after he sent his boss the ideas, he got a reply. The CEO was good with all the promos and wanted them out first thing Monday. "Are you sure?" Harold asked in what he called his cover-your-ass email. "Maybe we should think these through a bit more, have someone else read them." His boss said no. He wanted them out Monday. Period.

And that's how Harold set the hook. That Monday, he posted the promos exactly as approved to Seafare's social media accounts. Next day, the analytics team noticed traffic had exploded. Harold's boss started doing victory laps. But later that day, someone sent out an urgent email: the aroma promo was a top story on Reddit—and not in a good way. Had anyone proofread the posts? Only then was the problem discovered. In Harold's text, he'd made two crucial spelling errors. He'd meant for Steve to say, "The aroma of Seafare is so indescribably unique I can't put my finger on it." But he'd typed "pull my finger" instead. Then the hashtag, which was supposed to be *#seafarearoma*, came out *#seafartorama*. The internet was having a field day. Harold's boss panicked. He ordered the posts taken down. But the damage was done. When the CEO lit into him, he pointed the finger at Harold. Harold simply forwarded his email pleading for another set of eyes.

Nobody believed Harold hadn't done it on purpose. Pull my finger. Seafart-o-rama. It was just too perfect. But Harold maintained it was all a spellcheck issue, the predictable result of hastiness. And his boss had been the one to insist on moving so fast. The boss wanted Harold fired. Harold told him he'd lawyer up. In the end, nobody wanted a public spectacle on the fallout of Seafart-o-rama. So they paid Harold three years' salary and medical to leave. And that's how he went into early retirement. Not quite the crowning achievement of his career, but pretty darn clever.

I wish I could say things got better for Harold after that. He orchestrated his career exit brilliantly, but didn't have a clue what he was entering into. For days, it was the same story: wake up late, lie around watching TV, drink too much. Repeat. After he missed church a third time, I let him have it. Was this what he wanted his life to be? Moping around, wasting time, content with no purpose? "You think I'm content?" he yelled. "Do I look content?" He stormed out of the den, stomped around the house, then ditched into the basement. He didn't come up for hours. I could hear him down there, banging things around, swearing to himself. Finally, around dinner time, he called for me to open the door. When I did, he stumbled out, wobbling under the weight of a huge cardboard box. It only registered when he was dumping the box into our recycling bin that these were papers and mementos from his career. I asked: was he sure he wanted to get rid of all that? He leaned over the bin, rummaged through it, then pulled out the Noid doll. "What do you think?" he said, waggling it at me.

Harold didn't eat that night. He brought up three more boxes before I went to bed and kept at it. I tried to stay up but dozed off around midnight. When I woke at five, his side of the bed was unrumpled. I found him in the kitchen with the lights off, gazing out at the still-dark skies. When I asked if everything was alright, he gave a jolt, then a heavy sigh. "Pretty soon it will be," he said. "Another day and this old life will be gone." Before I could think of some encouraging way to respond to that, he asked if I'd been kidding about Father Bob, that he met people for lunch. I told him no, that it was true. "Even nonbelievers?" he asked.

"Especially nonbelievers," I answered.

"Good," he said. Then he cried out in this wounded, childlike voice I'd never heard from him: "Because I need a new life now. And I can't find it on my own." He came to me then, fell to his knees, wrapped his arms around my waist, and started weeping, muffled at first, then unrestrained, a shivering howl. I knew this moment would come for Harold. I was sure it would bring us closer together. But there in the murky dawn, I didn't feel the joy I expected. Mostly what I felt, if I'm honest, was fear. Selfish fear. I was afraid of his weakness. That was my sin. I knew it the instant it overtook me. The moment I'd been waiting for our whole married life wasn't a cause for rejoicing. It was a trial, a test of my courage. Careful what you wish for, right? Funny how God works.

So I reached out to Bob. We set up a lunch for a couple weeks away. In the meantime, Harold continued disposing of his old life. His dad would've been proud; he went about it efficiently, room by room, tossing out anything that wasn't a necessity—clothes he hadn't worn for years, books, souvenirs of trips we'd taken, old albums, financial papers, boxes of computer junk and disks and widgets and wires. He started taking things too far, insisting we sell off our decorations—furniture, wall hangings, knick-knacks. His mother would've rolled over in her grave.

The one thing he had trouble parting with was our photos. They were everywhere, not just in the shoeboxes we kept in our hall closet, but in drawers all over the house. Early on, Harold tossed loose pictures in a bucket he carried around. But there got to be too many. He started separating them into stacks on the dining room table, first by child, then when the stacks got un-wieldy, by occasion—births, vacations, school activities. Finally, he put sticky notes on the table for every year from when we met to the present. As he sorted photos, invariably the ones he set aside to show me were of our kids when they were their most innocent. "Look at how Brady cuddles up to me," he'd say. "Were we really that close back then?" Or, "This one of Jake and May at the beach is a gem. Big brother shares a peach with baby sister." Half the photos he showed me were of moments he couldn't place. Some-times I could jog his memory; other times, I couldn't. With every-one he couldn't recall, he'd get sadder, harder on himself. First it was, "How did I miss that?" Then, "I wish I could live that over." Finally, he came right out and declared, "I failed them, Joyce. God, I failed my own children." Those were painful days. Strange, mournful days. Here was Harold, grieving over a life he was sure he hadn't lived right, even as he was ridding himself of it. And there I was, on the verge of the life I'd always wanted—and dreading it.

I couldn't wait for Harold to meet with Bob. As the days drew nearer, Harold got more anxious. *What should I say? I don't want to lead him on. Maybe I'm not meant to have faith.* The day they were due to meet, Harold wanted to cancel. He floated the idea of sending an email to the church's "contact us" address and leaving it at that. I told him there was no way he could stand up Bob; I'd never be able to face him again. He finally gave in and went.

I expected him back in half an hour, 45 minutes tops. So it was a surprise when he was gone for an hour. Things must be going well, I thought. But after two hours, I figured he squirmed out of lunch and was killing time to put off facing me. About five, he came breezing in with two bags of groceries. Groceries! This is a man who only ever went to the store to research what he advertised. But there he was, emptying bags on the counter with all the urgency of someone minutes from a hurricane. I marveled at the crazy things he'd bought: granola bars, fruit chewies, Tootsie Pops, Purell and Bandaids, travel-sized soaps, lotions, and toothpaste. Did this have something to do with Bob? I asked.

"Sort of" was the extent of his explanation. I tried again, asking pointedly how lunch went. "Good," he said, separating his haul into piles with one of each item. "I told him I didn't believe and probably never would. And he said, okay." That was it? No way Bob gave up that easily. "He said people these days rarely come to Jesus in a bolt of lightning. I didn't have to have faith right away. But I could just start trying." That annoyed me. I'd been telling him that for years. "I guess it was just the way he said it," Harold explained. "If you admire what Christ did, whether he was the son of God or not, you could just try to be more like him. Like that woman said on the TED talk you liked so much—what was it?"

"Fake it till you make it." Another thing I'd told him.

Harold nodded. Then he informed me there was even a Bible verse for it, like I didn't know. "Something about walking in the same way he walked," Harold explained. "Anyway, the way Bob put it, it didn't seem so hard."

I couldn't hold back laughing. Sure, being like Christ was a breeze. Harold laughed along. But I don't think it was for the same reason. He was just giddy. *So what did all the groceries have to do with Christ?* I tried again. Harold cocked his head, like wasn't it obvious? Then he told me a story about how, after he left Bob, he was at a stoplight on Banksville when, out of nowhere, a woman started knocking on his window. "She was a mess," Harold said. "Hair flying everywhere, bad teeth, ratty coat, torn-up gloves. She asked if I could help her out." She was a panhandler, I clarified. Harold ignored me. "All I had in my wallet were twenties," he went on. "That seemed pretty steep. Then it suddenly popped into my head: what would Christ do? And right as I thought it, I realized I had a

doggy bag with half a sandwich and a pickle. So I gave it to her."
He shrugged and went back to working, as if everything now was
completely clear. I had to prod again. Was she grateful? "Not at
all!" Harold said. "She threw the Reuben at my back window as I
drove away. It's still cloudy with the Thousand Island dressing."

Now I was really confused. So what were all the groceries for?
I asked a third time. Harold said he didn't want to be doling out
money, because he'd read that most highway beggars were addicts
or scam artists. So he asked himself *what should I do?* How could he
walk the walk?' And that's when it came to him: care packages. A
little food, a few personal care items. Then, whenever he was driving around, if he saw a beggar, he'd just reach into the backseat and
grab a package. I had to admit: it wasn't a bad idea. "It wasn't
mine," Harold said. "Not by myself at least. I'm not that thoughtful. It was me pretending to be more like Christ." I didn't know
what to say. Honestly, I was still a bit befuddled by the whole thing.
I told him he should just…keep on pretending.

And that's exactly what he did from then on. You'd think playing Jesus would be a hard thing, that you'd find it unsustainable
and backslide into old habits. That wasn't the case with Harold. If
anything, he got better at it, more obsessive, more…efficient.
That's the best word for it. All that time management nonsense his
father had drilled into Harold, that he'd rebelled against for the
sake of his mother's fantasies, was finally being put to use propping
up the greatest fantasy of all—remember: Harold still didn't
believe. Even so, nearly every waking moment for him was pro-
pelled by a single question: *What would Jesus do now?* He taped a sign
on our bathroom mirror. *Walk the Walk.* Shorthand for 1 John 2:6.
But that wasn't enough. Before long, the sign was on every bathroom mirror in the house. Even then, when there was the slightest
pause in all his frenetic Christlikeness, he'd give a sigh and mutter,
"What now?" I can't tell you how many times I caught him saying
that. *What now.* Oh, I don't know, Harold. Take a seat. Relax. Have
a cocktail. Watch some TV. Take me to dinner once in a while.
How about that for "What now?"

If I sound bitter, you have to understand. This is a man who went from complete self-absorption to total surrender in days. One week, he wouldn't go to Sunday service. The next, he'd signed up for everything you could possibly do at St. Paul's—Friday Book Club, Monday night Men's Group, the Dickens Boys Chat 'n Chill, parish kitchen help, all the concerts. My friend said he even poked his head into their Purls of Wisdom meeting. He didn't know it was a knitting club. Honestly, it was embarrassing. I didn't want to spend all that time at St. Paul's. There was the Sunday service, the coffee break afterwards, Bible study, my Tuesday small group, then the occasional community event. That was enough. We're told to pray in private. Yet here was Harold, doing three times as much as that—and making me look like I was slacking off by comparison.

That wasn't even the worst of it. After he'd exhausted what he could do at St. Paul's, he started volunteering for outreach programs. Jeremiah's Place to help domestic abuse victims, Shepherd's Heart Ministry to feed the homeless, prison worship at Western Pen. All these were in sketchy areas downtown. I know how that sounds: white fear of the dark city. Look, I don't begrudge what Harold was doing. It was precisely what Christ would've done. But that doesn't mean it wasn't dangerous, that there weren't people who didn't give a damn about Harold's altruism and would've robbed him as soon as he hit the street.

Still, if Harold had stopped there, I could've lived with it. But being the world's most efficient Christ walker, Harold wasn't content with any spare time. Remember the care packages? They started as handouts for when he happened across beggars. Once he went downtown, though, he ran through them in a hurry. And he saw that people had bigger needs than a Ziploc bag could hold. So he took some of the coats, gloves, and hats gathering dust in our closets and crammed them in his car. Then, instead of handing them out when he came across people, Harold went hunting for them. Whenever he had a free daylight hour, whenever that *what now* look showed on his face, he got in his car and drove off. All he would tell me after he got home was what he'd given away, who had thanked him, and what he'd told them about God. The good stuff, in other words. But I knew bad things happened. I picked the shards of glass out of the windshield bay when the wipers wouldn't work. I found the bloody shirt he balled up and threw in the trash. I should've put my foot down. He could walk the walk just as easily around Mt. Lebanon as the ghettos.

Then one day, I breezed into the kitchen, and there was a toothless black man having tea in our breakfast nook. I had the presence not to scream, but I may have squeaked. That was enough for him to lurch back, bang his chair against the wall, and topple the kids' pictures off the shelf. Good thing they were in cardboard. The old man started bowing madly, mumbling apologies. Harold charged in, wielding a broom. I thought he'd swat the man with it. But no. "It's alright, Larry," he said. "It's just my wife, Joyce. Honey, this is Larry. He's a bit down on his luck. So he's going to stay with us for a few days."

That's how Harold broke the news we were taking in a home-less man. "But you going to put me to work," Larry was quick to add. "That's the deal. I ain't taking no handouts."

"That's why I got this." Harold handed Larry the broom. Larry stayed the weekend. Swept every inch of our house. And for that, we fed him, put him up in Brady's room, washed his clothes, outfit-ted him in winter gear, doled out a hundred dollars, and took him back to the city. Honestly, it wasn't that big an imposition. What rankled me was that Harold didn't talk to me in advance. I coaxed an admission out of him that, yes, he could've been a little more thoughtful.

So next time it happened, he had the courtesy to call ahead. By a whole half hour. This second of Harold's strays was a skittish, doll-eyed woman named Leah. She ran Harold down at a truck stop and begged him to take her away. We set her up in May's room, and she hardly ever came out. When I'd check on her, she'd be crouching in the corner, gazing out like a trapped feral cat. She'd been a sex slave to a trucker who kidnapped her a month before in Kansas City. I never heard the stories myself. But Harold said if I'd heard them, I would've believed her. She had this crude tattoo of a butterfly that had been carved into her neck. According to

Harold, that was how this monster branded her. Horrific. We found some of May's old clothes, packed a suitcase for her, got her washed up, trimmed her hair, gave her a little cover up, then Harold drove her to the Mt. Lebanon police.

Then there was Charles Tackett, a Vietnam vet who thought the CIA was after him because he had proof of being subjected to drug experiments in Saigon. Harold tried to convince him to go to a shelter, but all Charles wanted was to print off a copy of his memoir. He had this folder stuffed with old type-written pages. Wall-to-wall words. No paragraphs. Harold said it was indecipherable. Charles was so grateful, he cried. He said the new copy could not have come at a better time. He had a meeting with Mike Wallace from *60 Minutes* that week. I didn't have the heart to tell him Mike Wallace had been dead for two years.

The one who brought everything to a head was Dion Evisullio. Sounds like one of Harold's mother's fantasy characters now that I say it aloud. Harold found Dion on Carson Street. He was bleeding from a cut on his head he said he got when someone threw a brick at him. Dion was a kid, younger than May. He'd been hopping trains for two years, ever since his dad kicked him out of the house. He wanted to be done with it, though. The trains had gotten too dangerous, he said. People had lost the hobo spirit. He should have been south where it was warm by now, but they threw him off the last train he caught. He'd sprained his ankle and missed his chance. Now, here he was, stuck in Pittsburgh. To look at Dion, you wouldn't be inclined to take him in. He had demonic tattoos all over his body, skulls and flaming eyeballs, grinning goblins and fake wounds festering with snakes. One snake curled around his left eye. He had piercings in his nose and lips and eyebrows, a shaved head, and a scraggly red beard, with turquoise beads nestled in it. He was scary, not big, but lean and wiry like a wolf.

I don't know why, but that kid really got to me. He was so menacing on the outside, but once you offered the slightest kindness, his mask melted away. And underneath was all vulnerability. He was with us nearly four nights, and even in that little time, we fell into a routine. Every morning, he woke up early and made egg toast and coffee, his way of repaying us, he said. And at night, we'd sit in the den and watch TV, even Harold, who hadn't so much as glanced at the thing since he'd started walking his walk.

But it was during the days, when Harold was out driving, that I really got to know Dion. The first day, he asked if we had a U.S. map. He wanted to find the shortest way to a warm place. I dug out an old atlas, and Dion found the chart of driving times between cities. Then he asked for a piece of paper and started adding up times for different routes. Pittsburgh to Roanoke to Greensboro. Greensboro to Columbia to Charleston. When he started writing down times to Memphis, I grabbed my iPad. He was amazed to learn about Googlemaps. I was stunned he didn't already know about it. We spent the afternoon plotting routes, checking Amtrak schedules, talking about where he'd been and where he'd like to go. That night, I asked Harold if we could drive Dion south for a few hours when it was time for him to leave, just so he had a head start. Harold studied me, then laughed. "Someone finally got to you," he said. "Figures it would be the one in need of mothering."

Maybe he was right. Next day, I roped Dion into helping bake cookies, and I hadn't done that since the kids were in Boston. Then we spent a good three hours playing Yahtzee. The day after, Dion asked about our kids. I brought out the box of photos Harold had organized from our early years. At some point, Dion asked what Harold did for a living. When I said he was an ad man, you would have thought I said he was a hitman. Dion gasped like it was the worst thing in the world to be. "A pretty famous one too," I added, rattling off his successes. Dion still couldn't believe it. I led him into the foyer, opened our closet, and moved aside a stack of boxes on the top shelf. There was a souvenir of C-Rex staring down at Dion. "You can't tell Harold I showed you this," I warned. "I fished it out of the trash after he tossed out all his old work stuff."

"What the heck's that?" Dion asked. Peeking around a box was the Noid. I laughed. No way I could convince Dion this thing was a hallmark achievement. I just said it was the Noid—and was going to leave it at that. "The Noid," Dion echoed.

"The arch-villain of Domino's Pizza before you were born," I added. "It's a long story." Dion seemed impressed. He asked if he could hold it. "Just be careful," I told him as I handed him the doll. "That's the original puppet. Probably worth a fortune."

Dion cradled it like a newborn. It was that big too, minus the ears. Dion gazed at it with an odd sort of wonder. The Noid stared back with those crazy eyes and that buck-toothed grin. His white gloves were frozen, reaching up, forever seeking an embrace. "He's cool," Dion said, almost choked up. "And Harold made him?"

"A long time ago," I said. "Now remember: you can't say anything to Harold about this. If it were up to him, we wouldn't have it in the house." Dion nodded and set the Noid back up on the shelf. Then I spread out the boxes to hide it.

That night, we got a snowstorm. Within a few hours, there was a six-inch topping of snow on our patio grill. Harold went out to shovel. After a while, Dion suggested we go out and help lighten the load. I got him Harold's nice down coat, dug out a hat and some gloves, and we went out there. It was achingly cold. At one point, Dion said he wished he had better shoes. That's when we noticed he was wearing his ratty Converse. Harold told him he had a pair of boots in his closet that were practically brand new, and why didn't he go get those. Dion said it was okay; he'd just gut it out. I was the one who insisted. Dion finally relented. "I'll just be a minute," he said.

It was a good 10 minutes before Harold said, "Maybe he can't find them." And I waited a few more before going inside. When I called out, no one answered. I saw the foyer closet door open but thought Dion had just looked there for the boots. After another unanswered call, I went up to our room. My jewelry box was in the middle of the floor, laid open and cleaned out. That's when I knew why the foyer closet was open. I ran downstairs. The boxes had been pushed aside. The Noid was gone. *That snake.* I don't know if he'd been playing me the whole time or just saw too good an opportunity and couldn't help himself. What's the difference? It was a betrayal either way. It wasn't about what he'd taken. My jewelry I could get over. And Harold didn't even want the Noid. It was the fact that he'd opened up to me, gotten me to care, and that, ultimately, none of that meant anything to him.

I didn't even hurry outside to break the news to Harold. That's how much it shook me. When he asked where Dion was, I just said, "Gone." He had to press me before I added, as matter-of-factly as I'd tell the time, that Dion had stolen my jewelry and left.

It took a second to sink in. "What?" he bellowed finally and rushed into the house. He was back in minutes. "That little punk," he shouted into the whirling snow. "He stole all the money out of my wallet and took my car keys."

For some reason, that pushed my button. "You're the one who brings home these lowlifes," I snapped. "What did you expect?"

Harold stared me down, chest heaving, cheeks huffing. Then he stomped away, down the alley and across our front lawn, head down, tracking the footprints Dion had made in the snow with the boots he'd stolen. It was more than an hour before he got back home. I'd already gone to sleep. I wasn't ready for what happened next. The big light over our bed went on. Then something landed on me. "What the hell is this?" Harold thundered. I poked my head out of the covers and turned just enough to see one of the Noid's gloved hands reaching around my shoulder. "I found this in a ditch along Cedar," he said, "where Dion's footprints ended." What was there to say? I couldn't very well act like I had nothing to do with it. So I admitted that I'd fished it out of the trash. "I didn't want it, Joyce," Harold snapped. "That's why I tossed it out."

"Well I did," I fired back, sitting up. "Don't I get a say? I was there too. Looking after our kids while you chased your career." Harold reminded me that he was trying to forget that period of his life. He was trying to be better. Wasn't that what I wanted? I lost it. "What *I* want?!" I screamed back. "You pretending your life didn't happen? No. No! I want *this* Harold!" I grabbed the Noid and shook it at him like a voodoo doll, hands and ears wobbling. "The Harold who was passionate. The Harold who would've considered it a failure to wind up so damned sensible."

"That Harold is gone," he said, pointing at the Noid, his voice low and defeated. "I'm walking the walk now."

I couldn't hold back. "Screw your walk!" I yelled. "You don't even believe in God! You think all these good deeds are going to get you to heaven? They aren't! Read Ephesians. We're saved through faith. That's it. You can't earn it on your own."

Harold's head slumped. "I don't have any other way," he said. Then he left. I tossed the Noid aside and went after him. He already had a big stack of blankets, and he was walking down the hall. They were our kids' blankets. Harold said they needed them more in the city, then he disappeared down the stairs. I got my robe and slippers and hurried to catch up. By the time I got downstairs, the garage door was already whirring. I watched him back my car out into the snowy night. My car. Which he never drove. Because he didn't have the keys to his. As he was clocking the steering wheel to turn for Vernon, our eyes met. He stopped, gave something between a smile and a grimace, and waved. Then he drove off.

I went back to bed, woke up, and didn't start wondering about him until I needed my car after breakfast. When I called his cell phone, it went to voicemail. Still, I wasn't worried until after lunch. Another call, more voicemail. I tried the church; no one had seen him. I called Shepherd's Heart, where he helped feed the poor. Nobody there knew who I was talking about. After dinner, I called the police. They asked how long he'd been gone. When I answered about 18 hours, they told me I'd need to wait a full day before filing a formal report. "It isn't illegal for an adult to go missing," the detective pointed out.

"But I know something's wrong," I argued. "I know it."

Then he started digging into the details. Was there any reason he might've wanted to leave? Had we had a fight? I admitted that, yes, we'd argued, and maybe, in his mind, Harold had cause to stay away. "Give him a day," the detective said. "He probably just needed some space. Tomorrow, he'll come home, he'll apologize, and all will be forgiven."

Of course, that's not what happened. The next day, they took the report and started looking for him. A few people in Oakland remembered seeing him that morning, handing out blankets. But the police never found his car. "If the car was stolen," the detective said, "it's already been chopped up and sold for parts."

"What about his body?" I hesitated to ask.

He took his time before he answered that one. "Look," he finally replied, leaning in close, like he shouldn't be telling me what he was about to. "If you want to get rid of a body in this city, there are hundreds of abandoned houses. And three rivers." Then he asked me point blank, "Is it possible Harold wanted to disappear?"

At the time, I insisted, no, it wasn't. Now, I'm not so sure. I hate to say this, but I kind of hope he's dead. Otherwise, I don't think I could forgive him. A few months ago, I had a dream. I saw Harold again. We were in heaven—just ran into each other, like it was the mall. "What happened to you?" I asked. He shrugged and gave that same enigmatic smile he had before he drove away that night. He took a fisherman's cap out of his back pocket, exactly like the one the Gorton's guy wore, and put it on. Then he reached into his shirt pocket, pulled out a piece of sliced bread that somehow turned into a Polaroid, and handed it to me. As he walked away into the fog, I turned the Polaroid over. It was a picture of his dad, laughing hard, with this gleeful babyish face, like the babies in those videos Harold adored. Out of his head stuck the two long red ears of the Noid, and around one eye was Dion's snake tattoo. I woke up with a jolt—and all morning I couldn't shake that naked feeling you get when someone's played a really good prank on you.

I don't know what to believe anymore. I'd like to think God looked down on my Harold, saw how hard he was trying to find faith, and waved him into heaven. Then sometimes I'm so mad, I don't even know if I'll make it there myself. You know what I think about most? I shouldn't say it, but here it is: If we *do* both make it into heaven and I see him again, do I have to act like we're married still? Do I have to hang out with him? It's a stupid question, I know. I mean, I loved Harold—as much, at least, as is humanly possible. But this is heaven we're talking about.

Shouldn't it be better than that?

NEIGHBOR

DEREK NETHERY, 2017-Present
Told by Ilsa Page-Carlson, Derek Nethery, and Grace Page

Voicemail from Ilsa Page-Carlson to Grace Page, March 16, 2017

Grace, it's your mother. I just finished my—your book. I'm ready to talk now. Just so I understand: this is for my eyes only, right? You're not thinking anyone else could read this, are you? I'm sure you've already thought this through, so I don't need to tell you there's a lot in these interviews that could hurt people. I mean, if Granny Emma were alive, she'd never speak to you again. And Uncle Bobby won't like that you only told Grampa's side of the story either.

But it's more than family. I know some of these people. I have to live with them. Then, there are the ones we don't really know. Do you think they want the sort of details you uncovered to come out? I think about that man who was abusing the Asian girl. Kumi. I had a couple run-ins with him. He wasn't a nice person. It would not shock me if he sued you. After all, you don't know that what these people tell you is the truth. You're just listening to one voice. The only story where you interviewed two people, Bev and Clay across the street, showed how hard it is to get at the facts. We all see what we want to see. I mean, I know that bartender Josh. We dated. He wasn't kidding about being a bullshitter. Think about the story he gave you. There are at least three different versions of what happened to that girl. Who knows if any are true? That reminds me; Josh said he didn't want you to tell that he knew all along what happened to her. Unless he died, or she found Owen again. So which is it?

Then there are my feelings. I don't know that I like you putting all the details of my hospital stay in your story about Mary. I get that you're trying to keep these genuine—turn on the recorder, capture the interview, transcribe what was said. But couldn't you remove the extraneous stuff? I'm sure you're cutting out all the *um's* and *ah's* and verbal tics already. So there must be some grey area in what you decide to include and leave out.

And about Derek. Don't take this the wrong way—what he said, the parts I knew, they're all true. And reading it, imagining him with you, saying what he said…well…that's the real gift. But it's personal, Grace. It's not just Derek's story. It's mine too. I'm glad you found him, and it means the world to know he still thinks about me. I think about him. But that's between us. And it's nothing we can change. What's the point of telling the world about it?

Sorry to go on like this. I don't want you to think I don't appreciate what you've done. I do. I'm just not sure I want to share it. I hope you understand. Call me.

Email from Derek Nethery to Grace Page, March 19, 2017

I knew you were closer to this than you let on. How could you sit across from me and keep a straight face when I told you about the baby your grandparents were taking care of? It's a wonder you didn't blurt out, "That was me." If what you're saying is true, that you only learned about your mom and me a week before you came to visit, when she wrote my name down on a pad in the hospital, I'm going to have to reassess my belief in a divine power. I mean, out of the blue you decide to write this history; somehow, through no help of your family's, you find out about me; and you just so happen to be my childhood sweetheart's daughter. Incredible. Forgive me if the jaded explanation seems more convincing— that you knew what you were doing all along. I'm going to give you the benefit of the doubt. In the end, what does it matter? The important thing is, you gave me a chance to tell your mom how I feel about what happened. Has she read the interview yet?

As for the old house, 630 grand? Are you kidding? I've got the money. My dad left me a big chunk when he died. But that's way more than I can afford if I plan to be around another 20 years. Even if they took a half-million, like you say, what am I going to do with a house that big? And let me guess: your mom doesn't know you're twisting my arm to move back, does she? Maybe I'm misreading you. Maybe you were just floating the idea to see how I'd react. Well, I'm not dismissing it. Life is short. Learning about Ilsa's cancer has brought that fact home in a very real way. Please give her my best. *— Derek*

Lunch, Ilsa Page-Carlson and Grace Page, Bistro 19, March 28, 2017

Grace: It's just in case, Mom. If you really don't want me to go through with this, I'll erase the tape. Okay?

Ilsa: So you're not worried about anything I said—the pain you'll put people through, the lawsuits that might come your way, the whole thorny question of truth.

Grace: I think it's clear these are all one person's view, don't you?

Ilsa: So what's the point?

Grace: I don't know, Mom. It's just something I had to do. Don't worry. I'm self-publishing. Nobody's going to read it.

Ilsa: I wouldn't think so.

Grace: Mom!

Ilsa: You said so yourself. Who wants to read about the lives of a bunch of no-name people in some nowhere house?

Grace: If it makes you feel better to think that way—

Ilsa: I don't mean to be insulting. I know how much work you put into it. *I* love it. But I know the people and the places.

Grace: Well, I'm glad at least you aren't putting your foot down.

Ilsa: No. I suppose if you want to go through with this, that's up to you. But there *is* one part I'd like you to cut out.

Grace: I knew it—

Ilsa: You haven't even heard what I was going to say.

Grace. Go on.

Ilsa: The part in your story where you talk about your father. I don't want you mentioning his name. Can't you blank it out?

Grace: Why? My dad knows who he is. It's not a secret.

Ilsa: But we never went around announcing it either. Please, Grace. I'm asking for this one thing.

Grace: Fine. I just don't get why.

Ilsa: Well, let me ask you this: has Derek read all the interviews?

Grace: No. Just his.

Ilsa: That's why. Derek knows your dad. You knew that when he said his name. He shouldn't find that out in your book. It would hurt him.

Grace: I hadn't thought of that.

Ilsa: Really? I'm surprised. Maybe you should rethink—

Grace: Speaking of Derek. I was meaning to talk to you about him. He put an offer in on his old house.

. . .

Grace: Mom?

Ilsa: Turn that off.

Grace: I thought you'd be happy. It's a good thing. Isn't it?

Ilsa: *Turn it off!*

Interview, Derek Nethery, May 14, 2017, 138 Vernon Drive

Arifle in the garage. Two fifties in the crack between the front step and the landing. Any other secrets you want to tell me about? And what's with the *Walk the Walk* sign on the mirror in the basement bathroom? It's time you let me read all those interviews. I need to know the ghosts I'm up against here.

So, I'm the final chapter, eh? Full circle. First and last. If I didn't know better, I'd accuse you of planning the whole thing. I don't have any stories for you this time, though. Not yet. It's only been two days. All I've done is unpack and move my stuff in. *What stuff?* I know; have you ever seen such an empty house? Forty years of drifting hasn't exactly amounted to a wealth of possessions. Like

I told you when you first suggested this...madness, I don't need all this space. It's senseless really. Downright ridiculous.

Driving here, through downtown Mt. Lebanon, nothing felt right. There was a familiarity to things, but no connection, no substance. Everything might as well have been a cardboard façade. I felt like an interloper. Then I turned onto Vernon Drive and drifted past those houses, closer and closer to Virginia Way, then between the sidewalks I walked every day. And everything was suddenly as it used to be, infused with meaning and promise. I turned onto Parkridge, the place of my first memory, in a state of nearly unbearable gratitude.

I was thinking of Ilsa from the moment I got out of my van. But I was afraid to even glance across the lane. I walked the house before I unpacked a thing. Every room. Down the hallway to the basement, then back up to the kitchen, through the nook to the den, across the dining room, around the living room, out to the screened-in porch and upstairs, into every bedroom. It was all exactly like I remembered. I thought of turning the old sunroom, where I played my 45s, into my bedroom because of how it sits above the trees with three sides of windows. But the hardwood floors were in bad shape. The whole place smelled like sour booze. It must've been someone's party room. I couldn't bring myself to stay in my parents' room, so I set up the air mattress—yes, that's all I have—in my old room, facing the two dormer windows that looked down on Vernon, just like my bed did 50 years before.

It was only after I'd put away all my clothes that I remembered the carving in the bathroom. The window sill had been painted over, and it was hard to see the *IC DN*, but it was there, faint yet distinct to the touch. I was tempted to look out the window then, but there weren't any drapes. I didn't want to see Ilsa if it meant she'd think I was spying on her. Still, as I unpacked the van, I thought of her; when I'd see her, what I'd say, how she'd react.

Around sunset, I was brushing my teeth at the sink upstairs, and there she was, right across the lane, perfectly framed in the window. I was already in shadows, but I stepped back anyway. She was watering that flower bed along the side of your house. If I had passed her on the streets of Talkeetna, I wouldn't have recognized her. Yet the fact that she was there made it feel like I'd never taken my eyes off her. Of course, she was older. But the way she moved, the way she held her head and her hair swept off it, even though the blonde had turned white, it was her. Absolutely.

I couldn't get a long look at her face. She kept putting her head down to concentrate on the hose and the flowers. But now and then she'd straighten up and look off over the trees behind the lane, like she was thinking. Once, she glanced up at my window. For just a second, her eyes flashed the way I remembered them. But the smile I was used to seeing wasn't there. It was more of a wince, and I winced along with her, not so much for the pain she seemed to have, but for the loss of that sudden, easy joy I was expecting. For my loss. I know how selfish that sounds.

Then someone came toward her from the park side, an older woman your mother must've known well, because she went to meet her in the lane. And the two stopped close to each other and talked. The old woman motioned to my house. Ilsa broke eye contact with her, looked down, said something, and shrugged. The woman leaned in and cocked her head. Then your mom lifted her face, rolled her eyes, and smiled. It still wasn't her old smile, but I saw the trace of it. And in that moment, I understood. She was straining to contain that smile, like she didn't deserve it. And when I realized that, I welled up. And I was upset. At what, I don't know. Time. Loss. God. All of it, I suppose.

This morning, I went over to her house. It may not look it, but I dressed up for the occasion. Anything besides jeans and a flannel shirt is stepping out for me. You could've mentioned she worked at Markham. When she didn't answer the door and wasn't there after lunch either, I figured I'd scared her off. A while ago, I wrote a note, went over, and set it on the welcome mat. "Want to walk?" I forgot to sign it, but I think she'll know who it's from.

It's 20 to four now. Twenty minutes before you said she'd be off work. If you don't want to be here when she gets home, we ought to stop. Let's not cut it too close. Next time we talk, I hope you don't have that recorder. I hope the story's over and we're on to something new. Someday, maybe you'll tell me why you did this. Someday, maybe I can repay you for it. For now, all I can say is, thank you. It's not enough, I know. But gratitude is all I have. And that's more than I ever thought I'd feel again.

Email from Ilsa Page-Carlson to Grace Page, May 18, 2017

Five days. Five! I was beginning to think he was avoiding me. He'd taken one look at this ruined, 60-year-old version of the little girl he knew and had a change of heart, started plotting his escape back to Alaska. Even when the moment came, last night before sundown, it was me who had to force things. I heard this clattering in the lane, and when I looked out the window, Derek was hunched over the engine of his van, banging away at something with a wrench. I'm not a mechanic, but I know you can't fix much on a car using a wrench as a drumstick. I decided if this was some sort of first move, he was in desperate need of assistance. I went out on our back porch and leaned over the railing, peeking through our Korean lilac. Years ago, I couldn't have hidden behind our landscaping. After a flurry of clanging, I cleared my throat. He didn't hear. I cleared it harder. Nothing still. *Maybe he's hard of hearing*, I thought. At our age, it's a distinct possibility. "I was wondering who was making all the racket," I finally said, shouting a little through the rustling leaves. He jolted to attention, turned his head slowly, and tilted it to find me through the leaves.

"It's just me," he replied.

"You're taller," I said. It came out as a joke, but what I meant, the full thought those words didn't express, was that, essentially, he looked the same. I don't know how to describe it, just the way he stood, how his body inhabited space. There was a physical logic you could clearly trace back to the boy I had such a crush on.

"You look—" he started to reply, then stopped with his mouth hanging open. I might've been more anxious waiting for him to finish if he didn't look so openly awestruck.

"That bad, eh?"

"I was going to say 'prettier,'" he rushed the words out. "But that doesn't hardly do it."

Well. We could've ended the night right then. It took my breath away, for sure. "I don't know about that," I said, laughing him off. "But I'll take it. I'm just surprised that quiet boy next door turned into such a smooth talker."

He pushed his hair back and scratched his jaw, like he was trying to make sense of the change himself. "I don't spend much time around people. I've developed a bad habit of saying what I mean."

"That's hardly a flaw," I offered.

"It's gotten me in my share of trouble over the years." For just a moment, the gulf between us—the years, the distance, the history—was palpable, a chasm across that little lane. I couldn't think of anything to say that wouldn't plunge us into it. "Matter of fact," Derek finally said, "I may have overstepped my bounds asking you to go walking so soon."

I wasn't quite sure what he meant, but I wanted to help him out. "Oh, I don't think so."

"In any case, I'm sorry," he added.

"Sorry? What for?"

"The note I left. I shouldn't have put you on the spot like that."

"You left me a note?"

"At your front door, yeah. On the welcome mat."

I laughed. "The only time I open that door is when a stranger rings. I wouldn't have seen that note for weeks."

"Ah," he exclaimed with a slow nod, like everything suddenly made sense. But he didn't act on the discovery.

"Are you asking me to go for a walk?" I tried prompting.

"I'd understand if you didn't want to," he said.

"Why wouldn't I?"

"It occurred to me there were some unresolved issues from the last time we saw each other."

The way he spied at me then, sidewise, struggling to focus, I could tell my response mattered to him. And I knew why. "Derek," I said, "I can't remember what I had for lunch yesterday. How could I possibly hold a grudge for so long?"

He smiled at that, a quick sheepish grin, as if he wouldn't dare show more. "Well," he said, "I've done a pretty fair job of hanging onto guilt for 50 years." If he was trying to put me at ease, it didn't work. Not because what he'd said bothered me, but because it seemed to weigh on him so heavily. His eyes thrashed around the pavement between us.

"So, are we going to walk or not?" I interrupted.

That snapped him out of it. "Now?" he asked, like the idea had never occurred to him.

"Unless you'd rather not."

"No. No, that's fine," he said, waving me off. He noticed then how dirty his hands were. "Let me go wash up real quick."

"It's just a walk," I reminded him.

He didn't know quite what to make of that. "Right," he said, scrunching his brow, all serious. Then with a big huff and a quick shake of his head, he loosened up. "Right," he repeated. And he smiled again, only this time, it stayed longer.

We headed up Vernon the same way we did when we went to school. "I was afraid I wouldn't be able to get past how much things had changed," Derek said. "But the strange thing is, it all feels exactly the same. There's the Kinmans," he pointed at their house across the street. "And the Bensons. Then Wells, Caffey, and Jansen." He turned to our side. "And next to you the Ratsups, then Chadwick, Herron, and Brown."

"The Kinmans, Herrons, and Ratsups are still here," I said. "And me. And you."

"And me..." He laughed. "I still can't believe it. I can't believe I'm really here. And that I have *your* daughter to thank."

That's how he brought you up, Grace. I didn't know what to say. I wanted him to know I didn't put you up to it. But I thought the more I said, the more it would seem like I'd known about it. In the end, just to move past things, I said, "I can't believe it either."

By this time, we were at the top of Virginia Way, about to head down the hill. "The funny thing is," he said, "I've known about Grace for years, since I dropped out of college. And I've always wondered about her."

"I know," I let slip.

"That's right," he said. "You read the interview. The others too, right?" I just nodded. That's when he asked, "If I read the whole book, would I understand more? About Grace—why she wrote it, who she is, what drove her to do this?"

"Maybe," I conceded. I had to. He's going to read it some time.

We were nearly at the bottom of the hill by now, almost to Mayfair. That's when he brought up the subject I was dreading: "Would I find out more about you?"

"Not really," I replied. I knew what he was getting at. From the day you told me he was coming back, I knew I'd have to face this moment. I'd wrestled with how to handle it, even rehearsed what I'd say. Yet now that he was here in front of me, I sort of went empty. A kind of peace flushed through me.

"You don't have to tell me anything," he said.

"I think it would be better if I did, don't you?"

He didn't answer. Out of reflex, we turned up Mayfair, toward the church and the way to school. His silence went on. I thought, maybe he's considering the question. Or bracing for the truth. Then he asked me, point blank: "It's someone I know, isn't it?" I said yes. He guessed Ralph. I said no. We were right there on the same side of the street, just two houses away from where he lived when we were kids. He uttered his name, actually whispered it. "Ben." His best friend from half a century ago.

I could've said yes, but what would've been the point? Everything needed to be out in the open if we were going to move past it. So I told the truth. "Probably."

He stopped. His head snapped around. "Probably?"

I didn't want to stop there, not so close to Ben's house. But I did. I leaned close to catch his eye and said, "It was a bad time for me, Derek. A shameful time. There were others, but the timing with Ben makes the most sense. We were at a party. We got drunk. We'd known each other forever, and it happened. Once. Then it couldn't be undone. I wouldn't *let* it be undone. That's the only good decision I made back then."

The whole time I made my confession—that's what it was, Grace—Derek was slowly slumping. First, his head hung. Next, he bent over and put his hands on his knees. Then his breathing got harder. Here it was, the moment of finally knowing, and he was struggling to hold up to it. I couldn't blame him. Finding out it was Ben probably made things worse than he expected. Or maybe it was precisely what he dreaded. I don't know. But at the time, I just wanted to move past that first jolt. "Derek?" I asked gently. "Can we start walking again? Can we just keep walking?"

"*We'd known each other forever*," he repeated, then closed his eyes, shook his head, and straightened up. He let out a deep breath and said, "I wish I'd never left."

What could I say to that? "I wish you hadn't either?" How would that help? In the end, I took the practical way out. You know me. I said, "We can't change what happened."

"No. No, we can't," he agreed. And then he started walking again. As we passed Ben's house, he looked up at the high windows where I'm guessing his old friend's room was. Then, on the other side, he looked down the sloping driveway. I thought of his story, that last confrontation he'd had with Ben down there, when he hit him for telling about our moment in the storm drain.

"Is Ben still...in contact?" he asked. I said no. "Where is he now?" I told him Phoenix—married, kids of his own, a grandson. "So, do you hear from him?" he kept digging.

"No," I answered.

Then I asked, did it matter? We had turned onto Youngwood by this point, heading down the long slope to the woods. He didn't answer for a long time, so long I thought he either hadn't heard me or was too consumed in his own thoughts. But then he turned to me. And he mustered a smile. This soft, brave, and wounded smile. "No," he said. "Not at all."

And we walked the length of Youngwood, passing all the old paths we used to take to school. And we didn't say a word the whole time, just glanced at each other now and then, and smiled, like we were sharing a secret we'd only just discovered. At the end of the road, that dark path we'd taken so many years before, on that day when everything changed, was still there, no more worn than when we were afraid to venture down it. Derek stopped at the edge of the path and peered into the shadows that shifted and danced with the dying sunlight. He touched my shoulder. "Shall we?" he asked. And when I looked at him, it wasn't a smile anymore that I saw. It was deeper than that, a gaze of wonder and gratitude. And hope.

"Yes," I said. We stepped back into those woods. And as we walked, Grace, I had the strangest sensation. As we were taking that path along the creek, I felt like we were also high up on the hill, looking down from above, through the portal of that storm drain. The other end of the binoculars, as Derek called it. Two fragile children, confused by our world, yet falling in love. Still.

And again.

AUTHOR'S NOTE

I lived in seven different places before I was seven—Red Oak, Iowa, where I was born; Shenandoah, Iowa; Huntington, West Virginia; two houses in Bay Village, Ohio, one on Bassett Road just off the shore of Lake Erie (where my brother did, in fact, start a fire in the woods near the high school) and another on Lincoln Road; then Paoli, Pennsylvania outside of Philadelphia; and finally 138 Vernon Drive in Mt. Lebanon. As best as I can reconstruct, I lived there from the spring of 1966 to the spring of 1969, just about three years, from the ages of seven to 10. I came with a crew cut and left with a mop-top. Considering the short period of time I spent in that house, perched between the park and the woods, you wouldn't think it would take hold of me the way it did—and still does. But that was a special time, not just for a young boy awakening to the world, but also for a country struggling with the loss of its own innocence.

For years after I moved away, to Bloomfield Hills, Michigan, I would wonder what was happening to the friends I'd left in that neighborhood south of Pittsburgh. Even now, I have the most vivid dreams of walking up Vernon Drive, down Virginia Way, along Mayfair to Youngwood, and up into the woods that had been the sanctuary of my imagination for those three short years in the late sixties. In some way, it's like time split into two paths for me in 1969. While I followed the inevitable course that led me to where I am today, I've always felt there was this second path running somewhere alongside me, not too far off in the shadows of my mind.

This book was my effort to find that path, to connect what had actually transpired in my life to what I wondered had happened ever since the moment my dad pulled out of Parkridge Lane, and we left Pittsburgh nearly 50 years ago. Some of the moments in this book are real memories from my time in Mt. Lebanon; some happened in other places where I've lived; and most are simply the product of imagining who may have filled the absence after we moved out of the house on Vernon Drive.

Last fall, late in September of 2017, I had the occasion to go back to Mt. Lebanon. There was a 40-year high school reunion for the class I would've graduated with had I not moved away. A couple of my old grade-school friends who I've stayed in touch with through Facebook encouraged me to go. I reconnected with a dozen or so of the kids I'd gone to school with at Markham Elementary. It was amazing to me how much they were like what they'd been. We all got together at The Saloon in downtown Mt. Lebanon, pored over old class photographs, told stories of our time together so long ago, laughed, and marveled at how time hadn't taken us all that far away from the essence of who we were.

I hope some of those friends read this book and remember those times as fondly as I do. Every house, every family, every person has their own history. This is for all of us who feel the lure of their past and are compelled to step off the well-worn passage of their days in search of it.

Peter Tiernan, September 2018

Made in the USA
Middletown, DE
19 January 2021